ALSO BY ROBIN ACTON

The Taker

EMPTY BOXES

ROBIN ACTON

PRAISE FOR *THE TAKER*

"This writer ranks up there with my favorites James Patterson and Mary Higgins Clark when it come to suspense and intensity."

"The story line was great to follow and understand. I found my heart racing many many times throughout the chapters and felt I was too in the race to find Lindy."

"I highly recommend this book."

"Looking for a page-turner with surprising twists and turns? Then this is book for you. Acton is a superb storyteller. Her descriptions of police work and the courts are vivid and reflect a journalistic bent for details that lend credibility and authenticity to the story. The characters are multi-dimensional and rich in personality. Overall, a very good thriller that I hope makes it to the screen. I keep thinking it would be a great movie."

"I just finished this book. Couldn't put it down. It was a heart pounding exciting experience. Not a dull moment! I can't wait for the next one!!! Just Loved it."

"The Taker is not a run-of-the mill mystery. Unexpected twists and turns kept me in suspense throughout. I put you right up there with the best mystery writers of today."

There *is* something worse than death.

EMPTY BOXES

A Rita Locke Mystery

ROBIN ACTON

Author of *The Taker*

Blank Slate Press | Harrisonville, Missouri

Blank Slate Press
Harrisonville, MO 64701

Publisher's Note: This book is a work of the imagination. Names, characters, places and incidents either are products of the author's imagination or are used fictitiously. While some of the characters and incidents portrayed here can be found in historical or contemporary accounts, they have been altered and rearranged by the author to suit the strict purposes of storytelling. The book should be read solely as a work of fiction.

For information, contact:
Blank Slate Press
www.amphoraepublishing.com
Blank Slate Press is an imprint of
Amphorae Publishing Group, LLC
www.amphoraepublishing.com

Manufactured in the United States of America
Cover Design by Kristina Blank Makansi
Cover photos – bloody scalpel: Shutterstock, Maxew;
graveyard: Shutterstock, SkizoTV

Set in Bitstream Century Schoolbook

Library of Congress Control Number: 2025937341
ISBN: 9781966103004 paperback
ISBN: 9781966103011 eBook

For my father, Bob Acton, a kind and great man
who taught me and my brother Mark the meaning
of unconditional love while being the best dad ever.

CHAPTER ONE

Blood pooled around the body in a thick crimson puddle and dripped from the bottom step onto the polished hardwood floor. The drops beat a quiet rhythm with the ticking of the carved mahogany clock in the hallway. Flames licked the logs stacked high in the fireplace in the adjacent study, warming the killer who sat at a desk, oblivious to the muted late-night infomercial for whitening toothpaste. The TV cast a blue glow onto the flowered pattern of the Persian carpet.

One by one, he skimmed over papers pulled from files piled on the cluttered desktop and jammed into its drawers. Each folder was searched and then restored to its original position, albeit minus some incriminating contents. Unfortunately, the victim had kept meticulous, damaging records. The process proved tedious, but necessary.

Names. Dates. Locations. Huge mistake. So much of the information represented risk. Just as the man had to be silenced, the evidence had to be removed, but carefully to avoid future scrutiny from prying eyes.

When the clock chimed three times, he sat back, satisfied, and returned the last file to the bottom desk drawer before locking it and dropping the key back into its tray in the shallow center drawer. He stuffed the collected papers into a manila envelope and placed them in a leather briefcase.

The shotgun, wiped clean with a cloth already burning atop the crackling firewood, leaned against the wall in the corner of the room, precisely where it had been standing before the argument. He winced, remembering that the victim had purchased the weapon that killed him, believing it would provide protection. Not exactly money well spent. The desk appeared as it had two hours earlier. Nothing remained here that could link them to each other. No one had witnessed the fatal shot in the hour after midnight.

Over and done.

He got up, carried the briefcase into the hallway, and gave the body and the gruesome scene a final look.

"Fool," the killer murmured to the dead man. "It didn't have to end like this. You should have known I'd never let you quit."

Leaving the body and the blood and the warmth of the glowing fire behind, he peered into the dark, empty street, closed the door, and walked out into the freezing rain, pleased at a job well done.

Rita Locke opened her eyes and moved closer to her boyfriend, nuzzling his neck. She loved waking up next to him. It had been years since she felt this happy and content, and she enjoyed every minute of it. When the phone rang, she groaned and reached out from under her down comforter, slapping her hand along the edge of the nightstand through three rings before she found it.

He tugged gently at her free arm. "Don't answer it, babe. C'mon, let it go to voicemail," he mumbled, pulling her closer.

"You know I can't do that, David. It might be work." She yanked out the charger cord and swiped her finger across the screen to answer it.

"What?"

"Aw, what's the matter, Red, still getting your beauty sleep?"

Her head ached from too much wine at dinner the night before. Nevertheless, she sat up when she recognized the voice of one of her best news sources, an aide who worked for the county coroner.

"Jesus, Vince, it's Sunday! What the hell time is it, anyway? This better be good."

"Well, let's see. Let's just say there's a body that you're going to be interested in over at the Mason-Watson Funeral Home."

"A body at a funeral home? You've got to be kidding me, because I'm pretty sure the place is probably full of them. Seriously, you know I don't work weekends. Can't it wait?"

He snorted. "Nope, and it's not just *any* old body, either. It's Bob Watson, the funeral director."

She sat up straighter, pulling the comforter around her waist. "Get out! Something tells me it wasn't from natural causes, or you wouldn't be calling me at this godawful hour on a Sunday. What happened?"

"Someone blew him away last night, left him splattered on the front hallway steps in his silk pajamas. The hairdresser found him this morning when she came in to fix up one of his customers in the morgue downstairs. She called the cops. They called me. I called you. You, who ought to be thanking me and getting into your car instead of complaining right now."

"Shit. Thanks. I owe you. I'm on my way."

"Take your time. It's going to take a while to get this scene processed because the guys from the crime lab only got here about ten minutes ago. And Red?"

"Yeah?"

He hesitated a moment. "You might want to skip breakfast if you know what I mean. The poor guy's full of buckshot. Looks like a massacre here."

"Right, okay, see you later."

She hung up and slouched back down under the comforter, nudging the shoulder of the man lying next to her. She kissed his neck, and then his cheek, brushing her lips softly across his morning stubble. His eyes remained closed.

"I know you're awake, so quit faking. Hey, babe, c'mon. I gotta get up. I have to go to work."

He turned over and opened his eyes, now fully awake. "Ugh. I knew that as soon as I heard the phone. So, I guess our plans for today aren't going to happen?"

"No, I don't think they are from the sounds of this. There's been a murder. Bob Watson from the funeral home, and..."

"Watson? Huh, too bad. Yeah, yeah, I know the drill. There's a murder, and you're on the crime beat, and criminals and editors don't give a crap when it's your day off, yada, yada. We've been through this enough before, so I'm well aware of what this means."

She rolled closer to him. "Tell me, what does it mean?"

He brushed a long, red curl from her cheek and kissed her. A few seconds passed before he spoke in a monotone. "It means you're leaving, and I'm going to my sister's party without you because someone killed a guy who I wouldn't let bury my dog. Correct?"

She sighed. Unfortunately, he was right on target. Sensing his hurt feelings, she offered to compromise. "You could stick around here and wait for me. Maybe we could go to the party together a little later?"

"Are you kidding me? It's a gender reveal party, for chrissake! I'm not going to disappoint Chrissy by being late and missing the surprise."

She moaned. Knowing his sister, the party would be over the

top. She understood that he had to be there as the baby's uncle and godfather, but other than him, who would care if she missed it? When she received the invitation three weeks earlier, she'd agreed to go to the party because she loved David and had a good relationship with his family, but the very thought of the whole thing hit her in the pit of her stomach. Events like christenings and baby showers tore at her heart. The miscarriage she suffered a decade ago still haunted her, especially because having a child of her own seemed doubtful.

"What's the latest we could leave and make it in time? Maybe I could meet you there later," her voice trailed off with the suggestion.

"No. Look, I know this day was going to be hard for you, but I can't miss it, and I can't be late, so I'm leaving at one, just like we planned, with you or without you."

She looked at the clock on her nightstand. "It's almost nine now, so there's no way I'll be finished that early."

He nodded. "Honey, don't you see? I want us to go together. It's your choice as to how this plays out, though. I surely don't want anyone to die, but you know how I feel about Bob Watson."

"I know, I know. But it's my job, so I have no choice. Go without me."

He sat up against the headboard and ran his hands through his thick chestnut hair. "Okay. Like I said, I've been around long enough to know the drill."

When she moved closer to lean against him, his body tensed.

"David, I know –"

He cut her off. "Listen, Red, I can't keep on like this. I don't want to be with someone who jumps out of bed in the middle of the night to dash off to a crime scene, shows up late, and can't make plans more than two hours in advance. I want more than ruined parties and forgotten plans."

"What are you saying?" she asked. She held her breath.

"Maybe it's better if we cool things down, take a step back for a while."

His words stunned her because he'd been talking about the future, *their* future together, for the last several weeks. The night before, at dinner, she'd suspected he may have been hinting at a forthcoming proposal. She'd almost dared to hope for a diamond next week for Valentine's Day, no matter how corny that made her feel. She hesitated, not sure she wanted to know what he meant, but then blurted out, "All of a sudden after eight months, you wake up one morning and decide you don't want to be with me? How long is 'a while'?"

He groaned and looked at the ceiling, avoiding eye contact. "I don't know. I've felt like this off and on for a bit, and I probably should have said something before now, but as we got more serious and spent more time together, I thought things might change, and you would ease up a bit at work."

She sat up. "It's my *job*."

"Yes, but you've been there long enough that you don't have to jump at every story just to prove yourself." He ran his hands through his hair again in obvious desperation. "Or, put it this way. I *hoped* things might change because I love you and I want to be with you, wanted to make a life with you. Now, though, it's obvious to me that I'll always come second, or third, maybe even fourth, *after* the criminals, the editors, and the newspaper.

"You're married to that place, to your job, to your readers, and there's no room and precious little time left for me."

She stopped listening and flipped back the comforter to get out of bed. Now almost thirty-nine, she'd heard it all before, more times than she'd like to admit. She'd hoped he could handle the unpredictability of her career, but he obviously could not.

Her green eyes stung with tears, and she struggled to swallow the lump that had formed in her throat. She picked her jeans up from where she'd tossed them onto the floor the night before, pulled them on, and went into her closet to find a clean shirt. By the time she'd washed her face, brushed her teeth, and twisted her hair into a loose knot on top of her head, he'd left the bedroom without another word.

She fumbled through her purse for her makeup bag and quickly applied blush, mascara, and lipstick. When she went into the kitchen, she was shocked to see that the house key she'd given him lay on the counter. She grabbed her phone and keys, pulled on a leather jacket and boots, and went out the door. Icy rain that started the night before pelted the empty driveway where his car had been parked.

He was gone.

Nothing new to see here, folks. Nothing at all. It's happened before, too many times. Same story, different man.

Still, her heart hurt.

No matter how many times it happened, that aching, empty feeling always felt new.

Rita saw Pennsylvania State Police Lt. George Carr arrive at the funeral home, a stately, red brick Victorian mansion, just as the coroner and his aides carried the black zippered bag that held Bob Watson's body out of the door and down the concrete steps guarded by twin stone lions.

The rain had stopped, and Rita leaned against the hood of her Jeep that she'd parked across the street, sipping tepid coffee, and watched the photographer she'd called on her way to the scene.

He'd been snapping photos at various angles from across the street. The paper didn't use body photos, but the shots of the coroner's van being loaded in front of the business would help to tell the story. Rita looked back at Carr and smiled as he slid from behind the steering wheel of his unmarked patrol car and walked up the tree-lined sidewalk toward her. She'd written about lots of his cases in the past decade, and they'd become decent friends when she covered the deadly case of a serial kidnapper two years before.

"Hey Red, you're up early on a Sunday. Am I correct in guessing that a little bird told you something big happened?" When he grinned, his caramel skin creased into fine lines at the corners of his brown eyes. He waved at Vince Rogers, who was pushing the gurney that held the body toward the coroner's van. It was no secret that the coroner's aide tipped Rita on cases that would make headlines. She wasn't one to sensationalize, though, so they'd never tried to discourage him from helping her.

She waved at Rogers and winked at Carr. He'd just been promoted to lieutenant, so she was surprised to see him. "Now, George, you know I never burn a source. You know I've never done you wrong when you shared information with me," she joked. "I didn't expect to see you out here now that you're the big cheese. Congratulations, by the way."

"Thanks, but no promotion would have helped me today," he said.

She understood what he meant because she expected the killing would be a high-priority case. Almost everyone in Unity Township knew Watson either through his business or as the president of the local Rotary Club.

Carr looked toward the funeral home. "Guy like him gets blown away in the middle of the night in his fancy pajamas, and

I get to sleep in? No way the commander would let that happen."

She laughed and pulled a notebook and pen from her satchel. She doubted he knew much this early in the investigation, but she had to try to get something out of him. "Nah, wouldn't think so. I have a feeling the business community will be unnerved by this one until there's an arrest. What do you think? Robbery gone bad? Look, I know it's early, but can you tell me anything?"

He shook his head. "Not much, and right now, anything I do say is strictly off the record. From what the guys told me on the phone, it looks like Bob was walking upstairs to his second-floor apartment when someone shot him in the back at close range. He never made it to the top of the steps. They're processing things now, but they said there doesn't appear to be any sign of a struggle, or a break-in for that matter."

"What about his family? Did they hear anything? Are they okay?"

He pulled a notepad from his breast pocket and flipped it open. He read for a few seconds and then slapped it closed. "Cindy Ekas, the woman who found him, said his wife and son are out of town, visiting family somewhere in Ohio. We've got officers out there trying to track them down now."

"Why was the hairdresser here on a Sunday?"

"According to Ms. Ekas, Watson got a body yesterday afternoon. He called her last night and asked her to come in any time today to do the woman's hair and makeup for the viewing tomorrow. She had plans for later this afternoon, so she came in early, just after seven thirty."

He explained that the hairdresser had a key to use when the funeral director wasn't there, and that she frequently did the hair and makeup on bodies in between salon appointments or in the evenings or early mornings. "She let herself in when he didn't answer because she thought he might still be sleeping and didn't want to disturb him. She's hysterical right now but managed to tell our guys that it wasn't unusual for him to be gone or to sleep late, especially on a weekend when there are no funerals."

"I feel sorry for her. Not everyone can handle the gruesome reality of a murder."

He looked toward the steps. "That's all I've got for now, Red. I have to go inside and get the contact information for the family of the dead woman so they can make other arrangements for viewing and burying her. Man, I'm not looking forward to that call at all."

Rita nodded. Based on what the coroner's aide described to her earlier, she doubted the scene could be processed by state police investigators and cleaned up overnight.

He blew out a deep breath. "Yep, even if Bob's wife could get another funeral director to supervise things on short notice, the guys said it's going to take a professional restoration company to handle this one. Anyone coming in for visitation hours tomorrow would have to walk right past it all to get to the viewing rooms, and trust me, my guys say it isn't a pretty sight."

Rita looked toward the mansion and noticed that one of the cement guard lions had a chipped nose and splintering cracks in its mane. "Well, I can't say that I envy you on that one. I'm going to stick around here for a while, see what plays out. If I give you a call later, can you get me something on the record?"

Nodding, he put his notebook in the breast pocket of his coat. She thought he looked tired as he clicked his pen open and closed several times, which did not surprise her, given his age and the job's erratic schedule. He had to be nearing retirement.

"Sure, yeah. Just wait until we get his wife, okay? I don't know Amie well, but I feel for her with having to deal with this.

I met her at our Rotary picnic last year. Their son, I guess he's about eight now from what I remember, has some issues. Autistic, I think. Goes to an expensive special-needs school somewhere around Philadelphia."

She shook her head slowly before taking a sip of her coffee. She didn't envy him in that conversation either. No wonder he looked tired. "Oh, wow. That's too bad."

"Yep. Some people just never seem to get a break. It might be rumor, but from what I understand, they were having a bit of a rough time of things financially a while back because their insurance doesn't cover tuition. Seems like things have gotten better in the last year or so, though."

She looked beyond the lion's chipped nose and noticed peeling paint on the trim surrounding the porch roof and rotting wood around three large windows. "Look at this old place. The whole exterior of the mansion is in dire need of repairs. It probably costs a bundle to maintain, too. I can't imagine what it takes to heat it. Was the funeral business in trouble?"

He shrugged his shoulders and turned to go up the steps between the lions. Looking back at her, he said, "Hell, Red, I don't know. Funerals aren't cheap. I guess you'd have to count the bodies and do the math."

CHAPTER TWO

The two weeks after the murder dragged on.

She'd tried to make up with David during two phone calls the first week, but he steered her away from their problems with polite conversation about the weather and trivial small talk. At the beginning of the second week, he called her at work to seek permission to come over and pick up some of his belongings. She fought back tears, hoping no one in her Pittsburgh newsroom would notice her red, blotchy face. It had broken her heart when he'd left his key.

"David, you don't have to ask me that because you know you can come over anytime. I didn't ask you to leave your key. You stormed out the door without a word. I don't want things between us to be awkward. You know I love you, and you say you love me. Can't we work it out?"

She heard him sigh on the other end. "How would talking about things change anything?" he asked. "One of the things I love about you is your passion. I just wish it could be passion for me, not for the paper."

Ultimately, he agreed to come over that evening for dinner. She ordered takeout from their favorite Asian restaurant, and he brought a bottle of wine. Again, their conversation was stilted and polite, and after two hours they'd accomplished nothing toward repairing their relationship.

On his way out the door, his arms loaded with several shirts and a pair of sweatpants, he leaned toward her and pecked her cheek with a quick kiss. "I'll talk to you soon," he promised.

She closed the door behind him and slumped to the floor, sobbing.

Two weeks after the murder, Rita scanned the emailed press release from the Pennsylvania State Police, making sure she'd noted everything of importance. When she finished, she tossed it onto a stack of yellowing newspapers on the corner of her desk next to a jumble of chewed pens, two empty Diet Coke cans, and a half-eaten sandwich left from her lunch. The newsroom remained quiet that afternoon except for static communications on the police scanner and two beat reporters talking on their phones in distant cubicles. Swiveling her chair around, she saw the features staff reporters in a meeting with their editor in a glass-walled conference room. Three other editors sat alone at their desks reading copy. Another slow news day.

She turned back to her keyboard, grateful for something new to write about in connection with the Watson murder after such a long wait. She'd called Carr when she got the email, hoping for more information, but he had nothing much to add to the scant details. The release confirmed Watson's own shotgun killed him and that the only fingerprints on the weapon or any other surfaces in his office belonged to him, his wife, or their part-time employees. Because records verified the funeral director bought the weapon after several burglaries in his neighborhood, she included references to two recent crimes in her story. Police said although his wife told investigators he had kept the gun in his first-floor office, Amie Watson couldn't confirm whether it was loaded on the day of his murder. The police report indicated that she told investigators she hated firearms and had been against the purchase, but her husband had insisted they needed to be able to protect themselves from harm, should the situation arise.

State police had no leads and no suspects, according to the release. Nevertheless, Rita already knew, thanks to Carr, that police believed Watson recognized and opened the door for his killer because there was no sign of forced entry at any of the mansion's three entrance doors or two attached garages, and he'd apparently been comfortable enough to answer the door in his pajamas without putting on a robe. She couldn't imagine who would be angry enough with him to shoot him to death. Even though David hadn't liked the man, she'd never heard anyone else say anything negative about him.

David. She closed her eyes and took a breath.

"Hey, Tom, I'm going to have something on the Watson killing for tomorrow. Nothing earth-shattering, maybe ten inches of copy."

Tom Moore, her editor, turned away from his computer and wheeled his chair around to face her desk. "About time. No arrest yet?"

She shook her head and picked up her notes. "Nope. I talked to Carr when I got the email a little while ago. Said the wife, Amie, claims they have no enemies. She was out of town visiting her sister when he was killed, and police said her alibi holds up. I asked him whether there were signs of a robbery, but Carr said nothing points to that as a motive. Amie told the police nothing was missing, not even Bob's wallet, which the police found on his office desk not fifteen feet away from his body. And in their apartment upstairs, her diamond engagement ring was still sitting in a tray on her vanity, right out in the open, when she got home that Sunday evening."

Rita scanned her notes further. "From what Carr said, a few members in the Rotary Club claimed he could be a little standoffish at times. Still, they apparently liked him enough to vote him in as president about eight months ago."

She took a long gulp of Diet Coke from a third can on her desk and found it to be warm and flat as usual. The newsroom clock told her it had been sitting there for two hours. "I should add, though, that my boyf—, I mean, my friend David Hatfield, was at the funeral home last year when they had a viewing for his grandmother. Somehow, he got turned around in the wrong direction when he went looking for a restroom. Told me Watson bit his head off just as he was about to enter a door at the end of the hallway on the main floor. David's usually easy-going, but he was really irritated about it because he felt Watson acted as though he was a criminal when all he did was head the wrong way. He's despised him ever since."

Tom frowned and turned back to focus on the computer screen in front of him. He typed as he talked. "Could just have been a bad day. So, did this guy have a girlfriend? Maybe some honey on the side who got a little pissed at him? You know, the whole 'woman scorned' scenario?"

Rita shrugged as she read through the last of her notes and the log of phone calls she'd made. She'd called the hairdresser and Watson's wife a few times but hadn't heard back from either of them. Watson's partner and other employees were part-timers who helped him only during visitations and funerals because he did all the embalming for the deceased to cut costs, according to what his wife told police.

She explained that police believed the killer was a man based on the size and type of weapon used. "Anyway, if he had a girlfriend, he must have been discreet about it. Carr told me that friends, neighbors, family, just about everyone says he and his wife seemed as though they got along well when they went out together. Friends said the couple didn't entertain much and always appeared to keep things low key at home because of their son. The little boy has some problems and goes to a school in Philly for children with special needs. Most free weekends, they visited him at school, but he came home that weekend to go to Ohio with his mother to visit his aunt, who is his godmother." She closed her notebook. "That's about all the police could tell me."

He stopped typing, swiveled his chair around, and wheeled it closer to her desk. "Something will turn up, sooner or later. Always does. I know you've been calling and leaving messages for that hairdresser who found him, but maybe it's time you paid her a visit, don't you think? My gut tells me there's a reason she's dodging you. I can understand why the grieving widow isn't saying much, but not her."

She nodded as she reopened her notebook and skimmed through several more pages. She'd been thinking the same thing. The woman hadn't returned her calls, not even to say that she had no comment. "Hey, maybe I can get my nails done while I'm there, claim it on my expenses," she joked. She held out her right hand, displaying unpolished nails that were short and ragged from too much typing and too little care. "Think the publisher is good for a French manicure?"

He had been wheeling his chair away from her desk but stopped to shoot her a look over his shoulder. He rolled his eyes as he swept his arms open wide. "Oh, sure. Hey, go all out for the facial and full body massage while you're at it, princess, and when you come back, you can plan how you're going to handle your coverage of the next sewage authority meeting." He chuckled as he reached his desk, where he drank from a chipped mug.

She grabbed her notebook and stuffed it into her leather satchel before getting up from her chair. "Okay, I can take a hint. I'm out of here. If you need me, I'll be at Curl Up and Dye."

He snorted, choking on his coffee. He put his cup down and wiped his mouth with the back of his hand. "You're kidding me, right? That's the name of her salon? The woman who has a side job doing hair on corpses. Oh man, that's the best one I've heard today."

An hour later, Rita opened the door to Cindy Ekas' salon, where the acrid scent of permanent wave solution burned her nostrils as soon as she stepped inside. When she identified herself as a reporter, the woman's eyes widened with surprise.

"I'll be right with you," she stammered, closing her cash register. She turned to her customer, a platinum blonde with a sleek bob and collagen-plumped lips and said, "Honey, I'm gonna have to close things up here now. I'll call you next week to schedule your next appointment, okay?"

She walked the customer from the counter to the door, locked it behind her, and pulled a pleated blind down to cover the window. She motioned toward a stylist's empty chair, and when Rita took the offered seat, she sat in the chair at the next station. When Rita began to question her, Cindy started to wring her hands.

"Is there anything you can think of that would make someone want to hurt Bob Watson? Are you aware of any enemies he may have had?" Rita asked.

Cindy's voice shook as she spoke, avoiding direct eye contact. "No, and I told the police. He was a good guy, never hurt anyone."

Beads of perspiration formed above her upper lip, and she rocked nervously in her chair. Rita realized then that the woman wasn't hiding anything as mundane as an extramarital affair with her employer. She was visibly terrified.

"Please, I don't want to be involved in this. You can't put my name in the paper again, promise me," Cindy begged, her eyes wild. She moved to the plate glass window and peeked through the side of the blind, scanning the street and sidewalks outside the salon. "Look, I don't know anything. I can't tell you any more about what happened to Bob, other than what I told the police. I walked through the front door and found him lying there on the steps. That's all I know. It was awful, Miss Locke. It's the most horrible thing I've ever seen in my entire life."

They were alone, except for a little Yorkshire terrier that had been curled up on a plaid bed in one corner but now shuffled over to sniff Rita's shoes. Rita leaned forward to pet the dog, although she wondered how he could smell anything other than lingering odors of chemicals and hair spray that filled the room and made her eyes water. "Hey little guy. Aww, you're a sweetheart. What's his name?"

The woman relaxed her body and smiled at the inquisitive little fur ball. "Boomer. I got him two years ago as a puppy and fell in love. I don't have any family, so he's all I've got."

"He's so cute. What does he weigh?"

"He's eight pounds, but in his mind, he's not afraid of anything and thinks he's a tough guy the size of a Saint Bernard. The little ones always do."

Rita sat back in the chair when the dog moved over to his owner, licked her hand, and then wandered back to his bed. She'd never had a dog, or any pet for that matter. Thinking back to David's words during their last argument, she realized she'd spent all her life building a career rather than developing close relationships. "I don't know much about dogs, but I can tell he's a sweet baby. To get back to our conversation, please, call me Rita. And Cindy, I hope you understand that I'm not trying to pressure you into anything. I'm sure finding Bob like that was terrifying."

Cindy shivered visibly. "It was the worst thing ever."

Rita continued, "I thought you might be able to tell me something new, maybe something you may have forgotten to mention to the police when you gave your first statement. You were probably upset that morning. Maybe since then you've remembered…"

She didn't have a chance to finish her sentence before the other woman jumped up, scooped the dog out of the bed, and bolted toward the door, unlocking it and raising the blind with a loud snap. She looked up and down the sidewalks and then turned to Rita. "I said no. There's nothing else to remember, and I can't get involved in this. I'm sorry, but I need you to go, please, and don't come back here again."

Rita got up to leave and walked slowly toward the doorway. She hated to go before she could find out what frightened the woman so badly. "I'm not trying to force you into anything, and I'm sorry to have upset you." She pushed further. "Please, tell me what you're so afraid of. Has someone threatened you, Cindy? Do you know something that could put you in danger? Do you need help?"

The other woman shot her a terrified look and barreled toward her. "Please, just leave. Whoever killed Bob could be watching." She pushed Rita's shoulder with her free hand, nearly shoving her out the door and onto the sidewalk. "You want answers? Go to Watson's place. Be careful, though. That's all I'm saying."

She slammed the door, locked it, and switched the 'open' sign to 'closed' before pulling down the blind again and disappearing behind it.

Rita stood for a moment, stunned by the woman's remarks. What did she know about the murder? Why was she so afraid? She'd panicked so suddenly. Had she seen someone outside the salon? Rita looked up and down the street but saw only two passing cars and no one walking on either side. For a moment, she considered waiting for her to come outside, but then gave up and walked across the street, got into her Jeep, and drove away.

A black Toyota pulled out behind the Jeep and merged into the late afternoon traffic. The driver dialed his phone, and the call was answered on the second ring. There was static on the line.

"Now what?"

"I've been keeping tabs on Cindy for a while," he said. "Today, I got lucky. She had a visitor after hours, and it wasn't a customer in need of a dye job."

"Who? Tell me. We're in the middle of a thunderstorm and the power has been out for two hours. It's hot as hell here now, and I don't have the time or the patience for guessing games."

The driver chuckled. "Right now, I'm not in the mood for games myself. It was that reporter from *The Journal*, the red-head, you know, the one that was all over the news when she helped to save the little girl that got kidnapped a couple years back. Rita Locke. Anyway, they were alone in there for a while. Who knows what Cindy told her."

"Oh great, a reporter is just what we need right now. I know who she is, the nosy bitch."

The driver exhaled loudly. "Don't worry about it. I'm following her now. Hopefully she's on her way home so I can get a read on where she lives, see what her neighborhood looks like. Might come in handy later."

There was no response for a moment or two, but then, "Go ahead and check it out, but other than that I'm not sure. Messing with her could attract too much attention, and attention is something we don't need right now, or ever, for that matter."

"Okay, but what about Cindy?"

"This is *your* deal, not mine. It's up to you, and I don't want any part of it."

"Got it."

At that, the call ended with a faint click.

CHAPTER THREE

Rita drove to the Mason-Watson Funeral Home and parked her Jeep at the curb in front of a sleek black hearse. An older gentleman in a charcoal coat with a red carnation tucked into his lapel greeted her with a smile and a friendly wave. He looked to be at least eighty. She noticed that he wore white gloves, something that made her smile and wave in return.

"If you're going on to the cemetery after the service, please pull around to the back lot, and we'll get your car into the lineup," he said. "You're a little early, though. The family hasn't arrived yet."

She gulped. Good lord, it never occurred to her that she might be crashing a funeral. Rotten luck, but too late to turn back now. "No, sir. I'm so sorry, but I'm not here for that. I'd hoped to be able to speak to Mrs. Watson for a few minutes. Is she available?"

He checked his watch and waved his hand toward the front door. "She's in the office, just to the right of the entry hall. You can try, but I don't imagine she'll have much time. It's almost eight forty-five, and the family should be here by nine for the final viewing and service."

She nodded and went up the steps past the stone lions and through the wide oak double doors leading into the mansion. Faint chimes rang out as she stepped inside the hallway, where she glanced up at the staircase lined with fresh floral wallpaper that appeared a shade brighter than the matching covering on the opposite wall. It made sense, given Carr's vivid description of the murder scene. Almost immediately, the cloying fragrance of aging flowers mixed with the lemony scent of furniture polish and burning wood filled her lungs, so she moved toward the open doorway leading to the office. She tapped on the door frame.

"Hello, Mrs. Watson?"

A slim woman, dressed in a tailored black pantsuit, rose from her chair behind the desk and crossed the room warmed by the heat of a roaring fire. She smoothed her blonde hair, so light it appeared almost white, and smiled at Rita as she motioned for her to come in. "Yes, may I help you? Are you here for the service?"

Rita shook her head and smiled. Her timing couldn't have been worse. "No, ma'am, I'm sorry, but I didn't check to see whether you had a funeral today. I'm Rita Locke from *The Journal*, and I wondered if you might have a few minutes to talk to me. I'm working on a story in connection with your husband's death. And please, accept my sympathy for your loss."

The smile, plastered so expertly on Amie Watson's lips, disappeared. Her back straightened, and she glanced at the floor for a few seconds before meeting Rita's gaze. "Thank you, but no. I'm not going to talk about it. Really, I have nothing to say. Please, you must leave. I have a family coming in for a funeral soon, and you can't stay for that."

Rita stalled, unwilling to back down and leave empty-handed. Service or no service, she was a reporter working on a story, and she needed information. "Perhaps another time? Amie, your husband was a respected member of the community, and I'd like to do a story, maybe a feature, on how you're taking over the business and running it in his absence." She made a last-ditch effort. "People may think you're shutting things down without him, so this would be a chance for you to talk about your plans regarding the business."

Amie clasped her hands and looked around the room. Her voice didn't rise above a whisper. "God, I hope people realize we're staying open. I can't go out of business. I need this for my son." Her eyes brimmed with tears.

"Tell me about him," Rita prompted. "I gather he has some problems?"

"He's on the autism spectrum and had been largely non-verbal until about two years ago. He goes to a school across the state and is finally making progress, so I can't chance pulling him out now or he could regress."

Rita shook her head. "I can't imagine how much you might be worried about him. That's a lot for you to handle alone, isn't it?

Amie continued, "Yes, it's a bit daunting. I never finished college and haven't worked anywhere since Bob and I married fifteen years ago. I'm not a licensed funeral director, so I have my older brother, Daniel Mason, and my husband's friend, James Foster, helping me to stay open."

Rita spoke softly, "Oh, I see, so your late father and your brother represent the 'Mason' in your business name?"

Amie dabbed at the corners of her eyes with a handkerchief pulled from her jacket pocket. "Daniel, my sister, and I inherited the business from our father, but I had no interest in becoming licensed. Believe me, I'm better at handling families and visitations than dealing with bodies. My sister went to nursing school and didn't want any part of it at all, so Bob bought her share to give us two-thirds ownership of it when we got married. Daniel still owns a third, but he has another location in Washington County that he operates himself." She explained that although her brother had been helping her to understand the paperwork, he didn't have time to do the embalming.

Rita scribbled a few notes. "So, James is helping with that?"

Amie nodded. "Yes, thank God. He and Bob were best friends in mortuary school. He's made himself available whenever I need him even though he's busy with his own funeral home in Butler County. We've been working things out, but it's overwhelming."

Rita looked at the pile of file folders stacked on the cluttered desk not twenty steps from the hallway. *Every time she sits down at that desk, she faces the spot where her husband's body landed. It's no wonder she's nervous.* "I admire you for what you're doing. It can't be easy for you to be here after what happened."

Amie sighed. "I grew up in the apartment upstairs, so this is the only home I've ever known." She glanced toward the hall. "I'm not squeamish, but no, it isn't easy at all. That said, I need to keep the place going to support my son."

She looked around the office, her eyes lingering on the embers which had fallen below the fireplace grate and glowed red on the hearth. When the clock in the hall began to chime the nine o'clock hour, her eyebrows creased into a frown before she squared her shoulders and looked directly into Rita's eyes. "Okay, I'll talk to you, but not right away. I'm leaving tomorrow morning, and I won't be back for a few weeks. I need a little break from all of this, so my sister is taking me on a vacation. If you can wait until I get back, I'll do it."

Rita didn't want to wait, and really had no patience for it, but realized she had no choice. It was already near the end of February, so she threw out a date, hoping it would work.

"Great. How about March seventeenth? Will you be back by then?"

Before Amie could answer, there was a sharp knock on the

open door. A stocky man with ruddy cheeks walked into the room and stood between them with his back to Rita. "Excuse me, Amie? It's getting late, and I need to go over some things with you before the family arrives."

Amie nodded and gestured toward Rita. "This is my brother, Daniel Mason. Daniel, this is Rita Locke. She wants to do a story for the newspaper about how I'm keeping the business going without Bob to show people that we're still here." She lowered her eyes again.

He reached out to shake Rita's hand, holding it firmly for a few seconds too long as he stared into her eyes. Discomfited, she smiled but pulled away from his strong grip.

He said, "Miss Locke, it's nice to meet you. I've read many of your stories, and of course I was captivated by the drama surrounding that little girl's kidnapping a few years ago. You do very fine work, although I must say I can't imagine after such a sensational killing of a prominent businessman with no suspects, that a single news story will do much to dissuade people from taking their business elsewhere."

Something about him standing so close to her made Rita uncomfortable. She took a slight step backward. "Well, Mr. Mason, I'm not sure what it can or can't do. What I do know is that your brother-in-law was a respected member of the Unity Township business community, and people will be interested to see that everything he built here is going to continue. It'll be more of a feature story than anything else."

He smiled and shrugged his broad shoulders. "Whatever you say. You're the expert, Miss Locke. Not me. Now, if you'll excuse us so we can get to the morning's work?"

He strode out of the room and Amie moved closer to the doorway. "He's right, Rita, I have things to do now, and I don't want to leave everything for him." She looked up and down the hall. "He, uh, struggles a bit with PTSD."

"He's a veteran?"

Aimee nodded. "Yes, he served in the Army during the Persian Gulf War. Some days, he has a pretty short fuse, and I don't like to load him up with too much. I'll call you when I get back to set a time. You must understand, though, that I never know when we're going to have a visitation or service, so you'll have to be flexible."

Rita agreed without hesitation. "Oh, of course, thanks so much. I hope you get the rest you need." She heard the main entrance door open and voices in the hallway, so she turned to leave, but stopped short of going out the door. "If you don't mind, do you have a restroom I could use before I go? You know, too much tea this morning, and it'll take me at least forty minutes to get back to my office downtown."

The other woman motioned toward the rear of the corridor. "Yes, down the hall, first door past the stairs. You'll have to excuse me now so Daniel and I can meet with the family to go over some last-minute details for the service and open the visitation room for them. James is around here somewhere, but I have only one greeter this morning, and he's outside."

"Absolutely. I'll see myself out," Rita said. She followed the other woman into the hall and walked slowly to the ladies' restroom. She waited a few minutes, then poked her head out of the door to make sure that the hall was empty and the doors to the visitation room had been closed for the service. Hopefully, Amie and her brother were inside. Although she didn't know what she was looking for, this was her chance to poke around a bit undetected.

She crept down the hallway toward the back of the mansion, peering into two more lavishly decorated visitation rooms. A tiny kitchen held an apartment-sized refrigerator next to a counter with a microwave, a coffee maker, and a metal rack stocked with cups, tea bags, and packets of sugar and dry creamer. She kept going until she reached a door at the end of the hall, glancing backward twice to see if she remained alone. When she tried the knob, the door swung open, its hinges creaking. She stepped into a large room that could have functioned as a ballroom in the mansion's early days. It was dark, lit only by daylight filtering through two stained-glass windows, but once inside, she could make out three rows of coffins in the middle of the room below a row of three crystal chandeliers. A shiver traveled from her hairline down her spine as she mentally counted nine in the center and a dozen more that lined three walls.

Get a grip. They're nothing but empty boxes.

The coffins sat open, exposing lavish tufted linings and lace-trimmed pillows of soft velvet, crepe, and satin in delicate shades of white and cream. Fascinated, she ran her hand along the cool length of an ornate silver coffin with mirrored corners opposite a sleek one in steel blue and another in deep tones of carved wood. She walked between the rows, marveling at the variety of choices, morbidly wondering which she'd pick for herself. The mirrored one, with a white satin lining, she decided. Why not go out in style?

"What are you doing in here? Is there something I can help you with?"

Startled, she jumped when she heard the man's booming voice from behind her. Wheeling around, she turned to face the door, where a tall man in a dark blue suit stood glaring at her. "Oh, um, yes, I um, used the restroom, and I got turned around as I was trying to leave," she stammered, borrowing her excuse for snooping from David's recollection about his encounter with Watson. "I thought I'd come through this way, but I was mistaken. I, um, I've never seen a room like this."

His face softened a bit, and a slight smile creased his jawline. He was extraordinarily handsome, with hazel eyes, thick dark hair, and wide shoulders that filled out his suit perfectly, making her stomach flutter. "Yes, quite mistaken, I'd say. If you're looking for the main door, it's behind me at the end of the *front* of the hall. I'm sure you can see that this room is for storage of the products we sell, and there's no reason for you to be in here."

She nodded. "Oh, yes, so sorry, Mr....?"

"Foster. James Foster. And you are?"

She offered her hand, but he did not shake it. "Rita Locke from *The Journal*. I stopped in to talk to Mrs. Watson about a feature story on her business. She told me you're working with her."

The kindness in his smile faded into a deep frown and his jaw tensed. "Yes, she needs the services of a licensed funeral director to maintain the business legally since the... sudden death of her husband."

"So, you're working here, then?" she asked. "Amie suggested she'd be lost without you."

He blushed. "Yes, temporarily, but only when her brother can't make it, or when they have more than one service. At least until they can find someone locally to step in and take over. It's only been a few weeks since—"

Rita looked into his eyes when he stopped talking. "She's very lucky to have you for a friend."

He looked beyond her, focusing his gaze on the coffins. "Bob and I were very close, and I'd do anything for her, anything at all," he said, speaking in hushed tones. He raised his hand and gestured toward the door. "And now, I must ask you to leave. We're very busy this morning with a service and two viewings later, and you shouldn't be in here."

He stepped aside as she moved away from the coffins and

through the doorway. Without another word, he followed her out of the room and closed the door firmly behind him. She retraced her steps, past the kitchenette and visitation rooms and the front office, with him on her heels. When they reached the front entrance, he held the door for her and waved her out onto the wide porch.

She stepped outside and was turning around to thank him when he slammed the door in her face without another word.

Thrown out into the street twice in two days. Something was going on here that no one wanted to talk about. They were hiding something.

CHAPTER FOUR

The week after Rita's visit to the funeral home, the newsroom secretary tossed a padded envelope onto her desk as she sat reading wire service copy online. Police hadn't released anything new on the murder, and the court calendar was slow, so she was bored and killing time by searching for potential feature story ideas. When the envelope landed next to her keyboard, she jumped, startled.

"What's this?" Rita asked.

"It was too big to fit into your mail slot. Fan mail from one of your haters, I'm sure," the secretary joked before walking away. Over her shoulder, she added, "You know it's never a good thing when there's no return address, Red. Make sure it's not ticking."

Rita sliced open the envelope, noting the Pittsburgh postmark from three days earlier, and pulled out a single sheet of paper wrapped around a large metal key. Typed on the paper was a single sentence: "If anything happens to me, take this to the bank on the corner nearest the courthouse in Westmoreland County, and then go to the police."

Nothing else. No signature. No clue as to who sent it or why. She examined the key and saw that it was engraved on one side with the number 1951, and with the words 'Do Not Duplicate' on the other. She'd seen one like it several years before when helping her mother to clean out her grandmother's house after her death, and assumed it was for a bank safety deposit box. She knew the bank from a story she'd done when armed robbers held it up several years before.

"Get a load of this, Tom," she said. She pushed her chair back, got up, and walked over to her editor's desk. "Someone is playing secret spy games with me." She showed him the key and the note. "Looks like it's for a safety deposit box. Why is it that every crackpot in this city thinks I'm the person to solve the world's problems and fight the forces of evil? How am I supposed to know who sent this?"

He threw his head back and laughed. "You mean you're not? All you need now is a magic decoder ring, Red, and you'll be set. You're right, it's probably from one of your multitudes of nutty fans. You going to check it out?"

She looked at the clock and shook her head. It was after three o'clock. Things in the newsroom might be slow, but she wasn't bored enough to fall for the whole cloak and dagger bit and go rushing out the door to race into a bank just before closing time.

"Of course, I'm going to check it out, but it's too late today. Anyway, with my luck, if this key *would* open a safety deposit box, I guarantee you there's a dead mouse or snake or something equally disgusting in it. It'll keep overnight." She returned to her desk, shoved the key and the note back into the envelope, and tossed it into the top drawer where it landed on a jumble of notebooks and forgotten ketchup packets from too many lunches wolfed down at her desk. She turned back to her computer and was reading through her notes for a story on an upcoming homicide trial when two other reporters and three photographers began to gather near the door to the conference room.

Tom wheeled his chair around, stood up, and then bent over to stretch his back and legs. He straightened up and groaned when his left knee made a cracking sound. "You ready for the meeting?" he asked.

She looked up. "Meeting?"

He leaned over her desk and slapped her laptop closed. "Yessss, the one to discuss plans for the president's visit tomorrow. Or don't you read your emails? You've got the speech coverage. Andy has the airport arrival and departure, and Pete is doing opposition party reaction to whatever the president announces. As always, if anything happens and things go south, you're all on it together. This guy isn't the most popular around here, you know, and there are plenty of nuts out there who might want to cause a problem."

She reached for her can of Diet Coke and sighed, remembering an email from two days before about her upcoming assignment. She knew the protocol: speech coverage meant she should arrive at the convention center in Pittsburgh two hours before the president's arrival, submit to a search of her person and belongings by Secret Service, and then wait in a cordoned-off press area for what would feel like an eternity to hear a rambling speech full of promises about fixing the economy or some other hot-button topic of the day. Sometimes being the senior reporter on staff was more of a headache than an honor because she didn't relish the thought of covering events like this at all. She'd much rather be at a crime scene or in a courtroom, and she knew from sixteen years of experience that every sitting president, as always and no matter his political party affiliation, would be running behind schedule, she'd be starving for lunch, and without a doubt her bladder would be full. *Forget asking the Secret Service to use the restroom because once you're held captive in their pen, there's no getting out until the POTUS is gone.* She sighed and rose from her chair to join the group, but as she walked away from her desk, her phone rang. She answered it on the second ring, waving to Tom, who pointed his finger and glared at her as he closed the conference room door. She understood that she'd better make this quick.

"Rita, hey, I got your message the other day, but this is the first opportunity I've had to call you."

She broke into a wide smile and tossed her long red curls as she plopped back down into her chair and rocked backward. "George Carr, I swear you have perfect timing, and I'm forever grateful for your call, no matter when it is. You're now officially my favorite state police lieutenant because you've saved me from attending a boring meeting to discuss political coverage. If your wife ever dumps you, let me know."

"Fat chance. She's got her eye on my retirement checks already, even though it's two years away," he joked. "I figured you'd be busy planning for the presidential hoopla tomorrow, so what's up? Why'd you call?"

She told him about her visit to the funeral home and how Foster acted when he caught her snooping.

He groaned. Sometimes, he sounded too much like her father. "You know damn well we've interviewed everyone and picked that place clean already in our investigation and we came up with nothing. Tell me, exactly what were you looking for?"

She exhaled deeply and hesitated as she tried to find a reasonable explanation for doubting the investigators' findings, but she had nothing other than her own nagging intuition. "Truthfully, I have no idea. I've had a hunch that they're hiding something there. Anyway, there's nothing going on anywhere, other than the president tomorrow, so I wondered if there's anything new in the investigation. Help a girl out in a slow news week. You got anything for me?"

"Nope. Wish I did. However, I will tell you that I think you've got it wrong this time. Amie wasn't home when her husband was killed, so she saw nothing and knows nothing, particularly about their business, from what we've been able to determine."

She fished for more. "Money problems?"

"Nope, not that we can find. Apparently, Bob handled their money and paid the bills, leaving the kid and the household duties to her. We checked out their finances, and although they weren't making tons of money on funerals, there's no unreasonable debt. They got into a mess with credit cards a few years back, but everything has been paid in full."

There must be something.

"What about insurance?"

"Bob's insurance coverage wasn't anything out of the ordinary. It surprised me a little, because of the nature of his work, but actually he had a ridiculously small policy on himself."

He told her the widow would collect just a little over fifty thousand dollars from the claim, not enough to go very far or last very long.

She was shocked. "Well, that tells me she didn't hire anyone to kill him for cash."

"Nope. So far, we haven't found anything at all to cast suspicion on her brother or the other guy…Foster, isn't it? Looks like they all got along and worked together very well."

She huffed. "Yeah, James Foster. Easy on the eyes, but he's rude as hell. He all but pushed me out the door like he couldn't wait to get rid of me. I was only looking around, but he made it very clear that he was pissed when I stumbled into the coffin room where, I might add, I found a gorgeous mirrored one that I liked for future use."

"Good grief! Don't tell me you've picked out your coffin. You're not even forty yet, are you? I have more than twenty-five years on you. Red, seriously, let us do the detective work, okay? When we know something, you'll know." He blew out a deep breath and then spoke quietly. "Watson is planted six feet under right now because he apparently made someone mad enough to kill him with his own gun. Remember that because I don't want you to put that fancy box to use anytime soon. Until we make an arrest, whoever killed him is still out there."

Rita had no time the following day to think about her conversation with Carr or the safety deposit key because the president, true to form, was running more than an hour behind schedule for his mid-afternoon visit to Pittsburgh. By the time she listened to his speech on his administration's plans to address the nation's struggling economy, choked down a late lunch, and finished her story, it was nearly eight o'clock and she'd been working for twelve hours. She logged off her computer, grabbed her coat and keys, and drove straight home, where she soaked in a bubble bath before collapsing on her bed just before ten.

Three hours later, she sat straight up in bed, angry at herself for not pushing Cindy Ekas further into revealing what she knew. She resolved to dig a little deeper, prod more. She lay back down, her head sinking into the soft down of her pillow as her mind raced with questions. She glanced at the clock. Three-thirty.

Morning couldn't come soon enough.

Fumes from permanent wave solution assaulted Rita's nose again as soon as she stepped into the salon where Cindy stood behind her stylist's chair, winding an elderly woman's gray strands around small rollers. She looked toward the door and frowned but continued to work.

"I like them tight, honey," the woman said, smiling at the hairdresser's reflection in the mirror.

"I know, Mrs. Walters. You tell me this every time we do a perm, and don't I always manage to do exactly what you want?"

She turned away from her client and motioned to Rita. "I can't talk here, but if you wait until I'm done, I can meet you in the back." She gestured toward the back of the room, where a desk held a computer, two bowls of assorted candies, and a display of nail polish bottles.

Rita nodded and moved toward a chair in front of the desk, stopping on the way to pick up a magazine from a dusty metal rack bolted to the wall. She'd finished one article about flea market furniture makeovers and was starting on a second about inexpensive gardening plans when Cindy led her customer to a floor dryer, settled her in the chair, and turned on the heat. She joined Rita at the desk.

"Miss Locke, I told you I don't have anything else to say," she whispered. "You can't just show up here and think I can talk when I have customers to take care of."

Rita leaned forward. "Call me Rita, please. I'm sorry to barge in on you like this Cindy, because I know you're upset, but I think there's something you're afraid to tell me. Something you're hiding. Let me help you."

Cindy met her eyes but shook her head in refusal while twisting a silver filigree band around and around her right ring finger.

"All I can tell you is that it's not for me to talk about. I don't feel safe, and I won't until whoever killed Bob is behind bars," she whispered, glancing toward her customer, who appeared to have dozed off while listening to the hum of the dryer.

Rita touched her arm. "Who are you afraid of?"

When the woman didn't respond, Rita changed the subject. "Okay, tell me about your work at the funeral home. What was it like to work for Bob?"

Cindy broke into a wide smile at the memory. "He was kind. I liked him and I enjoyed working there, so much so that I haven't been able to bring myself to go back since he died. I miss him."

She glanced toward the woman under the dryer. "For one thing, nobody complained if they didn't like the way I did their hair," she said. "Oh, that sounded bad, didn't it? Seriously, I was honored to help families who trusted me with their loved ones."

Rita chuckled. "There's nothing wrong with a little humor to lighten things up. Reporters do it all the time. If we didn't, we'd be crushed by some of the awful things we see on a daily basis."

Cindy smiled and nodded her head. Her posture gave Rita the impression that she was becoming more relaxed. A quick glance told her the elderly woman had fallen asleep. Time to go for broke.

Rita leaned toward Cindy and stared directly into her eyes. "Let me just spill it out. I think you're holding back the truth. I'm not calling you a liar, but I feel as though there's a lot you're not saying. Tell me, do you know who killed Bob?"

The hairdresser looked at her hands in her lap. She didn't answer.

Rita continued, "I think you know, and it's not going to serve any good purpose by staying silent. If you won't talk to me, call Lieutenant Carr. He's a good man. Let someone help you."

A single tear trickled down the hairdresser's face and she brushed it from her cheek. "Please, leave. There's nothing I can say."

Rita nodded and turned to go but changed her mind. She pushed further. "I will, but before I go, I need to know if you sent me something, a safety deposit box key? I got a letter in the mail the other day with a key and a note inside telling me to go to the bank and to the police if whoever sent it was harmed. Did you send it? Does it have anything to do with Watson's?"

Cindy's head snapped up, but she said nothing. Her silence spoke volumes. Rita knew it had to have been her.

"Cindy, I want you to know that I'm going to the bank on Monday to use it. Is there anything you want to say before I go? Anything you'd like to explain? Tell me what you're afraid of. Is someone threatening you?"

The other woman let out a deep sigh and then stood and walked away. When she reached her sleeping customer, she shook the woman's shoulder gently and said, "C'mon Mrs. Walters. Let's get you rinsed out and styled. Your son will be here to pick you up soon."

Rita scribbled George Carr's cell phone number on her own business card and left it on the desk on her way out the door, hoping that Cindy would gather enough courage to use it.

CHAPTER FIVE

After an uneventful weekend with no calls from David, Rita spent the next four days covering a murder trial in Allegheny County for another reporter who had to undergo an emergency appendectomy. Missing David, she welcomed the opportunity to keep busy, but the long days in court meant she never had the chance to slip out early enough to get to the bank and delve into the safety deposit box. The trial ended late Thursday night with the jury's ultimate guilty verdict, so she planned to satisfy her curiosity and head to the bank early the following morning.

Tired and over-stimulated from the trial's dramatic conclusion, she tossed and turned for hours, finally drifting off just before dawn. She'd been out for an hour when her phone rang, startling her from a deep sleep. Groggy, she answered on the fourth ring and groaned when she heard her editor's voice.

"Geez, Red. You sound awful."

"This better be good, Tom," she said, squinting to look at her bedside clock. "It's not even seven thirty, and I'm not due in until ten."

He hesitated for a few seconds before answering. "Well, I thought maybe you'd like to know there's been an explosion and fire in..."

She cut him off. "You called me after I put in a twelve-hour day to tell me about a *fire*? It's been years since I covered spot news, or have you forgotten?"

"Hold on a minute, cranky. This one may interest you. Turn on the local news."

She fumbled around on her nightstand, grabbed her remote and clicked it on. When she could focus clearly, she saw a familiar Pittsburgh television reporter doing a live broadcast in front of a pile of rubble, with the shells of several burning buildings in the distance. "Okay, Tom, what am I looking at?"

"Jesus, Red, wake up, would you? Look closer before they move to another shot. Down to the bottom left. Look at the sign."

She scanned the screen. Bricks and charred debris littered the sidewalk and street, where the jagged remains of a storefront sign lay in a puddle of water and muck. She could make out the blackened letters "***url Up and Dy***," but the rest of the sign had been charred black. The ticker at the bottom of the screen read *Fatal blaze in Westmoreland County.*

She gasped. "Curl Up and Dye! Holy crap, that's Cindy Ekas' salon. What the hell happened?" Then the words on the screen sank in. "Wait a minute. Did they say fatal?"

"They pulled a woman's body from the rubble near the front door of the salon. Andy's down there now. He called me about ten minutes ago and said state police are saying it was some type of explosion overnight."

She scrambled out from beneath her comforter and headed to her closet for a clean pair of jeans. "I'm going over there. I'll call Cindy on my way in. Maybe I can…"

Tom cleared his throat and interrupted her mid-sentence. "Red, wait. Off the record, of course, but one of Andy's police sources says she had a purse, you know, one of those little across your body things that the young girl in features always wears, still strapped onto her shoulder. They checked the wallet inside and found Cindy's license and registration. The car parked in front was badly damaged, but cops told him it's registered in her name, too. Of course, there's nothing concrete yet, until the coroner says so, but it sure sounds like it's her."

Rita's stomach turned. The explosion and fire were no accident.

This was murder.

"Tom, someone did this to her. I know it. She knew something about Bob Watson's killing, and she was terrified that someone, although I don't know who, would find out."

He sighed and blew out a deep breath. "Red, I knew you were going to launch into this, but don't go jumping to conclusions. You don't know what caused this mess. It could have been something as simple as bad wiring, or a gas leak, or a paint can next to an old furnace. The buildings on that street are ancient."

"Well, then explain why she'd be there at the very moment in the middle of the night on the particular night that something would level the place. Give me one good reason. It's not like women wake up at three a.m. and suddenly need their gray roots done or their eyebrows waxed. There's no good explanation as to why she'd be there at that hour. I'm telling you, there's more to this."

He let out another long sigh. "I hate to admit it, but okay, you got me on that one. Go ahead down there and meet up with Andy, see what he needs, see what you can find out to give him a hand. Just don't go off spouting conspiracy theories until we get confirmation on what happened. For God's sake, don't put yourself in the position to get us sued."

Forty-five minutes later she was standing near the spot where the TV reporter had given the morning broadcast. Still in disbelief, her knees shook when she noticed the coroner's van parked at the end of the block and saw her friend and source, the coroner's aide Vince Rogers, taking photos of the rubble behind the yellow caution tape. He raised his hand and waved to her but said nothing before continuing his work. She was scribbling a description of the scene into her notebook when a familiar voice boomed behind her, "Hey, Red. Haven't seen you at a scene like this for ages. How are you?"

She turned to see a state trooper, Tyler Anthony, stepping across a fire hose to greet her. "Hey, Tyler. It's been too long. Seriously, you haven't been in court forever. How's the family?" She reached out to shake his hand and noticed a dark ball of shaking fur tucked under his arm.

Her heart broke when she recognized Cindy's dog. "Oh no, Boomer." She reached over to let the little dog lick her fingertips. "Tyler, is he hurt?"

He met her eyes. "You know this dog? I found him wandering around by my patrol car a few minutes ago."

She nodded. "I was in the salon recently to talk to the owner, Cindy Ekas. This is her dog."

"He seems to be limping a little, and some of his fur looks singed around his tail and the back of his neck by his collar, but I think he's okay." He shot a look at the coroner's van and scratched the shivering dog's ears as he cradled him close to his jacket. "Poor little guy. You know any of her family? Someone I could call?"

She shook her head and relayed what Cindy told her. "Not that we shared much personal information, but she didn't mention dating anyone, either."

He looked up to the sky and groaned. "That's just great, and of course, he comes right over to me. What am I supposed to do with him? I can't leave him here. You know how overcrowded those shelters are, even if I could find one willing to take him."

"Oh, this is so sad," she said, petting the dog's head. "I bet your kids would love him."

"Whoa, I can't take him. My wife is allergic to everything, and she'd kill me if I brought him home, cute or not, because my kids have been begging for a puppy for ages, and we'd never hear the end of it if they couldn't keep him. As it is, I'll probably send her into a sneezing fit when she gets a whiff of my jacket."

Deep down, she knew better, but reached out and took the quivering dog from him. Mentally, she ticked off reasons why this was such a bad idea. She'd never had a pet, couldn't keep a spider plant or a Christmas poinsettia alive longer than a month, and worked more hours than she ever spent at home. Years ago, she'd lost trust in her ability to take care of anything. The past few weeks and her failed relationship with David just reinforced those feelings.

She squeezed her eyes shut, recalling the darkest time in her life. Her chest still hurt when she thought about it. Just before her thirtieth birthday, she learned she was pregnant with her boyfriend's child not long after they'd ended their relationship. When she experienced some spotting, her doctor warned her to tell her editors she needed to rest if there was any hope of bringing the pregnancy to term. She refused, rationalizing that she could manage alone, so she told no one she was pregnant, not even the baby's father. One frigid evening, she fell on an icy sidewalk while on assignment and lost her baby.

Because she'd put her job above her health, she blamed her ambition for the loss of her child. She'd lived alone all her adult life without any responsibility to anyone or anything other than herself, and in her mind, her decision to ignore her doctor's advice confirmed she should stay that way. Although caring for a pet wasn't even close to having a child, she doubted her abilities. Still, she couldn't bear to see the poor little dog tossed into a shelter, so her heart won the battle against her common sense.

"Oh, crap. I'm probably going to regret saying this but leave him with me. It would be too cruel for him to lose his owner *and* get left at a shelter all in the same day. I'll think of something. Maybe I can find someone to take him," she mumbled. She opened her jacket and pulled the dog close to her chest. He whimpered, nuzzling into her neck, and she looked down as he reached up to lick her face. And just like that, she was hooked.

For pity's sake. I guess I have a dog now.

Two hours and nearly four hundred dollars later, after a trip to a walk-in veterinary clinic and a pet store with self-serve washing stations, a clean, healthy, and exhausted Boomer lay sleeping in a fluffy bed under Rita's desk. His charred collar had been replaced with a bright red one that matched the leash and harness tucked into her nearby satchel that lay next to a shopping bag filled with small breed food, a ball, an assortment of tiny chew toys, stainless steel food and water bowls, and a red blanket covered in black pawprints. Hoping to avoid ridicule, she'd left his new Pittsburgh Steelers sweater and red plaid pajamas in her Jeep. Although the newsroom staff had swarmed around him, she knew her coworkers would be merciless in their teasing if they saw Boomer's new clothes.

Deep down, though, she didn't care what they thought. She had no child of her own, no nieces or nephews to spoil with toys and gifts, so she couldn't help herself. She'd fallen in love just as Cindy described.

"What are you going to do with a dog?" Tom whispered as he crouched down and peered under her desk. He rubbed the little dog's ears. "You don't know anything about taking care of an animal, do you?"

She winced. "No, but I'm not a total imbecile. How hard can it be? If I don't know something, I'll look it up online. Tonight, I'm going to arrange doggie daycare or boarding or a dog sitter for long days when I'm really busy."

"Okay, don't get all huffy," he said.

She rolled her eyes. "I'm not, but how about we shift our focus to news now, okay? Someone deliberately blew up Cindy's salon with her in it, and while they were at it, destroyed two adjoining businesses and her car parked along the street. You know it, and I know it."

He patted the dog's head once more before he stood up. "Probably. But we can't print it yet, not until we get the reports from the coroner's office and the fire marshal."

"I know that. However, that doesn't change my mind because when I went to talk to Cindy, she was desperate to keep her name out of the Watson investigation and acted as though if she talked to me, she'd wind up dead."

She looked down at her hands. Her voice came in a whisper. "And now, she's dead, so there's that."

He shot her a warning look.

"Stop it. Geez Red, I know you're blaming yourself, but it's not your fault."

"Whatever," she mumbled as she wheeled her chair closer to her desk, careful to avoid the sleeping dog. Although she made several calls throughout the day to the coroner and the state police fire marshal, she ended up letting her colleague, Andy, write the story because it would be days before officials confirmed autopsy findings or the cause of the explosion. She typed up and emailed her notes to him. At the end of her shift, she gathered Boomer and his new belongings from beneath her desk to go home.

She'd started to walk out of the newsroom when she remembered the key in her drawer and froze in place. She turned and went back to her desk, pulled open the drawer, and scooped it up. If only she had found the time to use it sooner.

It all added up. Something had happened to someone she knew, someone who had been terrified. The explosion convinced her that it had to have been sent by Cindy. If not her, who else?

She shook her head, angry at herself, and slipped the key into the side pocket of her satchel. It was too late in the day to go now, but her first stop tomorrow would be the bank.

That's the only way to find out what's in the box and why she sent the key to me. There's the million-dollar question, though. Cindy warned me to be careful. Do I really want to open Pandora's box?

CHAPTER SIX

Rita went into the bank, her heels clicking on the ivory marble floor as she walked to the office doorway opposite the row of windows where tellers waited on customers. When the young woman behind the desk inside looked up, Rita asked, "Excuse me, but is there someone I could see about opening a safety deposit box?"

The woman stood, nodding as she came around to the front of her desk. "I'm Jamie. I can help you. I normally take new account applications, but we're a little shorthanded this morning, so give me a few minutes, and I'll take you back. Please, have a seat." She pointed to two chairs outside her door and walked to another doorway just past the bank of tellers before disappearing inside.

Rita looked around the massive room, admiring the painted frescoes above her on the ceiling from which were suspended two rows of gilded chandeliers dripping with crystals. This was not a typical modern strip mall bank of plasterboard cubicles with a drive-through lane and an automatic teller machine. No, this building stood tribute to days gone by, of carved wood and old money. She inhaled the familiar scents of musty paper, ink, and dust, recalling a similar bank building near her grandmother's home that she'd visited often as a child. Closing her eyes, she let her mind wander and remembered that her eight-year-old self once believed the bank to be a rich, magical place where Grandma stopped to get money when they were on their way to buy toys and ice cream on one of their shopping days together.

A few moments later, the young woman came back out and motioned for Rita to join her at the end of a hallway at the rear of the lobby. They walked together, exchanging small talk about the weather, until they came to a large room opposite the round entrance to the vault.

"What's the number?" Jamie asked.

Rita pulled out the key. It stuck to her sweaty palm as she read the number aloud, "1951." When the woman held out a clipboard, Rita scribbled her name and the date on a registry sheet. She held her breath, waiting to be turned away, or worse, for the young woman to alert a manager that she was trying to access someone else's property.

Instead, she nodded to Rita and moved to the center of the room lined on three sides with rows of recessed metal boxes. She stooped down, pulled out the box with the number corresponding to the key and handed it to Rita. "You can take it into one of the private booths to open it," she said, smiling as she pointed to four tiny spaces with open doors along the fourth wall. "When you're finished, come and get me, and I will put it back for you."

"Thanks Jamie, I'm sure I won't be long." Rita chose a cubicle and set her satchel and the box on a small wooden table before closing the door. Her heart pounded with a mix of anticipation and fear. Someone, in all probability Cindy, trusted her to see the contents of the box and to know what to do with whatever she found. She dug down into the bottom of her satchel, pulled out her leather gloves and tugged them over her sweating palms. *Sometimes, it helps to think like a criminal. All those years cov-*

ering court have finally paid off because no matter what I find in there, I surely don't want my fingerprints on it. Finally ready, she sat down in the straight-backed chair, leaned toward the table, and gripped the key with a shaking hand. When it turned in the lock, she heard a faint click.

She put down the key and slowly lifted the lid, bracing herself for the contents that ultimately left her speechless.

The padded box held piles of jewelry. Gold, silver, diamonds. At least two dozen rings, several pendants, chains, and at least six watches, each held in clear plastic sandwich bags, filled the box that contained a single sheet of plain white paper on which someone had printed in block letters Mason-Watson.

Had Cindy stolen the jewelry or witnessed the theft? The murder? Could she have identified the killer? Was Bob Watson a criminal or a victim? Or both?

With questions racing in her mind, she scooped the plastic bags out of the box and tossed them into her satchel. When the box was empty, she replaced the lid, locked it, and threw the key into her purse. She was pulling her gloves off when she heard voices in the outer room and looked up to see the clerk leading an elderly gentleman to the cubicle next to hers. Time to get out of here, she thought. When she stepped out into the larger room, her knees wobbling from sheer nerves, the clerk smiled. "All finished? Please make sure the box is locked."

She checked to make sure the box was locked and handed it over. "Yes, it's locked. Jamie, thanks so much for your help," Rita said. Her heart pounded in her chest as she waved to the man before going back into the hallway. Her heels once again clicked across the marble floor as she left the bank as quickly as if she'd robbed it. With so much jewelry in her purse, she felt as though she had.

Once outside, she got into her Jeep, pulled away from the curb, and at the corner, turned in the direction of the funeral home. Driving, she called her editor.

She spoke in a rush of rapid-fire sentences. Her voice shook. “Tom, it was full of jewelry. Probably three dozen or more pieces.” Breathless, she continued. “Soon as we hang up, I’ll call Carr out at the state police. I plan to turn it over to them, but right now I’m on my way to the funeral home to find out whatever is going on there.”

“Whoa, hold on Red, I don’t like this. Not at all. Why not wait for Carr? You’re already carrying around a bunch of jewelry that doesn’t belong to you, and I don’t need to get a call that you’ve been arrested for trespassing or theft, for God’s sake. And we both know this wouldn’t be the first time you’re getting into the story too deep, so don’t be stupid about this.”

She blew out a heavy sigh, frustrated at his warning. Two years earlier, she’d gotten personally involved in a story about the abduction of the pre-teen daughter of her former boyfriend, a police detective. While covering the story, she found herself in a life-or-death situation that ended with her shooting the kidnapper and rescuing the kidnapped girl and her badly wounded father from a burning cabin.

“Trust me, it’s nothing like that. I’m simply going to knock on the door, see who’s there, and try to get someone to talk to me about Bob Watson and Cindy. I have no idea what I’m going to ask, but two deaths and a cache of jewelry means there’s more to this, and I plan to find out what it is.”

She explained that she’d examined the rings. “I compared the sizes when I removed them from the box. No two appeared the same, and some were clearly designed for men rather than women, which led me to believe they were stolen. “They all couldn't have belonged to the same person."

Tom tried to reason with her. "You don't know for sure whether Cindy sent you that key and whether the jewelry you found has anything to do with her death or Bob Watson's murder at all. My suggestion is to turn the jewelry over to the police. They'll be able to get a court order to get information from the bank as to who rented that box. Once you do that, if it was indeed rented by Cindy, then you have something concrete to go on. Right now, it's all speculation."

"Agreed. Speculation and an extremely strong hunch. Questions, Tom. All I'm going to do is ask questions. I'm certainly not going to barge in there with a handful of gold and diamonds and start accusing people of theft. I'll most likely get the door slammed in my face and be back at my desk in an hour."

"Okay, okay. What do I know? I'm just the boss here," he cracked. "I'll see you later."

He hung up just as she parked in front of the mansion. Rita stepped out of her car and slid her phone into her pants pocket then reached in and gathered her things. She walked around it to open her trunk and saw no one on the street. She placed the satchel under a pile of bagged clothes she'd been planning to toss into a donation bin, locked the trunk, and slipped her keys into the pocket of her coat before climbing the steps between the concrete lions. Once on the porch, she rang the doorbell, and after a few minutes, rang it again in frustration. When no one came to the door, she turned and walked back to her car and drove off.

She called Carr but got his voicemail. She left a detailed message as to what she'd found and then called her editor again. He answered on the third ring. "Newsroom, Tom Moore."

"Hey, it's a no go here. No one answered at the funeral home, so if you don't mind, I'm going to use some of my comp time from the president's visit and try again tomorrow. I'm not quite sure how long Boomer can last in that crate without making a mess, so I'd like to head home if that's okay with you? My neighbor let him out yesterday for me, but I don't want to impose by asking her again."

"No problem," he said, chuckling. "I didn't take you for the dog mommy type, Red."

"Very funny. I'm simply not thrilled with the idea of cleaning up puddles if you get my meaning. I have no clue how long he can stay cooped up in there. I'm going to try Carr again about this jewelry, but I'll be at home if you need me. See you in the morning."

Traffic was light, so she made it back to her townhome within thirty minutes. Pulling into her driveway, she smiled when she saw the end-unit's brick facade and the L-shaped covered porch that would be shaded by a large oak tree come summer. She'd purchased it the year before after years of renting, and now with Boomer, she was grateful to have her own fenced back patio and tiny yard that wouldn't have worked for a large animal but had a patch of grass perfect for the little Yorkie.

I'd hate to have to trudge around in the cold while a dog looks for the perfect place to poop.

She turned the key in her lock and heard the dog whimpering in the crate she kept in her first-floor bedroom. "Hey buddy! How's my little man today?" He barked once in greeting and leapt into her arms after she released the latch to open the crate. He whimpered and licked her face. "Good boy. No accidents today. I'll take that as a sign that you're fully crate-trained and housebroken." She led him to the patio door, slid it open, and watched him go out to relieve himself. When he ran back inside, she rewarded him with a tiny biscuit and filled his bowl with food, feeling more than a little satisfied with her sudden conversion to domesticity.

An hour later, she tried Carr's number again but got his voicemail. When he didn't answer, she slipped the bags of jewelry from her satchel, pulled on her gloves once more. One by one, she removed the pieces from the bags, set them on her kitchen island, and photographed each piece with her cell phone camera, careful to replace it in the correct bag before placing them all in a larger bag that she planned to turn over to Carr in the morning.

Just as she finished packing them up, her phone buzzed, and Carr's name popped up. Glancing at the time, she saw it was after nine. She'd been working on the jewelry for hours. She put the bag down and picked up her dog before answering.

"Red, I hope I didn't wake you. I had my phone off during an early dinner and movie with my wife. What's up?"

She took a deep breath and launched into the details of her theory about the anonymous letter, the key, and the jewelry. "It had to have been sent by Cindy. Don't you see? She knew something and ended up dead. This jewelry could be the reason Bob ended up dead, too. Could be that he stole from the wrong person, or maybe he was working with someone and refused to share the rewards."

"Red, just hold on a minute. First, we don't know who rented the safety deposit box, although it could have been Ms. Ekas, based on what you told me about her fear and the note in the box. However, it'll take a court order to get the bank to tell us anything, you know that."

He sighed, sounding exhausted. "And yes, I'll call the district attorney's office to petition the court. Bring everything to the station first thing tomorrow morning. No detours, okay?"

"Absolutely," she promised.

"Once we get an inventory, I'll send some guys out to pawn shops to see whether Bob had ever tried to fence anything in or around the city. I can't see him as a thief, though, from what I knew of him. Although he didn't seem the criminal type, that doesn't mean anything. I guess anyone could be a criminal type and hide it if he's savvy enough."

She couldn't resist pushing her theories further. "Maybe he was desperate," she added. "If you remember, the day of the murder, you told me the Watsons' medical insurance doesn't cover the expensive school their son attends. His wife told me the same thing."

"And what does that mean," he prodded.

"Wanna bet that he was stealing to pay for it? You know very well that he wouldn't be the first parent to do something stupid to provide something his child needs."

"C'mon Red, aren't you getting a little ahead of yourself here?"

"Maybe, but it makes sense that this jewelry has something to do with his death. They could be running a theft ring out of there, and who would suspect it at a funeral home? Amie Watson said Foster was a friend since her husband's mortuary school days. Could be that this is the reason he all but dragged me to the door to get rid of me. For all we know, they could be hiding stuff in that coffin room."

Before they hung up, Carr promised to assign a trooper to start scouring recent theft reports to find any matches between the jewelry cache and reported stolen items in Pittsburgh and surrounding counties. "We'll get started as soon as you bring it in. We're going to have to get city police involved too because the funeral home serves a broad area. Keep it quiet until you hear from me, okay?"

"Sure, whatever you say. In the meantime, though, I might do a little quiet digging on my own."

He laughed. "So, what else is new? Just be careful. From the sound of it, some of this stuff is worth a lot of money. And money sometimes means trouble."

After they hung up, she had an easy dinner of frozen pizza and a glass of wine before she let Boomer out into the yard for a final time. She soaked in a tub full of bubbles before pulling on a pair of sweatpants and a fuzzy sweatshirt, hoping to finish a novel before bed. Although she tried to read, she couldn't concentrate on anything other than thoughts of Cindy's death, so she turned off the lamp on her bedside table and curled up with Boomer lying by her side.

As she drifted off to sleep, she thought about her conversation with Carr. *If money means trouble, it's time to follow the money.*

CHAPTER SEVEN

After two weeks, Rita's digging produced nothing new to advance her story and police offered no new leads with regard to the jewelry discovery or the deaths of Bob Watson and Cindy Ekas.

Frustrated, and still missing David, she took two ibuprofen tablets for a pounding headache and had fallen into a deep sleep when Boomer's whimpering woke her. Groggy, she looked at her phone and saw that it was just after two in the morning when she heard what sounded like footsteps in her living room. When he let out a low growl, she scooped him up, bolted from the bed, and locked her bedroom door before running with the phone into her bathroom. Shaking, she dialed 9-1-1 as she locked that door as well.

"Someone is in my house. Please, I need help," she whispered to the dispatcher. Her teeth chattering, she managed to give her name and address a few seconds before she heard the bedroom door swing open. "I'm alone in my bathroom, and they're getting closer. Please, help me."

She yanked a towel from the rack into the bathtub and placed the dog, now barking shrilly, on it before sliding the glass shower door shut. The dispatcher said something that she couldn't make out just as the doorknob rattled. She moved as far from the door as she could and held her breath. Wood splinters shot across the room as the door shattered and swung open to reveal the hooded figure of a broad-shouldered man. Dull rays from the bathroom nightlight illuminated the hammer he held in the air as he came toward her.

Boomer's barking drowned her scream as she dropped the phone and lunged forward to fight. The man swore when she connected with his stomach, headfirst, and knocked him backward into the bedroom. He quickly recovered and dragged her down onto the carpet, where he pummeled her head with the hammer twice. Stunned from the blows, she summoned all her strength to kick and claw at him, which sent the hammer back into the bathroom, where it clattered onto the tile floor. Blood streamed into her eyes as his gloved fist connected with her jaw, breaking it with one sharp blow. She howled in pain as her ribs cracked with another blow, her knee with a third. He grabbed a fistful of hair and pushed her down as blood filled her throat and mouth. She gasped for air as she tried in vain to snatch the hood from his face. *If I'm going to be killed, I want to see the bastard who does it.* He grabbed her right wrist and wrenched it away from his face, twisting it until it snapped. Searing pain shot up her arm. She let out a moan, unable to muster the strength to scream. He stood over her body as she crumpled to the carpet, face down. Laughing, he let loose several jolting, sharp kicks to her stomach and back until she stopped moving.

Is that Boomer, still snarling and barking? What a brave little guy. I already love him. Please, God, don't let him kill my dog.

"This is what happens to nosy reporters," he whispered, kicking her side one final time. "They go places where they're not wanted, and take jewelry that doesn't belong to them, and ask too many questions. And then, they die." He turned and left when she gurgled a faint moan.

Blinded with pain, blood soaking her clothes and spreading across the beige bedroom carpet, she lay there listening to whimpering from the bathroom until everything went black.

"Rita! Jesus, what happened? Rita, can you hear me?"

Trooper Tyler Anthony holstered his weapon and sprinted into the bedroom, where he sidestepped a bloody hammer and knelt on the floor beside her battered body. He felt her neck and shouted to his partner who was four steps behind him. "Get an ambulance here, now. She's alive, but barely." He looked around on the floor, where the weapon she'd been pummeled with lay covered in blood and strands of red hair. "Whoever did this used a hammer. It looks like she's been in a war, for God's sake."

She whispered something, and he kneeled at her side to hear her. "Boomer…bathtub. My phone…Kathy…"

"He's here. He's okay. Hear him barking? Rita, it's me, Tyler, I'll take care of him," the trooper promised. "Hold on, Rita. State police are here, and we're getting you help. An ambulance is coming. I just need you to hang on for me. Try to stay awake, honey. You're strong. You can do it."

Gasping, she tried to talk but gurgled and choked, wheezing through burning lungs. Did she know that voice? Who is barely alive? Is it me? Why does my mouth taste like copper?

"Boomer," she gasped, trying to reach for his hand. "Promise… Kathy."

"I promise. You want me to call Kathy to take care of Boomer, right? Is Kathy your sister?"

"Best…best friend," she mumbled.

"I promise, I'll call her. Help is on the way. Please, Rita, hang on."

He sounded kind, and she felt safe, comforted that Boomer would be looked after. She fought to answer, but the words didn't come. She knew she was dying. She wondered who would take her job, and for a moment, worried about her parents and how crushed they'd be over losing their only child. Fragmented scenes and a parade of faces, places she'd visited and people she'd loved, news assignments and college parties, all wound like a silent, slow-motion movie through her mind. *Maybe what they say is true, your whole life does flash in front of you right before you die.* She felt cold, and then comfortably warm and weightless, unable to hear the kind man's voice or the dog's cries any longer. She slipped into the merciful, pain-free peace, facing the light.

Darkness shrouded the room, where readings for her heartbeat, pulse, and blood pressure clicked and beeped in a faint, coordinated rhythm on bedside monitors, recording and charting the critical clinical details of her life. Clear plastic tubing sent oxygen hissing into her collapsed lungs and nutrition into her stomach while morphine and antibiotics dripped into her left arm. Her right arm had been casted to hold her shattered wrist. Her leg, held in traction, hovered above her body as she lay mute and still. Her right eye flickered open, the left swollen shut and crusted under bandages. She listened to the quiet symphony and scanned as much of the scene before her as she could without moving her head. She had no strength to shift or turn.

Closing her eye again, she relaxed and found peace and warmth once more in the blackness. She wanted to stay there forever.

The voices woke her.

Straining to listen, the voices comforted her. One was Kathy, maybe, and could it be her parents? She fought to open her eyes but couldn't summon the energy to awaken from her dream. She liked this place and wanted to remain there, safe and warm. She reasoned that it had to be a dream because her parents lived so far away, and after all, Dad didn't drive much since his heart surgery, so they couldn't be here with her. *Where is here? I don't even know where I am right now, not that I care.* Drifting off, she slipped away into the comfort of darkness once more.

She opened her right eye to bright sunlight, wincing from pain when she tried to open her left one, still swollen shut but free of bandages. She tried to raise her right hand, but it was heavy, casted to the elbow, so she dragged her left hand up to feel her face. Her fingertips traced her puffy cheek up to the stitches above her left eye. She felt the crusted threads along her eyebrow, absently wondering what kind of scar the wound would leave. How did she get it? She touched the tubes at her nose and felt her swollen lips, cracked and dry. Running her tongue around her mouth, she tasted metal but couldn't open her jaw. Her parched throat closed when she tried to swallow.

Her head ached. She reached up to her scalp and felt tangled patches of hair and spongy bandages, shaved areas, and only traces of her long, frothy curls. She looked above her leg, casted and suspended a foot above her body, to scan around the room. *Hospital. Must have been in an accident.* That explained the tubes running into her nose and arm, the beeping rhythm and whirring of machines. She tried to read the words on the whiteboard on the wall at the foot of her bed, but the letters jumbled together as she felt her head spin into a dizzy haze. Exhausted from the effort, she fell asleep.

When she awoke again, the moon cast a faint glow into the darkened room lit only by a dim bulb on the wall behind her head. She heard the machines once more, and the sounds of someone snoring close by. She moved her head to the left and saw him out of the corner of her eye. *David? I must be imagining things. Where did he come from? Why is he here?*

She tried to speak but her jaw wouldn't move. She slapped the blanket with her good hand, grunting, until he opened his eyes. He leaned forward and then leapt from the chair where he'd been sleeping. He rushed toward the bed.

"Rita! Oh God, Red, I thought you'd never wake up." His eyes filled with tears. "Oh honey, I'm so sorry this happened to you. I'm here with you now, and no one is going to hurt you again."

Relief flooded her body. He loved her after all.

She tried to speak but could only grunt. She raised her eyebrow, then whimpered and slapped the blanket once more to make him understand that she needed answers. He took a deep breath and began to talk, quickly rattling off a list of disturbing facts that would have brought her to her knees if she'd been able to stand.

"You're in UPMC Presbyterian Hospital, brought here by ambulance after someone attacked you with a hammer in your home, but you're going to be okay. Thank God you were able to call for help before the guy hit you because the state police getting there so quickly probably saved your life. You have two skull fractures that required twenty staples in your head to repair, your jaw is broken and wired shut, your leg and arm were shattered and are held together with pins and screws. You've had two extensive surgeries, but the doctor said you should be able to use them normally after you recover. It'll take a while because you're going to need physical therapy for your leg."

He brushed her forehead gently. "The orbital bone above your eye was broken, too, and you're probably going to need a bit of plastic surgery to fix a scar on the side of your forehead. You have two cracked ribs that punctured your right lung, and a bunch of bruises, and they removed your spleen, but your mom told me that the doctor said you can live normally without it." His voice broke, and he laid his hand gently beside hers.

She grasped his hand tightly, comforted by his touch.

He continued, "You've been in and out of things for the past six days, honey, but the doctors say you're going to be okay, I promise you."

She let his hand go and made a petting motion as she struggled to speak between clenched teeth. "Boomer," she croaked.

He nodded. "Boomer is fine. He's staying with Kathy. Apparently, you managed to tell one of the troopers who found you that you wanted her to take care of him, and he found her number in your phone. Your parents offered – they've been staying at your place since they got the call – but Kathy insisted she'd take the little guy because they've been here every day with you. They're exhausted, so I've been taking over here at night to give them a break to get some sleep," he said, his voice trailing off into a whisper. He looked away from her as if unable to meet her eyes. "We didn't want you to be alone if the worst happened because it was touch and go for the first two days, and then when you were stronger, we didn't want you to wake up here by yourself and be afraid."

He reached for her good hand, gently rubbing it with his thumb. "Red, I'm sorry. I've missed you, and I realized how much

I love you when Kathy called me the day after the attack to tell me you were hurt. Please don't be mad at her for calling me because she's been a mess worrying over you. I never should have left the way I did, and now, if you'll have me, I'll never leave you again. I've been crazy thinking I could have lost you forever."

She grasped his hand and nodded, closing her eye as she managed to say two words. "Love you." She was so tired. He was talking too fast, too much. She drifted off again, wondering if she'd been dreaming, or if he'd really been there, saying everything she'd always longed to hear.

CHAPTER EIGHT

Five weeks later, she neared the end of the nightmare that sent her from a peaceful evening at home with Boomer into a haze of agony and a screaming ambulance, followed by three pain-filled weeks in the hospital unable to talk, walk, or care for herself. Now, the swelling in her face was gone and her vision was getting better every day.

She'd been in a rehabilitation center for the past two weeks and would be there at least two, and possibly four more, before the casts were removed from her broken leg and arm and she could have any hope of being discharged. The cast would be removed from her arm the following week. Excruciating daily physical therapy sessions would continue on an outpatient basis when she returned home. However much she hated them, she forced herself through the exercises, determined to get back to work.

"I hate being unable to do things for myself," she complained to Kathy. "I guess it's an improvement that I can complain, though, now that they took the damn wires out of my jaw."

Kathy smiled, and shook her head, tossing her long blonde hair as she tucked a blanket around Rita's legs. "Maybe an improvement for you, but the rest of us are tired of hearing you whine." When Rita's eyes widened, she laughed. "Hey, you know I'm kidding, right? Girl, you're lucky to be alive."

Rita blew out a deep breath. "Yes, I know. I'm just anxious to get out of here and see Boomer and get back to work. I have too much to do. People *died*, Kath, and know I'm onto something that might tell us why. More than anything, I need to get back into it."

Kathy rolled her eyes in obvious disbelief. She drew her thin, six-foot frame down to Rita's level. "This 'thing' you're onto is the reason you were almost killed. Don't you get it? You know what your buddy Lt. Carr said. Do I need to remind you that nothing was taken from your house? No money, none of your jewelry, no electronics. Rita, that maniac, whoever he was, came there with a definite purpose in mind."

She lowered her voice. "He beat you to a pulp, for God's sake, and then left you for dead. It's a miracle that you're here today. Do you really want to get involved in it again? Is any story worth this agony?"

Kathy, who was more of a sister to her than a friend, made her think realistically about the ordeal she'd experienced. Rita reached up to touch her hair, once a mass of thick red curls and now a short, spiky pixie cut, thanks to a personal visit from her hair stylist. She'd cried over it, but Laura had said it was the best solution because doctors had to shave parts of her head when they stapled her fractured skull. She'd sobbed as Laura trimmed what was left. The loss of her long hair, more than anything else, exacerbated the trauma she'd endured.

In her official statement to police, Rita reported that the man who attacked her knew about the jewelry she'd found in the safety deposit box. Carr reminded her that the discovery was not much of a secret because authorities in and around Pittsburgh and Westmoreland County made much of the information public in their search for the owners. That, she realized, widened the field of suspects to just about anyone who watched television news, read newspapers, or knew someone in law enforcement.

She looked into Kathy's eyes and spoke with resolution. She'd come too far to quit. "Yes, I do. I'm going to finish this. It's my job…it's who I am…it's all I know. I'm not going to let this define me for the rest of my career and allow a thug to win. I can't hide from a story just because someone doesn't like it."

Kathy slapped her hands on her thighs and jumped to her feet, clearly exasperated as she shouted the words. "Doesn't like it? Listen to yourself. You were almost murdered. That's a little more serious than 'doesn't like it.'"

She didn't want to argue with her best friend. They'd had a serious disagreement once before when she wrote about a man Kathy was dating, and the story caused him to leave town. They repaired their friendship, and she didn't want to jeopardize it again.

Rita spoke softly, "Honey, I realize that. Look, I talked to Tom, and he's assigning a partner to work with me for a while on assignments when I go back to the newsroom. You remember Bill Martin, don't you, from that party I took you to last summer? He's a good guy, and smart. He's not going to do anything stupid to get us in trouble."

She reminded her friend that her father had a security system installed in her townhome with cameras inside and outside that she could monitor on her phone. "All I have to do is push a button for help. And David insists he'll be around more, although I'm not sure where we're heading with whatever our relationship is these days. I know he loves me, and I love him, but I'm not jumping into anything right now until I know we can work together and compromise to the point that he's here to stay this time."

She moved her wheelchair to the window and looked out across the lawn, where spring flowers had burst into beds of vibrant colors. When she turned toward her friend again, her jaw tightened with resolve as she clenched her fists. If she walked away from this story now, she should just throw in the towel and quit her job. She hated to upset her friend, and she knew the very thought of continuing to pursue this story would terrify David and her parents, but she was in too deep to turn and run.

"Please, understand why it's so important for me to do this. Thank God, I didn't die, but Bob Watson did. So did Cindy Ekas, and I'm going to find out why they died and who killed them and who tried to kill me if it's the last thing I do."

David held her door as she swung into the townhome on her crutches three weeks later. "Steady, babe, not so fast. You don't want to fall."

"Seriously, stop babying me, or I'll send you home right now," she said. "I'm not a toddler, and I know what to do and how much I can handle. God knows I spent enough time learning to walk with these damn things." She put them aside and rubbed her aching shoulders. "Two more weeks, and I'm rid of them."

She heard whimpering coming from her bedroom as she sunk down onto her couch. As promised, Kathy returned Boomer that morning before going to work, and he was scraping and crying to get out of his crate. Poor little guy had to be confused. "Oh, David, get him out for me, will you? I hope he remembers me."

He nodded and went into the bedroom, still carrying the overnight bag she'd had at the rehab center. She heard the lock on the crate click and a few seconds later Boomer leaped onto her lap, squealing while licking her face that was already wet with streaming tears. "There's my brave boy. You tried so hard to protect me, didn't you? We're home now, buddy, and we're going to be okay."

David sat next to them and began to scratch the dog's ears, causing Boomer's tail to wag even harder. "You know, I'll stay if you want me to, right?"

She nodded but then shook her head. No matter how much she feared being alone, she wanted her old life back, so it made sense that she had to start doing some things on her own. The night before, she'd convinced her parents to go home so her father wouldn't miss the doctor's appointment he'd already rescheduled twice during her lengthy recuperation. She tried to sound confident. "I won't always have someone here with me, so it's best I stay alone for a while to get used to it. Kathy and my mom filled the refrigerator before my parents left yesterday, the security system will be on the minute you walk out the door, and Boomer and I will be fine here getting reacquainted."

She also reminded him that the physical therapist would be there the next morning. Taking his hand, she smiled, adding, "However, if you'd like to come over tomorrow night after work, that would be great."

He leaned forward and brushed a short fluff of hair away before kissing her scarred forehead. "Ok, tough girl. By now, I should know better than to try to tell you what to do. Call me if you need anything. I don't care if it's in the middle of the night." He patted Boomer on the head and moved to the door, hesitating a moment before he turned back toward her. "Lock this behind me and get some rest. I'll see you tomorrow."

"Yes, boss," she joked. "Seriously, I'll be fine." She waved, and he closed the door. After a few minutes, Rita set Boomer down on the couch, picked up her crutches and hobbled over to lock the door. She pressed the code her father had given her into the panel next to it, listened for a 'beep,' and went back to the couch, catching Boomer when he jumped back onto her lap. She looked around the room that felt like home but looked surprisingly unfamiliar.

The blood-soaked carpet had been replaced with new wood flooring that she'd always wanted, thanks to a gift from her parents. The shattered bathroom door was gone and a new one stood in its place. A small table was missing, broken in the attack, according to her father. Her favorite armless chair, once in a corner near her bedroom door, had been removed because her blood had stained it too badly. Her mother had ordered another, but it wasn't due for delivery for another couple of weeks. Trooper Anthony suggested that she may have been thrown against it by her attacker or may have tried to raise herself up from the floor onto it, but even after several sessions with a therapist, she had few memories of the attack after dialing the phone and hiding in the bathroom with her dog. Thank God she'd put Boomer in the bathtub and closed the glass shower doors to keep him inside. Otherwise, he may have been hurt or killed by that maniac.

A cold chill ran from her neck down her back. *That's one memory I can live without. If I look back to every single detail of what happened, I'm done.*

She thought about the fact that nothing had been taken by her attacker, so it was clear, as Kathy insisted, his only goal was to hurt her. Although she hated the thought, maybe it was time to get a gun. She shuddered, recalling how awful she felt after shooting the kidnapper two years earlier. No, a gun was not an option.

She unlocked her phone. Carr, who visited her at the hospital with an armload of flowers, told her none of the jewelry pieces she had turned over before her attack meshed with local stolen jewelry reports so police were sharing the inventory lists and photos with other law enforcement agencies across Pennsylvania and in several surrounding states. Now, she scrolled through the photos she'd snapped before she turned the jewelry over to the police. One piece, a gold locket crusted with tiny pearls and diamonds, looked familiar to her for some reason. Had she seen it before, or was she imagining things?

That evening, she reheated her mother's homemade chicken soup, almost falling asleep as she took the last comforting spoonful. Exhausted, she struggled to the kitchen sink with the bowl, rinsed it, and placed it into the dishwasher with her spoon and teacup. Although she'd already locked the doors and checked the security system after letting Boomer out into the courtyard, she checked them again to make sure everything was locked and secure for the night. She pulled her living room curtain back a few inches to survey the empty street in front of her townhome, but let the curtain fall back into place when a car passed slowly down the block. A shiver ran through her, and for a few moments, she again regretted sending David home. *Is it always going to be like this? Staring at security camera footage? Hiding behind locked doors and heavy drapes in fear of what might be lurking beyond? No. That's not who I am. I'm not going to let him win, whoever he is. He's not going to beat me.*

Still, her heart pounded against the wall of her chest when she heard a car passing by a second time and peeked out to see it was the same dark sedan moving slowly past her door. Did she know that car?

She checked the lock a third time and left the living room lamps blazing brightly as she made her way into the bedroom. "C'mon Boomer." The little dog followed at her heels, waiting patiently while she locked the bedroom door behind them. She scooped him up onto the bed, and he curled into her arms.

She did not turn off the light.

Rita spent much of the next two weeks at home digging into everything she knew about the murders of Bob Watson and Cindy Ekas, convinced they were part of some type of jewelry theft operation. She scoured the newspaper's electronic library for hours each day, reading every burglary, robbery, and theft report that mentioned jewelry of any kind. She hoped to discover a connection between recent crimes and the items she'd recovered from the safety deposit box, something that police investigators overlooked.

She hit a dead end. None of the pieces she'd found were listed anywhere.

One afternoon, after two hours at her laptop, she decided to research Cindy Ekas and Bob Watson personally, grasping for anything in their past that might link them criminally or otherwise. Reading obituaries for Cindy's parents, she learned that the woman had no siblings and had lost her grandparents before she was born. She found a small blurb from the business pages announcing the grand opening for her salon fifteen years earlier, and several classified ads seeking to employ stylists in the time since.

Criminal records searches showed nothing more serious than a couple of speeding tickets two years earlier for her, while civil records indicated she was married in her early twenties but had no children. They were married for only eighteen months. She was indeed alone.

Researching Bob, Rita found nothing in a criminal records check, not even a speeding ticket. She read a feature in a business journal about him taking over the funeral home and several sports shorts from his career as a high school wrestler. Just as she was getting ready to take a break to let Boomer outside, something in the newspaper sports archives caught her eye.

Hah! Small world.

Bob Watson had gone to high school with Shane Gilliam, Kathy's former boyfriend.

Shane was tall, dark, and handsome, and the biggest fake she'd ever met. In fact, she'd wager that he might have been one of the most devious people she'd ever encountered in fifteen years as a crime reporter in Pittsburgh. Other than outright murderers, she doubted anyone could be more threatening than someone who claimed to be a doctor but never graduated from medical school, especially when that doctor hangs out a shingle and practices medicine on unsuspecting patients. She'd exposed him by her reporting, but he'd fled and never faced prosecution.

And to think he got away with it. That's going to haunt me forever, because I know in my heart that somewhere, someone suffered at his hands. Or worse. And even though my stories sent him packing, he never had to answer for what he'd done.

She let her thoughts wander.

Before he disappeared, Shane talked a good game, and when he talked, people listened. He charmed them with his wavy, black hair, ice blue eyes, and soft, deep voice that lulled them with traces of Irish brogue he'd perfected during a childhood spent at his grandmother's cottage in Ireland. With that appealing combination, he could persuade people to do just about anything: give him money, believe his lies, fall in love with him.

Sadly, Kathy fell victim to his charismatic allure.

And it was my fault.

Almost two years had passed since Rita met Shane on assignment while covering for a reporter on the features beat who was too sick to go to the opening of a new clinic outside Pittsburgh. At the time, he was working as the medical director for the general practice clinic that also promoted a new, controversial treatment for people with Parkinson's disease. Several weeks after her story was published, she and Kathy ran into him at a club. By the end of the evening, he'd taken her friend's phone number. They'd been dating for almost five months when everything crashed and he left town, devastating her friend when he disappeared.

Looking back, Rita was thankful Kathy recovered from the heartbreak and that their friendship survived. The weeks after her attack would have been unbearable without the comfort of her best friend.

She shut down her computer.

Oh Shane, I wonder where you landed. Who are you trying to con now?

CHAPTER NINE

Finally, after removal of her leg cast, Rita convinced her doctors to release her to go back to work because the publisher agreed to place her on desk duty for a month while she continued physical therapy. Her leg still ached when she was on it for too long, and she walked with a slight limp. Vanity took over, and she'd refused a cane.

Although she was happy to be out of the house and working, she hated being confined to the newsroom where the scanner above her desk blasted out emergency calls that normally would have sent her running to crime scenes. Her colleagues, tasting the excitement of the crime beat, willingly covered for her during several ongoing court cases, so she was stuck answering phone calls and handling mundane press releases. The frustration she felt made her want to scream, and one afternoon she looked across the newsroom to see how many people there were to listen.

A sportswriter sat punching the last evening's game scores into his computer, two fingers at a time, and three reporters on the features desk were huddled in a meeting. The editorial page editor, still trying to quit smoking, chomped on Nicotine gum as he read through page proofs for the weekend's papers. Everyone appeared engaged and busy, not bored to tears like her.

She pulled a couple of pretzels from the bag on her desk and ate them, washing the salty crumbs down with a long swig of Diet Coke before she maneuvered her chair toward her editor's desk, partially buried under a stack of the previous month's papers. "Tom, I swear this is going to kill me if I have to sit here for the next month," she complained. "Give me something, anything, with some meat to it, or I'm going to lose my mind."

"For God's sake, you've only been back two days, so quit your whining already. If you're looking for a story idea, find something to write about. Didn't you mention something the other day that you found out Shane Gilliam went to the same high school as Bob Watson? Until something breaks in the Watson case, maybe it's time to get your shovel out and do some digging, find out what scheme that rat is working now. Why not take another look at him? People like him are always up to something."

Rita wanted to kick herself for not thinking of it on her own. She turned to her computer and began to work. She hadn't thought about or looked for Shane in a long time, but the investigative journalist's first, simplest, and favorite tool, Google, led her directly to him.

It was almost too easy, and what she found was more than a little unbelievable. He'd opened a medical school on the island of Nevis, part of the Lesser Antilles chain located in the Caribbean about two hundred twenty miles south of Puerto Rico. He was serving as its president. Shane Gilliam was playing doctor again, and from what Rita remembered, he was a master of deception.

It had taken a lot of hard work to expose his lies two years earlier. Not long after she wrote about the clinic's opening, the newspaper ran several paid advertisements about the clinic's services, and four days later, she received an anonymous letter at work from someone who suggested Shane didn't have the qualifications to serve as the clinic's director. Her journalist's instinct kicked in, and she began to question tiny, but significant, inconsistencies in some of the things Kathy told her about him. Before long, her answers pointed toward fraud.

She did some digging, and a week later, she made an appointment and took a male reporter with her to the clinic, both for her personal safety and to help her to document the encounter. She remembered every detail of their meeting.

Shane, so handsome he was almost pretty, made Rita's heart pound when he walked into the examination room where she waited with her colleague. He wore a pale lavender shirt and charcoal gray pants under his white lab coat, which was embroidered in navy script, *Shane Gilliam, M.D.* He had a stethoscope casually slung around his neck and a thick gold Rolex watch circling his left wrist. She'd hated her body's response to him and had to remind herself to keep her cool. He may have been physically attractive, but he was a jerk, and by playing doctor without a license, he was also a criminal.

"Rita, how are you?" Smiling, he nodded at her companion, stepped over to the small sink, and washed his hands. As he was drying them on a paper towel, he turned to her and asked, "What brings you into the clinic today? You're not feeling sick, are you?"

She stammered a bit as she thanked him for seeing her so soon but stopped short before claiming any ailment. Drawing on her journalism training, she knew that, ethically, she couldn't lie about the purpose of her visit. She had to tell him the truth.

"Dr.…um… Shane, this is my writing partner, Bill Martin." She waited while the men shook hands and then said, "I wanted to talk to you for a few minutes about your work at the clinic, and I figured this was the best way to do it. I apologize if you thought I was here as a patient, but I assure you when I called for the appointment, I just gave my name and asked for a convenient time to see you. I wasn't trying to be deceptive."

His jaw clenched for a split second, but he quickly relaxed. When he grinned, his smile failed to reach his eyes. He glanced at his watch before moving toward the door, where he motioned for them to follow him down the hall. "Okay, let's go into my office so we can clear this exam room. You have fifteen minutes, which is the amount of time I normally spend with a patient. You already know that I'm a primary care physician in a clinic. I take care of people with chicken pox and diabetes and the flu, and on weekends I go out with your best friend, so what else is it about me that is so fascinating that you need to know?"

Walking briskly, he led them down a narrow corridor to a paneled office at the back of the building. Elaborately framed diplomas lined the walls behind the desk, where an engraved brass nameplate bore the inscription, *Dr. Shane Gilliam.* Another clean, white lab coat hung on a hall tree in a rear corner of the room, where one wall was lined with shelves of medical textbooks.

She asked him, point blank, when and where he graduated from medical school, where he did his internship and residency, and for proof of any prior places of employment. Still grinning, he waved his hand toward the diplomas and certificates.

"As you can see, my life is an open book," he said. He held his arms open wide as if to sweep the room. "Feel free to get up and look around. Hell, take photos if you want. Take notes."

Immediately, Bill pushed his chair back, pulled out a notebook, and began to scribble names of schools, graduation dates, and other information from the elaborate certificates decorated with gold foil seals. Shane's eyes followed him around the room, and he shifted in his chair to get a clear view.

Rita cleared her throat to get his attention. Immediately, he turned his gaze away from her colleague. "Shane, while he does that, maybe you can tell me a little about how you came to work here at the clinic. How is it that you're starting at the top?"

Shane stared at her with an icy smile. He hesitated, as if unsure whether he should answer, but then said, "Simple. I invested money in it. I'm the medical director."

"Do you have privileges at any hospitals? Do you have a private office elsewhere?"

"No, and no. This place takes up too much of my time as it is."

"So, then you can't admit any clinic patients to the hospital if necessary?"

The smile he'd plastered across his lips faded into a deep frown, and he shook his head. When he spoke, he sounded both angry and impatient. "No, I see them here. Listen, Rita, I've had about enough of your questions, and I have no idea where this is going. I'm busy, and I'm sure there are patients waiting for me. I appreciate your interest, but you're going to have to excuse me."

Bill cleared his throat and shot her a wary look as she leaned forward in her chair and placed both hands on the desk in front of her. She pretended not to notice and ignored the subtle warning. Realizing it was time to spell it out for the man, she held nothing back when she started to talk. "Shane, people are alleging that you aren't licensed or qualified to practice medicine, and that you aren't really a doctor. Is there anything you can tell me to clarify that? Why would someone make those accusations against you?"

When he jumped up, the force of his movement sent his chair rolling backward across the tile floor until it hit a file cabinet. His face went crimson, and veins bulged in his neck. "Get out. We're done here, Rita. I know you're Kathy's friend, but I'm not going to be ambushed in my own office and listen to false accusations that are nothing but total crap when I have sick patients, *legit-*

imate paying patients, who are waiting to see me." He stormed past Bill, swept out of the door, and stomped into the hall. She saw him take a chart from a plastic tray attached to another door, knock twice, and disappear inside without looking back.

Later, in the newsroom, she and Bill called all the schools listed on Shane's diplomas and learned none had records of his graduation. One medical school didn't exist, another turned out to be nothing more than a cheap diploma mill that offered realistic-looking, frameable documents. Online searches revealed that, although he'd graduated from college, he had never completed medical school, an internship, or a residency. He was not licensed to practice medicine in Pennsylvania or anywhere else in the United States, so the embroidered lab coat and stethoscope were nothing more than costume props used by a dangerous man playing doctor with patients' lives at stake. Frankly, the elaborately designed diplomas lining his walls weren't worth more than the paper they were printed on.

Three days later, they had gathered enough information for a story that would both end his charade and hurt her best friend, who had been hoping for a future with him. She warned Kathy before it went to print. It was a heart-wrenching conversation she'd never forget.

"Honey, I don't know how to tell you this, but you really must know before things go any further. He's a fake, not a real doctor. Hell, he never finished medical school, never had a residency. Nothing. He's playing doctor and treating real patients, for God's sake. He belongs in jail."

Kathy had shrieked back. "What are you saying? This can't be true. How can you say that? He loves me!"

"Honey, I checked. I double-checked. Bill checked, and double-checked, and we've got documents and confirmation from

officials, everything necessary to prove it. I just need you to understand that I love you, and I'm so sorry this is happening to you. I wanted this, I wanted us, to be wrong because I never wanted you to be hurt. But you should know that there's going to be a damaging story in tomorrow's paper. My editor approved it, and the paper's lawyer vetted it and cleared it for publication. I'm going to see Shane now to get a final comment. It's my job..."

Kathy interrupted her. "Whatever. Do your job if it's so important to you to ruin people's lives but leave me out of it. We're going to dinner tonight. I'll talk to him and let you know what he says, because I'm sure he has a perfectly good explanation for all of this. You're mistaken. He loves me, and he'd never lie to me."

Kathy had hung up without another word, leaving Rita feeling sick over their conversation because they'd never argued before in twenty years of friendship. They were closer than many sisters.

That evening, Rita confronted Shane outside the clinic as he was walking to his car. She'd secretly hoped, for Kathy's sake, that he had some reasonable justification for what they'd discovered. As the newspaper's photographer snapped pictures, he mumbled and lied, giving excuse after excuse for the inconsistencies between his resume and the documents proving it false. He gave conflicting answers when she'd asked him one final time to identify any medical schools he'd attended or graduated from and whether he'd ever held board certification, or board eligibility, in any field of medicine, in any country. He insisted he'd attended a Caribbean medical school while simultaneously earning a doctorate at a 'non-traditional' university in Ireland. She already knew that the Irish school was nothing more than an online diploma mill, and that the Caribbean school registrar confirmed he'd attended several classes there for a couple semesters but never graduated. He'd run out of chances to prove himself, and she told him so. The story was set for publication the next morning.

"Shane, I'm struggling to give you the benefit of the doubt here, so if there's anything you want to add, this is the time to do it. Is there any explanation you can offer for any of this?"

He'd glared at her but didn't say a word before getting into his car. His tires screamed as he floored the engine and drove out of the parking lot, leaving a black trail of rubber along the pavement in his wake.

By the time the story hit newsstands the next morning, he'd resigned from the clinic, cleared out his townhouse, and vanished without a trace, breaking Kathy's heart without so much as a phone call to say goodbye. The clinic's co-owner, a psychologist, disputed allegations that he'd known Shane falsely held himself out to be a practicing physician. The psychologist, most likely afraid he'd be drawn into a criminal investigation, claimed that although Shane invested a considerable sum of money into their partnership, he had never treated patients. None of the clinic's patients came forward with complaints against them before it closed its doors permanently.

Subsequently, Rita interviewed wealthy relatives who had given Shane over a hundred thousand dollars to invest in the clinic, and although they were furious, they refused to file criminal charges against him, fearing more scandal for the family. A male cousin, who admitted he'd given Shane twenty thousand dollars, told her that he held out no hope of ever recovering his money. An elderly aunt told Rita that the rest of the family knew he was on the run and could never repay them, so they cut their losses and remained silent.

He disappeared then, escaping arrest.

She looked again at his photo on her screen. *You can run, but you can't hide.*

There he stood in his white lab coat, boldly embroidered with the flowery script *Dr. Shane Gilliam*, smiling in photos with government officials, and shaking hands at a ribbon cutting ceremony with the prime minister. He boasted in press releases about his credentials and the stellar qualities of the colleagues on his medical school's teaching staff. He advertised that he'd welcome students from both the United States and Europe.

Within minutes, she found the school's website, faculty lists, schedules, tuition rates, and policies. Quickly, she printed page after page, fearing the information would disappear as fast as she found it. A paper trail would be crucial if she was going to find anything worth writing about him.

When she finished, she got up from her chair, stretched her legs, and limped to stand in front of her editor's desk.

"Tom, you're not going to believe what I found. Get a load of this."

She shoved the stack of papers onto his keyboard, forcing him to stop typing in mid-stroke. He scanned the first page briefly, shaking his head. She moved to the corner of his desk, pushed the morning paper aside, and sat down on the edge, facing him.

Tom whistled when he leafed through the printouts. He'd read through three pages when he set the rest down and looked up at her. "Are you kidding me? How in the hell…oh, no, why do I sense a request for a Caribbean vacation coming? Don't get any ideas. I gave you this to keep you busy and safe at your desk in the newsroom for a while, not to have you running to the nearest airport."

She laughed for a few seconds but then met his gaze. After more than a decade under his supervision, she knew that his first reaction would be negative, just as he probably knew she'd get her way in the end.

"Like it or not, you know damn well I'll have to go there sooner or later. I have to see this for myself, if we're going to run with it. Honestly, Tom, this is too good to let it go, especially since I'm the one that outed him in the first place as a fake."

He leaned back in his chair and looked across their Pittsburgh newsroom, where a round of layoffs the year before left several desks empty and sent many reporters scrambling to find other jobs and freelance work. Rita had been spared because of her investigative talents, but the once-burgeoning staff had been decimated. He shook his head. "No, Red. I'm not going to the publisher with this one, not the way things are now. You know how hard it would be to justify the expense this could entail. And right now, I can't imagine gaining approval from above, not with what happened to you."

She slapped her hands on her thighs in frustration. *This is good journalism. Why is there always a fight over money?*

"Yes, but I just gave you solid proof that he's running a school and advertising it. For pity's sake, he's listed as 'Dr. Gilliam.' I understand that things are bad, but we're a newspaper, and this is news that could stop someone who wants a legitimate medical education from getting caught up in his web of deception. In the end, we could save someone's life."

She paused to take a breath. She knew he couldn't send her immediately because of her physical condition and it would look bad, very bad, to her colleagues if she traipsed off to an island in the wake of layoffs with the threat of more to come. "But, as much as I hate to admit it, I probably won't be up to it physically for a while, so I'm not asking for anything except a little time to check it out further. Let me see if I can connect with students, or someone on his faculty first. I'll get as much as I can here in my free time. I promise to continue following the Watson and Ekas cases, but it doesn't look like there's much at all going on there now. Please, just free me up from sitting here typing up press releases for a couple of weeks, okay?"

When he didn't answer, she continued, "If nothing else comes of it, that's it, but if I can get people to talk, all I ask is that you go to the publisher and tell him what we know. Let him make the decision."

He rubbed his eyes with the palms of his hands and let out a long, tired sigh. "Okay, okay stop. You're like a hungry dog with a bone, aren't you? I have a feeling you're not going to let it go, so I'll give you until your stint on desk duty ends. After that, if you don't have anything, it's over. You've been away from your beat long enough. Deal?"

"Deal. I promise." She pushed her chair back to her desk. She reached for her drink, found it empty, and tossed the can into her wastebasket.

She clicked on file after file in the newspaper's electronic library, taking notes that filled nearly half of her reporter's notebook. Three hours passed by the time she'd read through the stories that had won a good number of statewide journalism awards after she and Bill exposed Shane's fraudulent activities. She did several online searches, checking to see whether he'd completed any medical training since his abrupt departure from western Pennsylvania, but learned that he remained unlicensed in the United States. By late afternoon, she'd placed phone calls to nearly a dozen people listed as faculty members of the new school that he'd named Celtic Cross Medical University. Three were in their offices but declined comment. She left messages for the others.

The next morning, two physicians on the faculty at medical schools in Philadelphia and Pittsburgh returned her calls and told her they were simply given 'courtesy titles' on the school's website but had never traveled to the Caribbean or taught a class there. "I signed a one-page contract to act as a consultant as needed. I didn't think the school ever got off the ground, though, because I haven't heard anything from Dr. Gilliam since I agreed to help," one of the physicians offered.

She scribbled his comments, thankfully made on the record, into her notebook. "So, you're saying you're not a professor there? You don't teach classes there, even though you're listed as adjunct faculty?"

"Hell no, I've got my hands full here. All I agreed to do was offer advice regarding curriculum, but he hasn't asked for any assistance. I still maintain my private medical practice, and I teach several classes at the University of Pittsburgh every semester. I haven't even taken a vacation in the last year."

Another semi-retired doctor from the state of Michigan told her he had never heard of the school and did not know a Dr. Shane Gilliam.

"Me, teaching in the Caribbean? Ha, that's a good one. What's this all about? Is this some kind of joke?"

"No sir, I'm gathering information for a story. Your name is listed on the school's website. You've been brought into this for that reason."

"Well, you can just take my name out of it because I have nothing to do with it and I don't know anything about any school's website. Like I said, I don't know Dr. Gilliam, and I don't teach anywhere."

Long before the end of her shift, she knew Shane was playing doctor again in a scheme built on lies and deception.

She told David about Shane that night over dinner at their favorite Italian restaurant. They'd fallen into a routine of seeing each other every other night, and their conversations were easy and comfortable, so much so that she'd begun to trust him again. She'd never stopped loving him. Two nights before, he'd stayed at her house, and she'd planned to ask him to go home with her again that evening.

They were midway through their second course when David put his fork down. "What's this guy look like? His name sounds familiar to me, but I can't place the face in my mind. I'm sure I've seen him in the paper before."

"Well, let's just say you'd recognize his face if you read the more than ten stories I wrote about him. We ran his photo with every one of them. Are you telling me you're not one of my loyal followers?"

His face reddened at her teasing. "Sure, yeah. Well, I, um, I probably read most of them, or some, at least," he stammered. "That was a while ago, though."

She smiled and picked up her phone and began to scroll through photos, searching for a picture she'd snapped of Kathy and Shane the year before. Had she deleted it?

He reached out and covered her hand with his to stop her from moving to the next photo. "Wait, hold it, what's that? Back up to the beginning. Where did you get that picture? That's my grandmother's locket."

She gasped. "It can't be. These are the photos of the jewelry I found in the safety deposit box that police traced to Cindy Ekas. The police have them now. Your grandmother's been gone for a year. There's no way…"

He cut her off. "Let me see that. Blow it up bigger." He took the phone from her, put his glasses on, and stared at the screen. "I'm telling you, Red, it's my grandmother's locket. My grandfather had it made for her before they were married. His uncle was a jeweler, and from what I remember, according to family stories, it was a one-of-a-kind piece. She wore it for her wedding jewelry. My mother insisted that even though it was valuable because of the pearls and diamonds in it, the piece belonged to no one else but Grandma, so she was buried wearing it. Or let's just say she wanted to be buried in it and *should* have been buried in it."

Rita's eyes widened and her words spilled over one another. "Do you know what this means? Carr said investigators questioned Amie Watson, her brother, and James Foster, but they all denied knowing anything about the jewelry, the safety deposit box, or Cindy Ekas, for that matter. They said Cindy dealt only with Bob when she came to the funeral home to do hair on bodies before viewings."

Her mind raced. This could be the first concrete piece of evidence to prove that the murdered funeral director was involved in stealing jewels. He may have been removing jewelry from people who were supposed to be buried with valuable pieces and hoarding them to sell later. That explained why Cindy's note instructed whoever opened the safety deposit box to go to the police. *Had she been afraid Bob's murderer would come for her because she knew too much?*

"He could have been stealing for years, and it's obvious Cindy knew about it and hid the items for him."

David set the phone down and looked directly into her eyes, his own glistening. He spoke just above a whisper as he gripped the sides of the table. "This is going to kill my mother when she finds out. Tomorrow morning, I'm going to the police. Then, I'm going to an attorney. I swear to you, somehow, I'll get that locket back and put it around my grandmother's neck if I have to dig up her grave myself."

They picked at the rest of their meal in silence before pushing their half-filled plates away and declining the waiter's offer of dessert. When they got back to her house, she fed Boomer, put him outside for a few minutes afterward, and then settled him in his crate when they went to bed. Most nights, when David slept at her house, they made love, but now he kissed her and turned away. She felt him tossing and turning for more than an hour before his even breathing signaled he'd fallen asleep. She lay there awake for most of the night, unable to quiet her thoughts about what they suspected.

What kind of man had Bob Watson been? And what could he have stolen to make someone angry enough to murder him?

CHAPTER TEN

Rita felt it was best that David call the police with his suspicions about the locket, fearing that she shouldn't let her personal life interfere with her work again. She'd almost lost her job a few years earlier over a conflict of interest in writing about her former boyfriend's daughter. Based on that humiliation, she reluctantly decided to step back from this situation for the sake of her career. As soon as she walked into the newsroom, she told her editor what she'd learned the night before, and they'd agreed that another reporter would cover anything that had to do with David's grandmother to avoid a conflict of interest.

"Better safe than sorry this time," Tom said. "I'm not saying you have to step away from the Watson homicide story altogether, but if anything comes of this jewelry thing, your byline isn't going to be on any story that involves David or anyone in his family."

She nodded and fired up her laptop. She'd expected his reaction. "I know. No need to worry. I've got other things to do. I'm focusing on Shane Gilliam today."

He turned back to his computer. "Good girl. Keep busy and stay out of trouble, not that you really get the concept of how to stay out of trouble."

Rita laughed, scrolling through her emails while sipping a cup of tea and breaking pieces off the cinnamon bagel she'd brought from home. She deleted most, answered several, and forwarded two to other departments. When she finished that, she thought about her next move with Gilliam and began to research information about medical school education.

One of the most important lessons she'd learned as a young journalism student was to follow the money when doing an investigative reporting piece, and she knew from experience that money, more than anything else, motivated Shane. As a result of his relationship with Kathy, she knew he loved fine wines and exotic vacations and wore only expensive clothes. Above all, he appeared to crave attention and lived to impress people, so she wasn't surprised when her research revealed that each year, astounding amounts of money flowed into dozens of offshore medical schools that were attended for the most part by desperate Americans who failed to get accepted into stateside institutions for reasons that varied from poor grades, low test scores, lack of money, or simply, lack of space.

As she read, she found that although there were several respectable offshore schools throughout the Caribbean nations, including the University of the Americas in Nevis, medical education experts consistently warned prospective students that studying offshore was a highly expensive gamble because, for every legitimate school, there were a handful of suspect ones. She learned that for many students, however, it was a risk they were more than willing to take because it was the only remote chance they had to be accepted into a medical school and achieve their dreams of practicing medicine. Within an hour, she'd gathered information online and was making calls to medical education professionals and organizational leaders to learn more.

Dr. Chloe Studer, a medical researcher and past president of the American Association of Medical Colleges, spent an hour explaining the pitfalls of offshore medical educational opportunities during a phone interview that afternoon.

"The schools in the Caribbean are unregulated, and time and again, it's been proven that most exist purely for profit," she said. "They're highly variable in the best-case scenarios, but in the worst examples, they fall far below any standards for medical education accepted in the United States. Large numbers of students who complete their coursework on these islands face huge obstacles when they take licensing examinations and try to secure residency placements when they return here because they simply aren't trained well enough in coursework or clinical experience. It's devastating to them, really, because the schools charge top dollar prices for bargain basement educations."

Rita scribbled furiously as the physician rattled off statistics citing offshore programs that operate on shoestring budgets without uniform application procedures, admission requirements, or academic standards. She found it difficult to believe what she was hearing. "So let me see if I have this straight. Anyone with enough startup cash can open a medical school offshore and begin to recruit students, and the people who operate these schools can accept anyone, charge any amount of money, and teach them anything, in any kind of setting?"

She heard the other woman exhale deeply before answering the question. "Yes, it's true—all of it. I've heard of them opening schools in houses, in warehouses, and even in old store fronts, but because it's outside the U.S. jurisdiction, well beyond our borders and government, nothing can be done to stop them as long as these desperate students ignore the risks and are willing to pay their prices."

"How can they get away with this?" Rita asked.

"Most of the tuition money goes right into the pockets of the owner or administrator, although I've heard anecdotally that some of it is used to pay off government officials on the islands, which are largely poor and dependent upon tourism dollars for survival. Government leaders there are more than happy to turn a blind eye to unscrupulous business activity and, in many cases, welcome these shady schools in order to line their coffers with cash."

Rita wondered how easy it would be for offshore students to gain placement in hospitals. "Should I worry the next time I go to see my doctor?" she asked.

"Not really," Dr. Studer replied. "The only good thing is that, although a few will make it, most of the so-called graduates of these schools never pass licensing tests to practice medicine here and don't get placed into traditional hospital residency programs. You're not going to find too many of them treating grandma after her heart attack, thank goodness."

Rita chuckled. "I guess that's fortunate for grandma in the grand scheme of things. But really, Dr. Studer, the whole thing seems a bit frightening to me considering what could happen if one of these poorly trained students manage to slip through." On the heels of her recent hospitalization, she shivered at the thought.

"Yes, I suppose it is. Thankfully, there are some safeguards here in the United States. For one thing, medical school graduates, no matter where they've gone to school, must be licensed to practice medicine before they can call themselves physicians, and unlicensed graduates are not allowed to teach certain clinical subjects in a medical school. However, the American Medical Association and state medical boards can't do anything to control what happens outside our borders. Law enforcement authorities can't reach down into the Caribbean and weed out the bad guys because of jurisdictional limitations."

Rita shook her head. No wonder Shane chose an offshore scheme this time. He could do whatever he wanted and get away with it while snubbing his nose at the law. "Dr. Studer, is there anything else you can tell me about these schools?"

Dr. Studer hesitated before she answered. "I don't want to be quoted on this, because I haven't seen it for myself, but I have heard anecdotal accounts from former students about some awful things they've witnessed in these places."

Rita put her pen down and leaned forward in her chair in anticipation. She wanted more. "What kind of things?"

The other woman paused again before replying. "Well, I've recently heard horror stories about their anatomy classes, for one thing. Let's just say that the people teaching the classes aren't always respectful when working with cadavers, something that medical schools here are very cognizant of. But then, I should remind you that because there's no oversight, nothing can be done to change things or to ensure that students are taught properly. Really, that's all I can tell you now. I have another meeting, so I have to go. I'd suggest you try to talk to some former students. There are a lot of chat rooms and discussion groups online that might point you toward someone willing to help you learn more."

An hour later, Rita felt physically sick. While trolling around online, she'd ventured into chat room groups for medical students past, present, and prospective, and couldn't believe what she'd learned while reading through several discussion threads that appeared to confirm what Dr. Studer told her. On one thread, participants talked of anatomy classes in which they dissected human bodies, some covered in mold and oozing fluids in unsanitary conditions, at the direction of instructors who read from textbooks. Commenters said the instructors appeared unsure as to how to use medical instruments, which led students to believe the instructors were not qualified to teach. Another former student compared her instructor to a butcher. Their comments made her blood run cold.

How can this be happening? This isn't education. If anything, it's borderline criminal.

She sent messages to five or six participants in the thread, hoping for a reply. Within minutes, she had responses from several who said they might be willing to talk to her for background material, but not until after the end of the current semester and then only anonymously. That wouldn't help. She needed confirmation *on the record*. She was ready to give up and look for more students when one young woman, who said her name was Lily, sent her a private message and agreed to a phone interview later that afternoon. Off the record, of course.

"I knew the minute I walked into the anatomy classroom that it was wrong, but I was afraid to say anything because I'd tried so hard to get into medical school in the United States. I applied just about everywhere, and even though I had the grades, there were no spots available," Lily said, adding that her parents took out a second mortgage on their home to pay for her classes in Nevis because it was nearly impossible to get government financial aid for offshore studies. She didn't want to let them down, so she tried to make the best of a bad situation.

"The body was in a black bag...the room was air conditioned, but not enough to keep a cadaver cool. I didn't know much, but to me, it was clear the body hadn't been preserved properly for medical school use."

She explained that bodies prepped for medical school use should carry an overwhelming smell of formaldehyde, while bodies embalmed for viewing in funeral homes do not. The bodies they worked on did not carry the telltale odor, she added. "There's no way the school was equipped well enough for us to work on them. I've heard since then that most offshore schools on the islands don't work with cadavers. Officially, that is."

Rita took a sip of Diet Coke to settle her queasy stomach. "Would you be willing to tell me, off the record of course, which school you attended? I won't use your name. I'm simply trying to get an accurate picture of the kind of place that something like this could happen."

Several seconds passed in silence before Lily answered. "You must promise that you won't ever tell anyone that I told you anything because the school's director is nuts, and he threatened us all the time. I'm trying to get some of my tuition refunded to help my parents pay off their debts."

Rita squeezed the phone in her damp palm, hoping that she'd convince Lily to tell her more because she had a hunch that this student could be her entry ticket into Shane Gilliam's latest scheme. His school was on Nevis, so her gut told her it had to be him. "I won't do anything to let anyone know who you are. I know that you don't know me, and probably have no reason to trust me, but I've never exposed a source. Please, tell me what you know, and I promise you that I won't use anything unless I see it for myself, or unless you or someone agrees to talk on the record."

She heard the young woman take a deep breath. "It was Celtic Cross, run by Dr. Shane Gilliam, that is, if you want to call him a doctor."

Rita shifted uncomfortably in her chair, rubbing her neck to relieve tension. "What else can you tell me?"

"Really, I can't talk anymore. I have to go now, or I'll be late for work. I'm waiting tables to make extra money to help my parents pay off their loan. Maybe we can talk again sometime."

Rita didn't want the call to end but hung up reluctantly after Lily agreed to talk again on her day off. When she read through her notes, she shook her head in disgust.

David called her as she was letting Boomer out of his crate that evening. He'd talked to Carr, who advised him to hire a personal attorney for his family to protect their interest in the matter should they decide to file suit against the Mason-Watson Funeral Home.

"He's also setting up a meeting with the district attorney to discuss the possibility of exhuming my grandmother's body to determine whether a crime has been committed, whether there's evidence of theft," he explained. He sounded defeated. "I already know there's theft. I showed my mother the photo of the locket, and she started bawling. Red, it broke my heart seeing Mom that upset, knowing that her mother's final resting place isn't exactly what she wanted for her. She agreed that we should cooperate with the district attorney and file the petition for exhumation. She wanted Grandma buried with the locket, the most precious possession she'd ever owned, not because it was valuable, but because it was from my grandpa."

He said Carr told him it might take a few weeks to get the petition filed, after which there would most likely be a court hearing. "Carr promised to try to impress upon the district attorney and the judge that the petition should be sealed, and the hearing be closed to preserve confidentiality during the investigation. I know you're not going to like that."

She winced. Of course, she didn't like it, but she understood the pain publicity could cause for the family on such a sensitive issue. "I can't cover it anyway because of the potential conflict of interest. If it's made public, another reporter will do it, but trust me, I'll find out what I need to know even if it's sealed."

"No doubt about that," he said, chuckling. "I don't doubt you on much, if anything."

Before they hung up, she told him about her conversations regarding Shane's medical school and said that story would keep her busy while another reporter covered his case. He whistled in disbelief. "Good lord, Red. How can anyone get away with that kind of shit?"

"Nothing surprises me anymore. David, seriously, you've been around me long enough to know that people try to and sometimes do get away with anything and everything, including murder."

CHAPTER ELEVEN

A week after the ruling, Rita joined David's family members and their attorney, as well as two state troopers, the county detective, two assistant district attorneys, and her *Journal* colleague Bill Martin, when they gathered in the cemetery shortly after dawn to witness the exhumation of David's grandmother. It had taken four weeks to reach this point. A closed hearing preceded the decision that cleared the way for the process.

No other news outlets picked up on the ruling, to Rita's relief. It wasn't unusual for a clerk in the prothonotary's office, the court office where civil filings are made, to place an order in a file and shelve it before reporters noticed it, particularly if it was an order they weren't anticipating. Although police and county officials tried to discourage the family from attending, they wouldn't hear of it. Facing his grandmother's grave, David stood behind his mother, who sat on a folding chair with her legs crossed at the ankles, while his sister Chrissy stood with her husband next to her mother's chair. His father had died four years earlier.

The Mason-Watson Funeral Home management had been informed by certified mail, which Amie Watson signed for, but neither she nor her brother appeared to witness the process. Rita, who had taken a vacation day to support David, reached up from her chair to squeeze his hand as they waited under a canopy in an area that had been cordoned off with yellow tape to ensure the family's privacy. Because the forecast called for sunshine and much warmer temperatures later that day, the cemetery owner also put up a small tent adjacent to the canopy where a cooler of water and some paper cups had been placed on a small table next to a semi-circle of six folding chairs. The family's attorney, the county detective, and the two assistant district attorneys occupied four of those chairs, while the troopers stood a few feet away from the family. Rita couldn't see where Bill waited.

Now, watching David's mother sniffling into a tissue, Rita wished she could be anywhere else on the planet. No one should have to go through this. A funeral is bad enough, but to witness removal and unsealing of a coffin after burial seemed brutally cruel to everyone involved.

She shifted in her chair when she heard a piece of the excavator's equipment, a backhoe, start up behind them. As it rumbled across the grass, she tried to focus on the man's burly arms working the hand controls, rather than look at the grave where the headstone and two metal vases of plastic flowers had already been moved aside. Headstones and vases had also been moved away from several adjacent graves on either side, and in front and back, to avoid potential damage from the machinery.

She watched the bright yellow backhoe scoop the first load of dirt, lift it up, and swing around before dropping it on a nearby patch of grass. She reached over and grasped David's hand again, glancing sideways at his pale cheeks. He'd adored his grandmother, so she couldn't imagine his pain at this moment. Her heart pounded with fear as to what they might learn. She hoped and prayed they were mistaken, that there was another locket like his grandmother's, and that they'd find hers exactly where it had been hung on her neck as she'd wished. Her thoughts wandered, and she mused that possibly the jeweler who designed the piece had made a copy of it without David's grandfather's permission.

Bucket after rumbling bucket, the dirt pile grew as the machine dug deeper, sending puffs of dry soil blowing into the breeze. Finally, she heard a scraping sound and knew the man had reached the cement vault that contained the coffin. She held her breath as he rolled backward several feet and two gravediggers employed by the cemetery lowered themselves into the hole with shovels to clear the remaining dirt away from the top of the vault.

When the dirt was cleared, the backhoe operator hooked chains to his machine, and then lowered them into the hole, where the gravediggers attached them to four 'o' rings on top of the vault. They climbed out of the hole and gave a thumbs up signal to the man, who slowly moved away from the hole, lifting the top of the vault up and onto the ground, exposing the dark wood coffin inside.

David drew a sharp breath, and his mother gasped before bursting into tears at the sight of her mother's coffin. He put his arm around her, and one of the troopers moved to her side while the other filled a paper cup with water from the cooler and handed it to her. Rita watched her take a small sip and wince as though she couldn't swallow it. She placed the cup onto the grass at her feet and it tipped over, sending water trickling into the ground near her son's foot.

No one spoke. Beads of perspiration slid from Rita's hairline down her neck and into her shirt. She feared what the body might look like, wondering how much decomposition had ravaged it in the last year. She noticed David had begun to breathe heavily.

Chrissy, who had given birth to her first child several months earlier and still carried some baby weight, fanned herself with an old theater program she'd pulled from the black diaper bag she used as a purse. The two assistant district attorneys, one male and one female, shifted uncomfortably in their chairs. The county detective snapped several photos of the uncovered coffin. Out of the corner of her eye, Rita saw Bill move closer to the grave and peer inside for a better look. If it had been her assignment, she'd have done the same thing.

The excavator removed the chains from the concrete vault lid and handed them to the gravediggers, who once again lowered themselves into the hole to attach them to the handles on either side of the coffin. Again, they climbed out and gave the thumbs up sign to the man, who turned on his machine, moving it away and slowly lifting the coffin above ground. Just as he was about to set it down, he hit a bump in the ground and the coffin swung in the air, causing David's mother to hide her face in her hands. The operator held the controls still for a moment and the swaying stopped before he lowered the coffin onto the grass. Finally, the painstaking process was complete.

David gripped her hand tightly as one of the cemetery employees pulled a thin metal rod from a toolbox and approached the coffin. He used the rod first to dislodge a small, round plug that covered a hole at the head of the coffin, and then inserted the hook into the hole, using it as a crank. He turned it several times to loosen the seal at that end and then repeated the process at the foot of the coffin. Finished, he nodded to his partner and then to the county detective before he stepped backward.

Its seal broken, the coffin sat ready to be opened. The county detective moved forward with his camera, as did the two attorneys, Bill, and the troopers, but the family and Rita remained still, as if frozen in their seats. She held her breath, terrified of what the coffin would reveal and how it would affect David and his family.

When the gravediggers lifted the lid, Rita heard a collective intake of breath from the witnesses standing closest to the coffin. She caught Bill's eye. With his mouth open wide, he appeared shocked. Her stomach clenched. *Oh damn, the locket must not be there. Now what?*

No one close enough to see inside said a word as they turned to face the family. "What, what is it? I can't look. Tell me what you see," David's mother begged, holding her hands over her eyes. "Tell me what you see!"

Despite her pleas, no one spoke.

Finally, David couldn't stand it any longer, so he jumped from his chair, tripping over Rita's foot as he scrambled to the graveside, where he peered into his grandmother's open casket. He moaned when he looked inside.

"Oh my God. It's empty." His face went white, and he sank down on his knees into the grass as his mother and sister screamed. Rita jumped from her chair and lunged toward David, who appeared ready to faint. She knelt on the grass and put her arms around him as he rocked back and forth. When he buried his head on her lap, sobbing, she looked over his shoulder and into the empty coffin. She saw only the quilted blanket, a spray of dried flowers, and a family photo placed inside during the visitation at the funeral home.

David's mother stood, clutching her chest, and slowly walked toward the coffin. Peering inside, she gasped, and the color drained from her face when she saw that her mother wasn't there. She turned back toward her seat, swaying as she walked. She raised her hand toward Chrissy, who had risen from her chair, as if to stop her daughter from coming closer. Before she reached her own chair, she collapsed backward into a heap on the grass and lay there unmoving.

Rita, David and Chrissy scrambled to her side.

"Mom, Mom, can you hear me?" David checked her pulse and leaned down toward her chest. "She's breathing. Someone, please, call an ambulance. I think she fainted, but I'm not sure. It could be her heart again."

One of the troopers pulled out his phone and dialed 911. Rita moved over to him and explained that the woman had a long history of heart disease. "Please, tell them to hurry," she said.

By the time paramedics arrived, the distraught woman was alert and sitting up but breathing heavily. Her face appeared flushed, and her skin glistened with perspiration. Paramedics immediately began to administer oxygen and then loaded her onto a stretcher for transport to the hospital. Rita's knees wobbled from nerves at the unfolding drama as she watched them pull away.

Chrissy and her husband followed the ambulance out of the cemetery, but Rita and David remained in the shade of the tent to watch the county detective and police, who had placed yellow crime scene tape around the gravesite as they photographed the empty coffin. Bill shook David's hand and then gave her a quick hug before he got into his car to return to work and file his story, and she promised to call him with any new information. She was sipping tepid water from a paper cup when Lt. Carr drove up, got out of his car, and walked into the tent.

David, his eyes swollen from tears, stood to face him. "Now what happens?" When Carr didn't respond, his voice took on a pleading tone. "Somebody needs to tell me what happens next. Bad enough her locket's been stolen, but where is my grandmother? Why didn't they bury her? Are you going to file charges against the funeral home?"

Carr, his face grim, held up his hands in desperation. "Whoa. Calm down a bit, David. I know this is hard to take, and I want answers to every one of these questions myself, but we need to gather some information here first." Patiently, he explained that the state police crime lab team would process the scene and determine whether there was concrete evidence—fingerprints, or whatever, to go on before anything further is done.

"I have no clue, after all these months, what they might find in the way of evidence here, because the science of this is beyond me. Absolutely, we'll be questioning Amie Watson and her staff. Two of my guys are there with her now, and she will be escorted to the station to give a full statement later."

Carr explained that Amie was shocked by the news and promised her full cooperation. "She insisted that she and her brother would do everything in their power to help us discover how this mistake, which is what we're calling it now, could have happened." He added that the investigation could be hampered because of the deaths of two key players at the funeral home, Bob and Cindy.

"I have two guys watching Amie collect and box up their records from last year. When she heard what happened here today, she offered them up without a warrant. I need to warn you though, she said Bob most likely would have been the person to have sealed the coffin, so without him, we may never know the truth," he cautioned. Nevertheless, he said, police would review the records to determine who may have been in the funeral home when David's grandmother's body was on the premises.

"David, I'm not sure who was there at the time of your grandmother's visitation and services, but we'll be looking at florists and other vendors who may have come into the building. I'd also like to see the guest book, if you had one, that would list signatures of anyone who attended the viewing hours for visitation or the funeral service for your grandmother. Pallbearers, too. It's possible that someone may have seen something or noticed something out of the ordinary, maybe something you or the staff there may have missed."

David turned to Rita. "Do you remember what I told you? The reason I couldn't stand Bob Watson?" As she nodded in agreement, he wheeled around to face Carr.

He told Carr about his encounter with the funeral director. "Now, I know that *he* was the criminal, and something was going on there that he didn't want me to see. You'll never convince me otherwise. This was not a mistake."

He punched his right fist into his left hand. His voice broke and he swiped a tear from his cheek, avoiding Rita's gaze. "I nearly caught him."

He promised that Carr would have the guest logs from his grandmother's viewing the following morning. "I'll do anything you want, but I want to know where my grandmother is, and whether she has been buried elsewhere, or God forbid, cremated by mistake. That would kill my mother."

He explained that his mother's religion frowned upon cremation. "And I want my grandmother's locket. I need to give it to my mother, to give her some measure of comfort in this mess."

Carr listened to the distraught man's pleas with his eyes downcast as if focusing on the blades of grass beneath his feet. He spoke slowly, his voice low and calm with resolve. "I understand, and you will get the locket back at some point. I can't give it to you yet, though. Right now, it's considered evidence in an ongoing theft investigation. And because of what we found today, it's party to an investigation as to the whereabouts of your grandmother's remains."

David thanked him and trudged toward his car. Rita stood and slung her purse strap over her shoulder before she held her hand out to Carr. "George, thank you for coming out here. You know I can't write about this case, but if there's anything you find out that you can share with us, pass it along to Bill, or me, and I'll give it to Bill. I'm still assigned to cover the Watson and Ekas killings, though, so if there's anything new..."

Carr smiled and chuckled a bit. "Yes, Rita, I get it. You've trained me well. When I know, you'll know. Be careful, though, because I don't like the way things are adding up here. Someone out there is playing a deadly game."

Two days after the exhumation, a county judge approved a search warrant for a more extensive collection of records and evidence at the Mason-Watson Funeral Home. The following morning, a Friday, Rita had a nasty phone call from James Foster, who did nothing to hide his fury.

"Well Miss Locke, are you happy now? It's bad enough that you've been writing about Bob's murder, and Cindy's unfortunate death, but now you have to stir up trouble that's going to cause Amie to lose this business," he shouted.

"Please, calm down Mr. Foster. I'm not trying to stir up anything," she insisted.

He wouldn't listen. "This will be splattered all over the Sunday front pages again, and God knows what's going to play out on the evening newscasts because those vultures will be out in full force when they get wind of this. Amie had nothing to do with that woman's burial, and she damn sure doesn't know what happened to her jewelry or why she isn't in her grave for God's sake. That would have been Bob's doing, and only Bob's doing, and he's dead."

She'd tried again to calm him, but he wouldn't hear of it. Based on her first awkward encounter with him, she'd expected this would set him off. "Mr. Foster, we're only doing our jobs as journalists. We write about murders every day, and we don't single anyone out to try and ruin their livelihoods or their lives."

He shouted that she cared only about selling papers. "Your goal is to get on the front page and make a name for yourself."

"It's not personal with us," she insisted. "It's purely the business of good journalism. The family filed the petition for exhumation. When the grave turned up empty, it became news, *especially* after Bob Watson's death."

He cut her off. "I don't care what you say, Miss Locke. You're playing with fire when you mess with Amie Watson."

Something in his tone told Rita he had more on his mind than friendship with Amie Watson. She'd wondered then if he was protective of her out of a sense of loyalty to honor his friend, or because he was in love with her. To her, he definitely sounded like a man in love, and she knew from her own experiences that love could make anyone behave irrationally.

"I'm not trying to mess with anyone," she countered.

He huffed. "I guess you haven't learned your lesson. If she loses her business over this, you're going to have hell to pay. I owe it to my friend's memory to protect his wife, and I'm going to do just that. Any way I can."

He hung up on her before she could ask him what he meant by referring to the attack she'd endured. The veiled threat made her stomach turn.

Two hours later, she leaned against her Jeep parked across the street from the mansion, where Bill and several other reporters and photographers from local television stations and newspapers gathered to watch state troopers haul dozens of boxes and several computers down the steps and past the lion guard before loading them into a waiting van. Amie Watson, her face pale and drawn, stood on the porch watching the procession along with her brother, Daniel, who had his arm around her shoulders. He stared at Rita, unable to mask his hatred. Standing with them was James Foster, whose tightly folded arms and clenched jaw led Rita to believe he was still boiling with anger at her as the scene played out before him.

Now, watching his blood-red face from across the street, she studied the muscular outline of his body as he stood close to Amie on the porch. He towered over her by at least a foot. He was broad-shouldered, fit, and built like someone who worked out regularly. If appearances meant anything, he looked to be very strong. Hadn't Amie told her he'd been a wrestler when he was young? His comment about learning her lesson chilled her blood and made her mind race with frightening questions.

Was he making an idle threat simply because he was furious? Lovestruck? Or was he the hooded man who attacked her, leaving her battered and near death in a pool of blood? If it had been him who'd invaded her home with murder on his mind, was he crazed enough to try it again?

CHAPTER TWELVE

James Foster's angry premonition about the weekend's news coverage came true, and when Rita walked into the newsroom on Monday morning, it seemed as though everyone in Allegheny and Westmoreland counties and the surrounding area decided to call with questions about dead loved ones whose burials had been entrusted to the Mason-Watson Funeral Home. The red message light on her desk phone flashed a warning that there were already seventeen voicemails waiting for her. She pushed the button and began to listen to the messages. As she put her satchel down, the phone rang again.

"Don't answer it," Tom said.

She stopped herself from reaching for the phone and turned to face him. Her eyes widened with shock because she'd never seen her editor so frustrated. "Why not? What's going on?"

He shook his head. "We need to talk about the Mason-Watson murder. Let it go to voicemail, and we'll sort things out later when Bill gets in. I've been fielding calls for the last hour, and I've referred most of them to state police and the district attorney's office. We're not here to give legal advice, so watch what you say about this if you do take a call, although I'd rather you forward them to me or to Bill."

She shot him a look. "What do you mean, give it to Bill? This Mason-Watson story has been mine since I climbed out of bed early on a Sunday morning to cover the killing, and now you're going to make me hand *everything* over to Bill?"

He ran his hands through his hair and swore as his phone rang again. He didn't answer it. "Red, seriously, I'm your friend, not your enemy. We've been working together long enough for you to know that I respect you and value your work, but I can't have you covering anything to do with the murder now that David's family is front and center in whatever this mess turns out to be. You know, and I know, and from the phone call I got this morning from the publisher, *he* knows that there's a direct conflict of interest here. I had to tell him last week that you were not going to be covering the exhumation because of your relationship with David and that you would be there as an observer only, and not as part of your job. I'm on the hotseat with the publisher, and I don't have the time or energy to deal with your temper or your ego on this right now."

She started to answer, but he cut her short with one look. He raised his hand to stop her from speaking. "My decision is final, so save your arguments. I'll take your advice as to which direction we should pursue, and I'll gladly take and appreciate any inside information you can feed us as a background *source* for stories that Bill will be writing, but other than that, I have to take you off the story. I'm sorry, because I know how hard you've worked on this, and what you've suffered personally and physically because of your involvement." He looked into her eyes. "Red, please understand, I'm also concerned for your safety here."

"I assume this means Cindy's death as well?"

"Yes, Red. I'm sorry but that's the way it must be."

She knew he was right, She willed herself not to show him how upset she was, but her eyes burned with angry tears as she recalled the late-night invasion at her home, which had always been her refuge, a safe place away from covering the ugliness of crimes and courtroom dramas. Tom was right, although she hated to admit it even to herself because she desperately wanted to write this story. She ached to be the one to find out who was responsible for traumatizing her and for hurting David and his family.

Rita was grateful that David's mother had suffered a panic attack, and not another heart attack, when she collapsed at the sight of her mother's grave during the exhumation. After two days in the hospital undergoing tests, she was recovering at home. David and his sister each confessed that they hadn't been sleeping well since the ordeal, and if Rita was truthful with herself, she hadn't had a solid night's sleep either.

Her therapist had suggested she should leave the story to another reporter. Well, now it wasn't her decision to make so she accepted the bitter realization that it was time to back off. She threw her hands up in mock surrender as if to acknowledge certain defeat. "Okay, okay, you win. I'll listen to these messages and then pass the numbers on to Bill."

Tom's forehead wrinkled with worry lines. "Are you okay? What are you going to do?"

She met his eyes, her lips pressed together, her tone cool. "I'm going to do my job and find another story. Right now, I'm going to work on the Shane Gilliam story, try to get a few more interviews with students."

He appeared relieved to have avoided further confrontation over the issue. Turning to his computer, he bobbed his head up and down. "Sounds good. Do that. Let me know what you find out."

Rita's follow-up interview the next day with the young medical student left her stunned. As she read back through her notes, she couldn't believe what Lily, often crying, told her about the first weeks of the semester she spent at Celtic Cross. The school consisted only of several rooms in a small house in a residential neighborhood on the tiny island of Nevis, a sister to the nearby larger island of St. Kitts. She explained that she and seven others, two women and five men, started at the same time the past September, joining six others who had enrolled several months before. There were just two instructors, Shane Gilliam, who taught anatomy and pharmacology, and a female nurse, Susan Potter, who served dual roles as the school's vice president and taught microbiology and biochemistry classes. Lily said Potter mostly read aloud from textbooks or websites rather than offering practical lectures of any value. She described classrooms as sparse, with the largest one, most likely a former living room, adjacent to a small kitchen where the students stored their lunches in an old refrigerator with a broken ice maker and a noisy compressor. The reference library, clearly once a bedroom with a small closet, contained about thirty medical dictionaries, obsolete textbooks on anatomy and various sciences, and outdated medication guides. "Nothing was up to date or modern, not the materials or the equipment. It wasn't a library. The shelves were cheap plastic, like you'd get at Walmart and put together yourself," Lily added. "To me, the books looked like they'd come from used bookstores or flea markets. Our textbooks were new, of course, because we had to buy them ourselves before we got to the island, but everything else was pretty shabby.

"Instruction was unstructured and informal to the point that it was often confusing," she said. "The worst, however, were the anatomy classes taught by Dr. Gilliam." Elaborating, she said that although they were in their very first semester and had no prior clinical experience, the students participated in several sessions in which they dissected human body parts. She recalled one instance in her third week when body parts were removed from a male cadaver and tossed into an empty five-gallon bucket before the bucket was emptied into the regular garbage bin in an alley behind the "school."

"The poor guy had been overweight, and Dr. Gilliam had us remove layers of fatty tissue from his body and put it in the bucket. I'm not even sure what we were supposed to be looking for, and I'm not sure he knew either."

At Rita's gasp, Lily apologized. "I'm sorry if I'm grossing you out, but that's what happened. Anyway, we worked on the body for a couple of days, an hour at a time, which is all we could stand because it was really starting to smell bad from the decay. We had to put bleach in a spray bottle and squirt the body before we could work on it. I almost couldn't take it. On the last day, he had us remove the face. There was no need to do it." She paused and sniffled before blowing her nose. "My friend Valerie had to pull the face off. It went into the bucket, too, and I swear we both almost threw up."

She blew her nose again. "That's when I realized Dr. Gilliam is a fake. Even if someone consents to donate his body to science, he has a right to be treated with respect, and this poor guy wasn't. I didn't know much, but I knew enough to understand that there's no way this stuff happens in legitimate medical schools."

Rita asked, "Did you tell anyone?"

"No, and I should have. I knew right then and there that I wasn't going to get the education I wanted or had paid for, and Valerie felt the same way. She left school the week after he made her do that."

Before their conversation ended, Rita asked whether that event, or something else, served as the catalyst for Lily's ultimate withdrawal from the medical school.

"I'd like to say that the anatomy class sent me packing, but I was too desperate for a degree, so I kept going for a few more weeks after Val left, and I'm ashamed of myself for it now. No, I got really sick from an infection in my arm," Lily said. "We didn't know what we were doing with the surgical instruments we were using to dissect cadavers, and he surely didn't show us any safety precautions beforehand."

Rita drew a sharp breath. "No scrubbing up? No protective gear or gloves?"

"I doubt that anything was sterile. About a week after the face incident, we were working on the body of an older woman when another student moved his hand as I was spraying bleach, and he accidentally slashed me with a dirty scalpel." She explained that it wasn't the student's fault because no one knew for sure how to use the surgical instruments.

"Dr. Gilliam didn't offer us much help. Believe me, the cut was deep, and I bled all over the place. Anyway, I asked him to stitch it up, and he wanted me to go to the island's emergency clinic instead." She said she was surprised when he refused. "After all, what kind of doctor can't stitch up a simple cut?"

She said she tied the sleeve of her bloodied lab coat over her arm and found first aid supplies in the school's tiny bathroom, poured peroxide on the cut and wrapped bandages around her arm. When classes ended two hours later, Dr. Gilliam dropped her off at the emergency room, where she received twenty stitches for the deep wound that became infected a few days later. "I told my parents what happened. They bought me a plane ticket, and I cleared out my things. I applied for financial aid, and I'm going to start nursing school next fall. I guess I'll never be a doctor, but hopefully, someday I'll be a nurse practitioner."

She expressed regret at failing to become a doctor, blaming Shane Gilliam for building up her hopes by accepting her into his school and then shattering her dreams. "This school was my last resort, and it turned out to be a sham. He's ruined so many lives, just to make money. He loves money so much that it's made him dangerous. Personally, I think he's a monster. A twisted monster."

Early the next morning, Rita decided to take her notes to her editor to plead her case. She wanted permission to travel to the medical school but had no idea how to begin to ask for it because the timing couldn't have been worse —she'd been off for months, and now she spent her days sitting at her desk. Why did Shane have to do this on a sunny island? Anyone and everyone from the obituary clerks to the publisher himself would suspect her of using a potential story as a ruse to escape Pittsburgh and enjoy a vacation on the paper's dime. How could she convince them to let her go after all the time she'd been off work following her attack?

If she wanted this story, she had to try.

When she'd finished recounting everything she'd learned the previous day, Tom wiped his hand across the graying stubble on his chin. He said nothing for a full minute while she awaited, and expected, his immediate refusal to consider the matter. Finally, he looked up at her. "I can't believe I'm saying this, but I'm going to talk to John. He may or may not agree to anything, but I agree that it's worth a try because of this guy's history here in Pittsburgh. If this pans out, Rita, it's a hell of a story. Could be that Pulitzer you've been chasing for the last ten years."

She doubted that their executive editor would part with the cash to send her chasing Gilliam again. He'd been wooed from his Dallas newsroom several years earlier to lead their Pittsburgh news staff, and it was no secret that he favored local coverage, and in her opinion, the work of male reporters. He'd barely acknowledged her when she was listed as a Pulitzer finalist two years earlier for her body of work on a serial killer. For those reasons, he wasn't her favorite, and behind his back she referred to him as "Tex" or "the cowboy" because he regularly wore leather western boots with expensive designer suits, which in her opinion, appeared totally ridiculous in the city of Pittsburgh. She couldn't hide her disdain for the man, and never really tried.

"Oh great, if it's up to Tex, I'm not going to get anywhere near that island unless it's by rowboat," she said.

Tom's head snapped up. "How many times do I have to tell you not to call him that? It's all up to him, all of this. Your job, my job, everything you see in this newsroom is up to him because he's the one who decides when to go to the publisher to get the money to do what we need to do." He spread his arms wide to enforce his point. "It's not up to me. This is business, Red. And business costs money, something the paper doesn't have much of right now. I said I'm going to try to get you there." He lowered his voice to a whisper. "Hopefully, he'll let me pull money from somewhere in our measly budget to get you where you need to go. Be patient, and while you're at it, it wouldn't kill you to be respectful for a change, until I get an answer from him."

She nodded, her face hot with embarrassment, hoping that no one else heard him. She looked around the room and saw two feature writers chatting near the copy machine and the city government reporter talking on his cell phone. Had they been listening? Other than the three of them, the newsroom stood empty at that hour. Grateful for that, she leaned toward him to apologize. They were friends, but she'd been way out of line talking to him like that.

Her voice shook when she spoke. "I'm sorry, Tom. I know it's been hard here these past few months, and I'm not trying to be a pain in the ass. You've all been great to me through this. Trust me, this wouldn't be a vacation. Put me on the worst flights, book the lowest budget hotel. Just get me there, and I'll bring back something good. I know it."

Tom rubbed his eyes and ran his hand down his chin. "I have no doubt about that, Red, seriously I don't. Aside from the cost, part of my problem with this whole thing starts with the fact that you'd be poking around in things outside the country, away from the protection of the paper, the police, and the government here. You already claim that this guy is a wacko, and you know he has it in for you since the last time you wrote about his scheme..."

She stopped him. "Yeah, I think he's dangerous, but only to people who fall for his lies about being a doctor, and I'm not one of them. I don't trust him, but I don't believe he'd do anything to hurt me other than call and complain to the publisher. I'd be more afraid of him stealing my wallet or credit cards than anything else."

He ran his hands through his hair and leaned back in his chair, closing his eyes for a minute. "I hope you're right because if something goes wrong, there's little we can do to help you from here, and who knows what kind of law enforcement operations there are on such a small island. From the cash these students are pouring into the place, it sounds like there's a lot of money involved, and if you push this guy into a corner, he might be desperate enough to do something stupid to get out of it. If we get approval for this, you're going to be putting yourself at risk, and you're going to be alone because I can't afford to send a photographer with you. After all that you've gone through already, I'd never forgive myself if something else happened to you."

CHAPTER THIRTEEN

When the argument started, David sounded so much like her editor that she did a double take as he leaned across the dinner table toward her. They'd had a great dinner in an expensive restaurant, and as she'd expected, he'd proposed. It wasn't quite the down-on-one-knee romantic scene from the movies, but it was heartfelt, and they'd both shed a few quiet tears when he slipped a blazing emerald cut diamond on her left ring finger after they shared a piece of chocolate cake for dessert.

"I love you, Red, and I want to spend the rest of my life with you. I realized when you were hurt and lying in that hospital bed that my life would never be the same, would never be right again, if I lost you," he'd whispered.

Before she accepted, she reminded him that they might never be able to have children. "What if it's just us? I know you want kids," she said. He'd known about her miscarriage since the beginning of their relationship, but she wanted to reinforce the effect it could have upon their future together.

When she'd finished, he took her hand and said, "As long as you're not still in love with the baby's father, that's all I need to know. I just want to be with you. We can be a great aunt and uncle to my sister's kids. Braxton isn't even a year old yet, and she's already talking about having another one."

"Then, yes. I love you, David, and I promise that even if it's just us, I'll do everything I can to make you happy." She gave him a wry grin. "I might even turn down an assignment or two, you know, to compromise with my husband."

He laughed out loud, causing their waiter to turn away from another table and look at them.

"Red, I appreciate the sentiment behind that comment, but we already know that isn't going to happen. I'm going to try to be patient and live with it."

As they finished their champagne, a gift from the waiter when he witnessed the proposal, Rita told David about her plans to travel to Nevis. "I'm going to visit the medical school, maybe take a look at some of the other schools there and on the neighboring island of St. Kitts." She took a sip of her drink. "I'm hoping that I can meet some of the students."

She watched his mood switch instantly from euphoria to disbelief. His face reddened, and his eyes blazed. "Are you crazy? After all you've been through?"

Stunned by his reaction, she sat back in her chair when he began to protest the trip. He ran through ten fingers worth of objections. "You know nothing about his place, you're barely finished with your physical therapy, and whether you want to admit it or not, you're suffering from PTSD as the result of what you went through."

She leaned forward, ready to argue as he rattled on, but he stopped her with a tender look. "Honey, I sleep with you. I listen to you crying from nightmares more often than you'll ever confess to me, your therapist, or yourself. What happened to you is real, and you're not over it yet."

She said nothing. He was right but she'd never admit it. When he finished, he sank back into his chair and ran his hands over his face. "You're dead set on this, aren't you?"

"That's an interesting way of phrasing it."

He gave a wry laugh. "If you're going to go, I'll take some time off and go with you. I'd never forgive myself if something else happened to you."

She twisted the diamond on her finger, imagining that it tightened as he spoke. Was this their future? She had no desire to argue every time she went on a difficult assignment. As firmly and kindly as possible, she said, "No, I'm going alone. It's not a vacation; it's my job, and I don't want or need a babysitter to watch over me. David, is this what it's going to be like after we're married? We haven't even been engaged for ten minutes, and you're trying to tell me what to do."

He mumbled an apology. "I'm not trying to tell you what to do or how to perform your job. I'm worried about you, that's all. I want you to be safe."

Afterward, Rita felt the magic of the evening fade away. They said little on the drive home, and when they got to her townhouse, he made an excuse that he couldn't stay overnight because of an early meeting. He left after an awkward kiss goodnight.

For days, as David's roller coaster emotions reeled back and forth between worry and anger over Rita's trip, she almost felt guilty enough to cancel it. Nevertheless, she ultimately decided to go for the story. She might not have another chance to catch Shane at his game.

On the day she was to leave, she woke up tired from another sleepless night after arguing once more with David over his concerns for her safety. He insisted again that he should tag along, and she'd refused, even though she'd almost given in because he'd been under so much stress in recent days.

Three other families had filed petitions for exhumation of their loved ones buried from the Mason-Watson Funeral Home. Based on what had happened in the case of David's grandmother, the court granted the requests immediately without holding hearings. Two exhumations, at two different cemeteries, resulted in the discovery of two more empty coffins and reports of four missing pieces of jewelry: two wedding rings, a pocket watch on a chain, and a cherished diamond brooch. When the third was opened, the woman's body was inside, and her wedding ring remained on her finger. Rita didn't know what was worse, knowing the depth of grief these families faced or seeing Bill's byline on the coverage that should have been hers.

Although David drove her to the airport, he said little on the ride there. As she got out of the car, she wondered whether she'd still be engaged when she returned. It wouldn't shock her if he changed his mind. "I love you," she said, squeezing his hand after he unloaded her bag from the back seat. He mumbled the same in return and pecked a light kiss on her cheek. Defeated, she turned to walk away, but he stopped her.

"Red, wait. You're a risk taker. I get that. I don't know if I can ever get used to it, though, but I love you. More than anyone or anything." He reached for her hand and stared into her eyes. "I'm also proud of you for the work that you do. Please, be safe and come back to me."

The lump in her throat left her unable to speak. She watched him drive away before she walked through the revolving door into the terminal.

Six hours later, she was grateful to be safely on the ground. It had been a rough ride from Pittsburgh to Miami, and even rougher from Miami to the island of St. Kitts, with turbulence that left her gripping the armrests with white knuckles. She didn't hate flying but didn't enjoy it enough to love it. To her, being in the air was simply the means to an end, a way to get from one place to another and nothing more. And now, because of her recent injuries, her legs and back ached from sitting so long in one position in the cramped seat and tightening her muscles during the turbulence.

She checked her lipstick and ran her fingers through her hair to fluff the spiky cut she'd grown accustomed to during her recovery. When the plane rolled to a stop, she gathered her satchel, pulled her wheeled carry-on bag from the overhead compartment, and hobbled up the long aisle behind a blonde woman dragging a bright pink roller bag decorated with palm trees. She noticed that the woman's expertly manicured fingernails, toenails, and capri pants all matched the pink on the bag. *She's ready for fun in the sun, which doesn't sound half bad right now. But no, it's time to go to work.*

A blast of hot air smacked Rita's face when she got to the door of the plane and stepped across the threshold onto the jetway leading into the Robert Llewellyn Bradshaw International Airport, a few miles northeast of the capital city of Basseterre. Thankfully, it was air conditioned, so the walk to find a taxi wasn't as miserable as she'd anticipated. Her leg, held together with pins and screws, throbbed from walking long distances between airport gates. She still had a slight limp but refused to admit even to herself that she could have benefitted from airport assistance that would have meant an easy ride in a wheelchair or electric golf cart rather than walking.

She stopped to use the restroom before looking for a taxi stand. From what she'd read about St. Kitts, she knew she'd have to take ground transportation from the airport to Reggae Beach, where she'd board either a ferry or a water taxi that would take her to Nevis, the tiny island where Shane Gilliam based his medical school. After a short taxi ride through town, she paid twenty dollars for a water taxi ride and boarded the small craft for the two-mile journey that sadly took only ten minutes. The passenger ferry between the islands would have taken longer, so she made a mental note to try it before she went home. The brief ride in the sea air, late afternoon sunshine, and turquoise water left her wanting more, and she was reluctant to get off the boat when it pulled alongside the pier in Charlestown, the capital of Nevis. She looked around with appreciation. The stunning surroundings surely boosted the island's tourism-based economy.

"Welcome to Nevis, my lady," boomed the elderly water taxi operator as he lifted her suitcase onto the wooden dock. He had several missing teeth and hands gnarled with arthritis but smiled as he helped her out of the boat. "Enjoy your stay on our beautiful island. May you find love and happiness here."

I'd like to find love and happiness here or anywhere. Why is it that all I ever seem to find are heartaches and arguments like the one David and I had last night?

She pushed those thoughts of David out of her mind and rolled her bag to the end of the dock, where she hailed a taxi to drive her to the hotel the newsroom secretary booked for her for the next week. It was described online as a beachfront villa with private terraces, but she doubted there would be time to put her toes in the glistening white sand. She had only seven short days to find out everything she could about the island, Shane Gilliam, and his medical school scheme. In the past week, she'd set up interviews with two medical school administrators on Nevis and one on St. Kitts, all of whom offered to let her tour their operations and talk with willing students. She had not reached out to Shane or to anyone listed on his website with connections to his school, hoping that the element of surprise might work to her advantage if she showed up unannounced.

After a dinner of grilled shrimp and rice on the outdoor patio at her hotel, she drank a glass of wine while watching the fiery orange sunset over the water. She'd planned to call David but decided against it and texted him instead because she didn't want to argue. *Arrived safely. Love you and see you soon.* She immediately powered her phone down. Despite his last words at the airport, she was afraid that she either wouldn't get an answer or wouldn't like his answer. *Coward, you didn't even wait a few seconds for a reply.* Exhausted, she went back to her room, showered, and fell asleep within minutes.

By late afternoon the next day, the tropical heat and humidity sent rivulets of sweat running down the base of Rita's neck, and for the first time ever, she didn't miss her long curls. She'd toured two medical schools – one on Nevis and the other across the channel in St. Kitts – and interviewed the chancellors at both, as well as a handful of students. These institutions, although clearly not as modern as their counterparts in the United States, appeared respectable, and the administrators willingly gave her proof of decent graduation rates and positive outcomes for residency placements. The graduating students she spoke with seemed to be both busy and happy, and several talked about their upcoming residency assignments in American hospitals.

"When your students work with cadavers in their anatomy classes, can you tell me how those classes are handled?" she asked the administrator in Nevis.

He paused for a moment. "Here, we have eight students per cadaver, and their classes are strictly regulated, following guidelines at leading medical schools around the world."

She pushed further. "Do your faculty instructors live and work here on the island?"

"Of course. Not everyone lives here full-time, however. Some are practicing physicians or educational professionals who split their time between here and the United States or Europe, depending on the semester and their caseloads," he explained.

When she asked several more questions about clinical coursework, directing her focus once more on the use of cadavers, he drew an impatient breath before answering. "*Our* anatomy classes are taught by qualified clinical instructors under sterile conditions. Unfortunately, you won't find that everywhere on the islands. Most medical schools don't work with cadavers because they simply aren't equipped well-enough to do so."

He hesitated and looked away before locking his eyes with hers. "Of course, the lack of equipment doesn't always stop them."

She wanted more. She needed specifics, so she continued to probe. "Can you give me some examples of those schools and the names of who I should talk to about them?" she asked.

He looked away again, refusing to meet her eyes. "No, my lady. I cannot."

She put down her pen. Her intuition told her he was hiding something. "Cannot or will not?"

Frowning, he pursed his lips. "Whatever you think, my lady. Take it how you will. That's all I'm going to say on the matter."

CHAPTER FOURTEEN

Rita reserved the second full day of her work week to talk with government leaders in the Ministry of Education and Ministry of Health for the Federation of St. Kitts and Nevis, a dual-island parliamentary democracy that gained independence from the United Kingdom in 1983. Her research showed that although the reigning monarch continued to serve as the ceremonial figurehead with a governor-general as the monarch's representative, the islands were governed by a prime minister and appointed cabinet ministers.

She had arranged interviews with a few of the ministers prior to leaving Pittsburgh. Secretaries for the two of them said she could anticipate waiting a while once she reached their offices. She'd arrived at the education headquarters located in Basseterre on St. Kitts shortly after nine, and at noon, still waited alone in a sweltering hallway. A few minutes before one, the secretary stepped out into the hall and waved her through the door.

A welcome blast of air conditioning from a humming window unit chilled her face when she entered the office where she met Saundra Hook, chairman of the Ministry of Education's accreditation board. "How can I help you, Miss Locke?"

From her tone, Rita could tell the woman was irritated at the interruption, so she wasted no time in getting to the purpose of her visit. She explained what she had learned about Shane Gilliam and his lack of credentials and licensing, as well as his history of fraudulent activity at the clinic in the United States. "I have copies of everything for you to review so you can see that my information is accurate," she said.

Rita relayed the story about Lily's injury while attending the school. "I have reason to believe that he may be jeopardizing students' health, not to mention providing them with a less than adequate medical school education. Did you or anyone else from the board investigate him or look into his professional background before the school opened? Have you visited the premises or talked with any students?"

The other woman clicked her tongue and shook her head as she skimmed the pages Rita had given her. "No, I did not, and neither have any of my colleagues because we had no reason to suspect Dr. Gilliam was anything other than what he'd represented himself to be – a licensed professional. I will tell you, however, now that you've brought this to my attention, that if this school and Dr. Gilliam are not legitimate, there will have to be an investigation." She shuffled the papers into a neat pile and pulled a manila folder from a drawer in her desk. "If these allegations are true, I'd not hesitate for a moment to pull the plug on this thing. Medical education is a rather big money-making venture on the islands, and we have several very reputable schools within St. Kitts and Nevis that are doing wonderful things and graduating well-qualified students who have gone on to very gratifying careers. We have a responsibility to every student, and I take it very seriously."

She explained that although the dean of a medical school isn't necessarily required to be a practicing physician, he or she should at the very least have a solid medical background and possess the appropriate credentials and licensing.

Because she'd heard rumors of kickbacks, Rita pushed further, asking whether the government's officials made a practice of accepting money from the medical schools.

The other woman's nostrils flared in anger, and she glared at Rita. "You're probably aware that Caribbean medical schools are targets for criticism, so we must work to ensure that everything is handled appropriately, and I do just that. Your comment is offensive to me because I personally have worked very hard to maintain objectivity and professionalism," Hook concluded. "If it is true, what you've told me about Dr. Gilliam tells me he is not someone we want in charge of a medical school, and there's no amount of money that could persuade me to look the other way." She motioned toward the door. "However, I cannot take your word for it, so I will be investigating it myself. Now, I'm very busy, and I must get back to work. Good day, Miss Locke."

Rita smiled as she stood. She respected the woman's no-nonsense, direct style. "Thank you for listening to me. When you've completed your investigation, I'd love to talk to you again to hear what you've discovered. Unfortunately, I'm only here until the end of the week, so it will have to be over the phone."

Two hours later, Rita's meeting with Dr. Martin Simms, the chief medical officer of the Ministry of Health, ended abruptly when she broached the subject of the use of cadavers in the country's schools. She related what she'd learned in her discussion with medical students and described what she'd heard about Shane's practices.

He frowned and pointed his index finger at her. "You're making very serious allegations, Miss Locke. I am unaware that

Celtic Cross uses cadavers in anatomy studies. For one thing, it is the health ministry's role to regulate the transport and use of cadavers in the country and approve the necessary documents – the donor's death certificate, the embalming certificate, and the transport certificate. I have none of those documents for this university, so I doubt you are correct in saying they are cutting people to shreds and disposing of their body parts in buckets. I don't know where you're getting that false information from, therefore I think this conversation must come to an end right here."

Based on research she'd done prior to arriving, she knew the island federation practiced 'citizenship by investment,' a system in which residents of other countries, largely the United States, who wanted to gain dual citizenship, could purchase a passport from the federation by investing money, usually a couple hundred thousand dollars. Dual citizenship opened the doors to various benefits, such as tax breaks and visa-free travel abroad. She wondered whether investors could gain similar favor from government officials by funneling money into the federation's ministries. Taking a gamble, she rose from her chair as if ready to leave, but stood in front of his desk, facing him as she locked her gaze with his. "Dr. Simms, may I ask you why you're so upset with me? Do you have something to do with this school? Do you have some financial stake in it?"

He jumped up, shouting, "No, I do not. However, I will tell you that a number of very prominent people on the island have invested money in this school to get it off the ground." He explained that the schools are vital to the island's economy because students pay rent and utilities to live here, and shop at local businesses for food and things they need.

"The people who run businesses in the area where the school

is located will not be happy to hear your annoying accusations based on tales from disgruntled students who could not handle the rigors of medical school. Good afternoon."

He strode to the door, opened it, and walked out into the reception area. He held that door open as well, leaving her no choice but to follow him and exit into the steamy hallway. The door slammed behind her as she made her way down the stairs and out of the building.

Rita wandered aimlessly around the shops in Charlestown after exiting the water taxi. It had been a long, hot day, and she wanted to unwind a bit before heading to her villa to type up her notes. Despite the fact that she was traveling alone, she felt safe as she walked through the vendors' stalls, comforted by the realization that she could blend into the crowd of tourists. She bought a brightly colored sarong for Kathy, dangly beaded earrings for herself, and for David, a t-shirt with a picture of a monkey on it. He'd get a kick out of it. She'd read about the hundreds of chickens and small African vervet monkeys that roamed the islands, but she'd been unnerved to encounter them running freely on the streets and around the resort, even though the hotel desk clerk told her the monkeys are harmless and fed off leaves, berries, fruit, and insects.

"Chickens, they run away. Monkeys, they won't hurt you either, Missy," the clerk said, smiling. "Unless they hurt your wallet." He explained that some enterprising islanders charge tourists ten dollars to hold and have their photo taken with a tame monkey. He held his head back and laughed. When he finished, he wiped his eyes with a handkerchief pulled from his shirt pocket. "Tourists don't know that if you hold out some food, any monkey will do it for free."

On the third day, after completing nearly a dozen interviews, Rita felt she had enough information to call on Shane at the school. She used the three-mile taxi ride to steel herself to face him, well aware that the confrontation would be uncomfortable, and possibly downright ugly. She knew he blamed her for uncovering his fraud at the medical clinic in Pennsylvania. He had to hate her for exposing him because it resulted in the loss of his livelihood, reputation, and all the money his family had invested in his scheme. When he learned she'd followed him to the Caribbean, he'd be furious.

And with Shane Gilliam, money was the religion he worshipped. The clinic was small change compared to what he could rake in at this school even with a few students, based on his tuition rates.

Dr. Gilliam was away for the day, according to the receptionist who greeted her when she walked into the front entryway of the school in a one-story home with faded pink siding. The young woman, Omaima Alwen, according to the sparkling brass nameplate on her desk, sat in front of a sixteen-by-twenty portrait of a smiling Dr. Gilliam in his embroidered white lab coat and holding a stethoscope. She'd seen it on the school's website. He was costumed and playing the role here, just as he had stateside. It inspired her, so she decided that this time, she'd do some acting, too. Immediately, she put on a bright smile and launched into some fast-talking, serious flattery.

"I'm Rita Locke, from Pennsylvania in the United States, where Dr. Gilliam is from. I wonder, since he isn't available, would you be willing to show me around your lovely school? I may not be able to return because I'm flying home in a few days." She doubted that the young woman, who appeared to be no more than twenty, would grant her request. Nevertheless, she had to see more, and with Shane away from the premises, this might be her only chance to gain an accurate picture of his operation.

Omaima beamed with pride and stood with her arms wide and welcoming. "Oh, yes, Missy Locke. We are most proud of the school. It is getting bigger and better with more students coming every month. Please, follow me."

She took Rita through a narrow hallway and proudly pointed out two classrooms, one of which appeared to have been a living room at one time because it had a picture window facing the street. The other may have been an office or den, Rita imagined. Each of the rooms held two long tables, surrounded by eight chairs, and a desk facing them. At the end of the hall was a kitchen area with a table for six, an apartment-sized refrigerator, a stove, and a microwave oven on a chipped laminate counter above a row of white wooden cabinets.

"Here is our library and computer area," the young woman said, gesturing toward a room that appeared to have been a bedroom at one time. Cheap plastic shelving took up two walls but contained at most forty worn-looking books. There were two six-foot tables and a dozen folding chairs in the center of the room. It was just as Lily described.

"Oh, nice," Rita exaggerated, pulling out her phone. "May I take some photos to remember this?"

Her escort hesitated but then broke into a wide smile. "Yes, please do. I'm sure the people of Pennsylvania would love to see this fine place and possibly come here to learn."

Rita snapped picture after picture of the books, the shelves, and the single computer on a small table on one side of the room before following Omaima down the hall to what she referred to as the "student lounging room." Inside, Rita saw five students, two male and three female, who appeared to be in their late teens or early twenties. All were engrossed in reading on their books or tablets. Two looked up briefly but did not acknowledge her.

"Where are the other students and instructors," Rita asked. "It's very quiet here today, isn't it?"

"There are five or six more students out in the courtyard on a break, and more are coming later in the week. We start a new semester Monday, but we have no instructors other than Dr. Gilliam and Miss Potter. Maybe more, someday."

She turned to Rita and smiled. "This is all I can show you."

"What about that room? What's in there," Rita asked, pointing to a closed door opposite the lounge.

The young woman's eyes widened, and she shook her head as she took a few steps backward away from the doorway. "Oh, no, Missy Locke, I don't like that room. I don't look at the dead people." She crossed her arms over body and said, "I don't go in there. Never will I go in there."

Rita smiled as she turned the doorknob and opened the door. She had to see it for herself. "I'm not afraid. I'll just peek inside. I'll tell you what, why don't I meet you back at your desk in a minute? I'm sure you're busy, and it won't take me long at all. Do you have a brochure or some information about the school I can take back with me?"

Omaima shuddered and backed away. "I'll get it for you. Please, Missy Locke, don't be too long in there. It's not good."

Inside, Rita gasped.

The room, no more than nine by twelve feet, was dimly lit and cold with the blinds drawn down on its single window, where an air conditioner air set to its lowest temperature reading blasted frigid air at maximum force. A worn black body bag lay on a long metal table with a large coffee can underneath it. Unzipped, the vinyl bag leaked some type of foul-smelling fluid into the can, drop by drop. She caught a whiff of chlorine bleach and noticed two spray bottles and a box of plastic gloves on a smaller metal table on the opposite wall. A tray of surgical instruments sat on a rolling cart next to a single chair. Although she'd seen corpses before, this time she couldn't force herself to look in the bag. She reasoned that she'd seen enough. Her hands shook, both from the icy blast of air and rattled nerves, as she snapped several photos and slipped out of the room that had no sink or source of running water for simple handwashing.

Walking down the hall on rubbery legs, she texted the photos to her editor and emailed them to herself. If she lost her phone, she needed proof of what she'd discovered behind that closed door. Without photos, who would believe her? She almost didn't believe it herself.

On her way back to the reception area, she snapped several more photos of the lounge, library, and classrooms. She thanked the receptionist and collected a colorful, professionally printed brochure. Gilliam apparently spared no expense when it came to promoting his operation. "Omaima, thank you for your hospitality. On my way out, I'm going to take a few photos of your lovely courtyard. I appreciate the tour."

Just then, the phone rang, and the receptionist smiled and waved at Rita before answering it. She walked down the three steps off the front porch and circled around the building, hoping to find a student to talk with. When she reached the back of the building, she saw a long wooden crate, coffin-size, on the rear porch. No students were in sight, so she leaned over the porch railing, snapped a photo of the empty crate, and looked for a shipping label or identifying marking. When she found nothing to identify where it had come from, she left the yard, walked down the street, and hailed a taxi. Her leg dragged from the long day, and she needed to take a break.

As she was sliding onto the split leather seat, her phone buzzed with an incoming call.

"What in the fresh hell is in that photo?" Tom shouted into the phone, ignoring the static on the line. "Is that a body bag?"

She described the scene in gruesome details that caused the wide-eyed driver to shake his head and look at her in his rear view mirror several times. "I told you if I came down here, I'd get the goods. The young lady in the photos is my new young friend Omaima Alwen, a very cooperative but not very savvy receptionist. She led me on a tour of the school this morning, if that's what you'd like me to call it. Shane wasn't around, and there were only a handful of students. Omaima claims more are coming, but I think that's just the party line of what she's supposed to say if anyone asks for details. Anyway, she's afraid of the dead, so she let me go into the room by myself. I sent the pictures to have stuff documented, you know, in case my plane goes down or something," she said. "I'll email you my notes later after I type them up. I'm on my way back to my hotel now."

"What about Gilliam? You need to get something from him on the record."

She blew out a deep breath. She'd anticipated that demand. "I know. I know I do. Now that I've seen what I've seen, I can call him. If he agrees to see me, I'll go back. I have a few more days left here. If not, I'll try for a phone interview."

"Red, if you go back, watch yourself. Make sure it's during daylight hours and let someone at the hotel know where you are.

In fact, call me on your way if you go back. The deeper you get into this mess, the more I don't like it."

She laughed. "Tom Moore, when do you ever like anything? I swear, you're getting more nervous and crankier every year. I will be careful. I promise. Tom, he's a fraud, and I think I'm beginning to understand what he's doing here. The more I see, I think the school is a front for something much bigger."

"Like what?"

"I don't have proof yet, so I'm not going out on a limb."

She didn't want to tell her editor yet what she suspected.

"Listen, this connection is bad because the cell service is awful here. I'm at my hotel now. I'm going to shower to get today's grime off and order an expensive dinner on the company's dime because I've earned it today. I'll call you tomorrow."

He stopped her before she could end the call. "Order anything you want, Red. But promise me you'll be careful. This guy is more than a nut case. In fact, he sounds like a menace. You ruined him once, and I doubt he'll take it lightly if you do it again."

CHAPTER FIFTEEN

Rita phoned Celtic Cross early the next morning, hoping to catch Shane before classes started. The receptionist, friendly and accommodating the day before, sounded stiff and cool when she agreed to relay her message to her employer, and hung up without saying goodbye.

Something tells me Shane wasn't thrilled to hear she gave me the grand tour. I hope the poor kid doesn't get fired for it.

While she waited for a call back, she called Carr to see whether state police had anything new on any of the jewelry recovered after Cindy Ekas' death other than the pieces on the most recently exhumed bodies. She might not be able to write about it, but she could pass the information along to her colleague. And by now, she surmised, the fire marshal should have a final ruling on the cause of the explosion and fire that killed the hairdresser.

"Nope, nothing new here," Carr said. "Our regular arson guy has been out for back surgery for five months now since that roof collapsed on him, and we're sharing fire investigation duties with Washington County. Ought to be back any day now, though."

She groaned with frustration. "What about the Watson case? Anything more on the jewelry?"

"No, nothing other than your boyfriend, David is organizing a group of family members of people who were laid out and buried from the funeral home. They're scheduled for a meeting with the district attorney next week, but I'm sure he's told you that already."

"No, not yet. On that subject, I haven't had the chance to tell you that he's a little more than a boyfriend, at least I think he is. He asked me to marry him before I left, and I accepted. Although that might be in doubt right now because we had a little argument before I left town. He's in a huff because I didn't let him fly down here to babysit me."

She stopped talking when she heard Carr laughing on the other end. "Red, when will these guys ever learn that you're a force to be reckoned with? You remind me a lot of my wife. She takes no crap from anyone, and I'd be the last person on the planet to try and control her or tell her what to do." He lowered his voice and spoke in a more serious tone. "Congratulations, honey. I hope it works out for you, and that you finally get the happiness you deserve."

She remembered that he knew the sad details of her love affair with the father of the baby she'd lost so long ago. "We've texted a few times, so I guess all is not lost," she said. "I wouldn't be allowed to write that story about the family group anyway."

He chuckled. "Oh, all of a sudden Miss Rita Locke is worried about a little conflict of interest? There's a news flash for the wire services."

"Very funny. I'm not, but you know how picky my editors can be. I never let trivial details like that get in my way," she joked. "I'll be back at my desk on Monday, but in the meantime, give me a call if you find out anything we *can* write about, okay?"

"Now who's being funny? Call me when you get back."

By the early evening, Shane Gilliam hadn't returned her call. She had dinner on the hotel's restaurant patio, enjoying the warm air and the music from a steel drum band setup near some huts on the beach. She lingered over two frozen margaritas and felt relaxed and drowsy when she made her way back to her room. She washed her face, slipped into a nightgown, and curled up on the bed, where she fell asleep quickly, lulled by the sound of the ocean waves.

Sometime in the middle of the night, she woke up, chilled, so she slipped under the comforter and between the sheets. As she rolled over to get comfortable, her hand felt something warm and sticky on the sheet next to her. She reached over, turned on the bedside lamp, and pulled back the covers, screaming when she saw the bloodied head of a bird.

An hour later, Inspector Wade Stringer shook his head as if disgusted. "This is a sad day for our island for someone to have done this to a visitor. I'm so sorry this happened to you, my lady."

Her teeth chattered with fear. The thin cotton robe wrapping her body provided no warmth, despite the sultry night air on the terrace. She wasn't ready to go back into her room, and in fact, she'd asked the hotel to find her another one. However, she doubted the staff would mobilize to accommodate her at three in the morning. She'd debated calling David, but she knew him well enough to realize he'd be on the next plane to take her home.

"What does it mean? Why would someone kill a parrot and leave the head in my bed? Things like this happen in bad gangster movies, not in real life."

The inspector hesitated before answering. “I’m not sure who would do this to you, but maybe you can clarify things for me. Do you know anyone here on the island? Any enemy who might want to frighten you or hurt you?”

“I told you. I’m a journalist, and I’m here working on a story about Caribbean medical schools. Other than you and the people I’ve interviewed, I know no one here, unless you count Shane Gilliam, the administrator of Celtic Cross Medical University, and I’m not even sure he knows I’m here. I have a call in to his office to set up an appointment, but he hasn’t responded yet. I have no idea as to whether he’s even gotten the message I left with his receptionist earlier.”

The inspector’s shoulders stiffened, and he glanced behind her into the room where two other officers were taking photos of her bed and the bloody mess left in it. “Where did you go this evening? You said you had a few drinks. Did you meet anyone? A man, perhaps? Possibly you refused someone’s advances. Were you intoxicated?”

She flared her nostrils. “I had dinner and *two* watered down margaritas in the hotel restaurant before I came back to my room, alone, and fell asleep. I didn’t talk with anyone, and I certainly didn’t make anyone mad enough to murder a bird and put it under the sheets with me.”

He looked out over the water, shimmering in the moonlight. “Well, it appears as though someone is sending you a warning. Parrots are known for their ability to talk. Maybe your practice of talking and asking too many questions…” His voice trailed off, and he didn’t finish his sentence. He looked directly into her eyes. “Have you ever heard of *obeah*?

She hadn’t and didn’t recognize the language. “No, what’s that?”

"Obeah is an old belief that an individual can be supernaturally harmed by someone for something such as an awful wrong or something as simple as being jealous or envious of them," he explained. "Some people refer to it as a type of witchcraft or sorcery."

Her eyes widened. He either had to be kidding, or he was trying to make her afraid enough to leave. For a moment, she wondered whether she should trust him. "Like voodoo? Are you telling me I've been cursed or something? Is there a red-haired doll with pins in it somewhere?"

He squirmed in his chair but smiled at her feeble attempt at humor. "No, nothing like that, although there are some similarities to Haitian voodoo. Obeah is an Afro-Caribbean belief, in which the practitioners, known as *Obeah men*, often use plant-based potions and poisons to do good or, in some cases, evil. It was practiced by many West Indian slaves until it was outlawed in the late 1700's, first in Jamaica, I think, and then throughout most of the islands because the white European colonials likened it to witchcraft or sorcery."

"So, it's illegal," she said.

"There are those here who still practice obeah covertly because they believe it can protect people from harm or help them find happiness or healing. Almost everyone here practices Christianity, but some of the older people, and now a growing group of the young people, still believe in obeah."

"How widespread is it?"

"You'll find it in all the islands, on some scale, but particularly in Jamaica. No obeah man or woman does it out in the open, though, and we don't go around looking for people who practice it. Usually, there's a sign placed, like special oils, sometimes a feather, but I've never seen a bird slaughtered..."

She leaned forward and cut him off. "If this *was* obeah, what does it mean to me?"

He stood. "Well, Miss Locke, if you do not know anyone here who would believe you need some type of healing, I'm thinking in your case, it could be a threat of some sort or a warning meant to protect you, maybe something to do with the story you are working on, something with regard to questions you have asked. The parrot, silenced, cannot speak or question, so it may have been placed there by someone who wanted to frighten you into silence."

He looked at his watch. "Right now, my suggestion to you would be that you wrap up your business here and go home to your country. I'm concerned by the fact that someone managed to enter your room and do this while you were out, and I will address that with the hotel's chief of security who is waiting for me in the manager's office right now. The first thing my officers learned when they arrived is that the security cameras on this side of the building malfunctioned."

She huffed and jumped up from her chair. "Could malfunctioned be a polite word for tampered with inspector?"

He frowned as he went through the motion of checking his watch again. "That, my dear, is something we do not yet know. You are upset and jumping to conclusions. I'll meet with the head of security and get to the root of the problem. It may simply be an unfortunate coincidence. I'm sure you're aware of the electrical outages that occur here periodically."

She remembered the first morning when she was midway through drying her hair and the power cut out. Yes, it could have caused the cameras to malfunction. As she began to reconcile that in her mind, he spoke again.

"But I must repeat myself, it might be best if you took a flight out later this morning. I believe there is always a flight leaving for Miami at eleven. In my humble opinion, for your safety, you should be on it."

She shook her head. He obviously wanted rid of her, but there was no way she'd run home in fear without getting the information she needed. "I have a few more days here, and I plan to use them to do the job I came to do. If someone wants to scare me away, it'll take a lot more than a dead parrot."

Moving to another room, a hot shower, and two cups of tea helped to ease her nerves from the long, sleepless night. She organized her notes, sent several emails and more photos to her editor, and planned her day.

Shane Gilliam. She had to confront him about what she'd seen at the school if she hoped to write anything about what American students experienced there. He was the key to this whole story, and she needed to hear his side of it to see if he could offer any credible explanation for anything—including the dead parrot. She imagined he'd stop at nothing to try to frighten her away and discourage her from writing about him again.

Just before noon, she took a taxi to the school where she had the driver drop her off directly in front. Today, there was no need to try to approach the school without being seen first because she was sure he'd know she'd be coming. She rang the bell, and the door swept open a few moments later.

"Can I help you?"

She smiled when she recognized the young man who answered it as one of the medical students she'd seen in the courtyard during her tour of the school the day before. "Yes, I'm Rita Locke. I'm looking for Shane Gilliam." She couldn't bring herself to refer to him as a doctor when she knew the truth about his charade.

When the young man shook his head, she noticed beads of perspiration forming on his upper lip. He appeared uncomfortable, clearly nervous about something, and he shifted his weight back and forth on his feet. "I'm sorry, but Dr. Gilliam's not here."

"Do you expect him soon?"

He shook his head again. "Ma'am, I'm sorry but I don't know. He goes back to the United States a lot, and he doesn't always tell us when. Maybe you should come back some other time. We're in a mess here today."

"Maybe his secretary, Omaima, can help me. Will you please tell her I'm here?"

His face went white, and he looked at the floor. When he raised his eyes to meet hers, his voice crackled in a whisper. "Ma'am, I'm sorry, but that's why we're in a mess. Dr. Gilliam is nowhere to be found, Dr. Potter is away, and there are no other instructors working here right now, and we're not sure what to do because the anatomy lab has been cleared out, our specimens are missing, and our written reports are gone. The police just left."

Her body tensed, uneasy with anticipation. The poor kid looked like he was about to faint. "Maybe we can call her at home?"

He looked like a frightened child when he used the back of his trembling hand to wipe a tear that streamed down his cheek and closed his eyes. "No, ma'am, we can't call her. The ferry operator found her body on the beach this morning. She's dead."

Inspector Stringer met her at the doorway of his office and waved her inside. His demeanor had changed from their meeting earlier at her hotel when he was nothing but kind and polite. Now, unsmiling, he spoke sternly when he leaned into her face and began to fire questions at her. "I see you've ignored my advice to take your leave. Tell me, Miss Locke, exactly what kind of story are you working on with regard to Celtic Cross? The school has been here for nearly a year without any issues or problems, and now, a few days after your arrival to do a story about it, we have a slaughtered parrot in your bed and the school receptionist is dead. I can't seem to find anyone at the school with any information or authority. That said, would you like to tell me what's going on?"

She stepped back, shocked at his wrath. She hadn't caused these problems. "Sir, I have no idea. In fact, I came here to get information from you about Omaima's death. She was very kind to me when I met her at the school, and I'm sorry something happened to her." She hesitated and then spoke just above a whisper. "I will admit though, I'm afraid someone may have hurt her because she helped me."

He glared at her. "Helped you with what? What did she do for you? Something illegal?"

She gripped the handle of her purse and tried to remain calm when she answered him. It took all her willpower to maintain an even keel and keep her emotions out of the conversation. It worked for a few seconds, but then she let loose with a tirade and described what she'd seen at the school the day before.

She swiped her phone and scrolled to the photos she'd taken. "They're time stamped, and you can tell they are original, not doctored or photoshopped. I sent them to my editors yesterday afternoon."

She told him the gross details of what she'd seen. "Don't you think you should be looking for him and asking him questions, instead of screaming at me? I came here to find out what's going on at the school and with him, things that are going on right under your nose. Did you know he's not even a licensed physician? Do you care, or is the money from the school too important to this island to care about what is really going on there? How much of a kickback is the government getting from this place?"

His eyes widened, and he appeared shocked. "I've seen no evidence of any of this at the school. Why didn't you tell me this at the hotel?"

She stared at him in defiance. She knew he would have dismissed it as unfounded allegations if she'd mentioned it earlier. "At the hotel, all you did was tell me to leave Nevis as quickly as possible. You weren't concerned about me, or my story, or what was going on at the school. You looked at me as an irritation, a problem that would be removed when I stepped onto a plane and off the island and away from your jurisdiction."

She held out her phone to him, thankful that she'd documented everything she'd seen the day before. He took it and swiped from photo to photo, saying nothing.

"You want evidence, Inspector? Well, now you have it. As I explained, I took these photos yesterday. I didn't get past the poor kid who answered the door at the school this morning, but something tells me you didn't see any of this when you were there because he told me everything has been cleared out and removed sometime between my visit and this morning. Am I right?"

He blew out a deep breath and shook his head. "No, I saw nothing of the sort. This is barbaric. Whoever is allowing this to go on isn't a doctor. He's nothing short of a butcher, and you may have my word that I will do everything in my power to make it stop if I have to shut this school down for good."

She smiled, finally relieved that he believed her. "I think finding Shane Gilliam is your first step. He managed to avoid prosecution in the United States for practicing medicine without a license, so I hope you can do something here to stop him, once and for all. He's cheating these unsuspecting students out of their money and their education. No one who attends this school, as primitive as it is, has any chance of ever passing medical licensing tests or getting a residency placement."

He interrupted her. "Miss Locke, are you forgetting something?"

She paused for a moment, thinking. "Such as?"

"It's not only the students and the school operations that I am concerned about. If what you said is true, and from these photos, I believe it is, Omaima Alwen most definitely may have been targeted for letting you see for yourself the inside workings of the school. The poor girl was left to die face down in the sand with her hands tied behind her back. Right now, the medical examiner is trying to determine whether she was already dead or drowned when the tide swept up onto the beach."

Rita shuddered with a sudden chill. Had Omaima tried to protect her by placing the bird in her bed as a warning?

"I believe whoever killed her may want to silence you as well, Miss Locke," he continued.

Shaking her head, she interrupted him. "Too late for that because I've already sent the photos and a lot of information back to my editors. Silencing me won't prevent this story from getting slapped onto the front page. Trust me, there's always another writer waiting in the wings."

He cleared his throat and waited a few seconds before he locked his gaze with hers. "Pray tell, how would the person who killed her know anything about your newspaper policies? Miss Locke, you may be in grave danger every moment you are here."

She gulped and looked away when she realized there was more to worry about if Shane Gilliam had anything to do with the girl's death. She knew that leaving the island wouldn't guarantee her safety at all because if Shane is the person who killed Omaima, she'd be in danger at home, too.

CHAPTER SIXTEEN

After a sleepless night riddled with nightmares, Rita decided to go home. Her interviews were finished, Shane Gilliam had vanished, and police were awaiting autopsy results on Omaima's body, something the inspector told her could take a few weeks. She'd supposed he wouldn't tell her even if the results had been available immediately because he clearly wanted her gone.

Her room at the resort was paid in full for three more days. She didn't want anyone to know she'd opted to leave the island and risk being followed, so she did not formally check out.

She called David to let him know she'd be arriving in Pittsburgh later that evening and then made a final call to the police inspector while waiting for a taxi to take her to the ferry. The inspector's tone was icy when he told her that police were unable to determine what caused the security cameras on the resort to malfunction, and that they had no leads as to who placed the dead bird in her bed. He said a second extensive search at the medical school produced nothing close to what she'd shown him in photos.

"Based on that, I must assume that the things you photographed simply were medical student pranks. Possibly some type of hazing. Nothing as far-fetched as you would have had me believe," he suggested.

When she hung up the phone, she felt as though he did not believe her at all. He'd brushed her off as if she were nothing more than a nuisance, a hysterical female who liked to make up sensational stories.

Her anger at the inspector grew exponentially during the nearly thirty-minute wait before the watercraft pulled alongside the dock.

"Good morning, my lady." The same elderly man who brought her to the island greeted her when she stepped onto the water taxi. "I see you are leaving us."

She forced herself to be polite. The inspector's attitude wasn't this man's fault. "Yes, it's time to go home. I'll always miss your beautiful island," she said.

He appeared tired, and she saw that his eyes were red rimmed when he looked at her knowingly. "Better for you to be gone home, though. Not good to be here alone much longer."

Her head snapped up. What did he know? "What do you mean by that?"

He looked out across the aqua waves into the distance shielding his face from the morning sun with brown, weathered hands. "Nothing, my lady. Nothing at all. Just not safe. Not for any young woman on her own." She wondered what he knew about Omaima's death and tried several times to nudge him into conversation.

He ignored further questions and said nothing more for the rest of the ride.

Rita bought a bottle of Diet Coke and two bridal magazines in the airport lounge, reasoning that no one she knew would see her indulging in fantasy wedding planning while waiting for her departing plane. She skimmed through page after page of gowns, samples of bouquets, and pre-wedding checklists billed as the ultimate guide to a stress-free wedding celebration. Ideally, she wanted a small ceremony with family and a few close friends, and she hoped David would agree. Nothing terrified her more than having to take the time to plan a huge celebration. *Not worth the hassle for one day. I'm not sold on the idea of a big, beaded dress, either.*

She heard double doors opening at the gate next to hers and glanced up at the monitor to see that a flight had arrived from Miami, where she would be headed forty-five minutes later for a brief layover before her connecting flight back to Pittsburgh. She went back to her reading but looked up again as people exiting the plane started to file into the room. A young mother with a toddler, two middle-aged men, and a couple wearing 'bride' and 'groom' t-shirts passed by her row of seats. She smiled at the honeymooners and continued to skim through another article, not looking up again until something caught the corner of her eye. A slim woman with white-blonde hair wheeled a black leather carry-on bag down the hallway and disappeared through double doors leading to baggage claim. She'd only ever seen that hair color on one person – Amie Watson.

Forgetting all about her flight, she tossed the magazines aside, threw her drink bottle into her satchel, and jumped from her chair, dragging her carry-on bag behind her as she tried to follow the woman. Although the airport was small, compared to behemoth terminals in Atlanta, Chicago, and Miami, she had trouble weaving her way through throngs of arriving passengers from two flights. The crowd, coupled with her throbbing leg and a flat wheel on her carry-on bag, slowed her down until she lost sight of the blonde a few feet from the security gates.

She pushed ahead and went through the gates, making a split-second decision to stay on the island. By the time she reached the airport's automatic doors, she was breathing heavily and in excruciating pain. A hot rush of air blasted her face when the doors opened in front of her, and she saw the woman getting into a taxi.

"Wait," she shouted. "Wait!" When the taxi drove off, another one pulled to the curb in front of Rita. She opened the door, threw her carryon into the back seat, and jumped inside. "Please, follow that car, and hurry," she directed the driver.

Rita's frustration mounted as the taxi weaved through traffic in St. Kitt's downtown area, where a group of school children crossing the street forced her driver to stop. She lost sight of the other car as they waited for the children to pass in front of them.

"Where to now, my lady?" The driver hung his head in apology. "I'm sorry, but I cannot follow because I do not know where they have gone."

Defeated, Rita went back to the dock and caught the water taxi to return to Nevis. This time, a young man ferried her from St. Kitts to the smaller island. Back at the resort, she returned to her room and stowed her carryon bag in the closet, unsure as to what she should do next.

First, she texted David and told him of her decision to stay, promising to call him later. Then, she tried Amie's cell phone, which went directly to voicemail. Frustrated, she opened her laptop and began to research hotels and resorts in the main tourist areas of the two sister islands. When she had a list, she called them, one by one, reasoning that Amie Watson had to be registered to sleep somewhere. On the eighth call, to the Marriott on St. Kitts, she breathed a sigh of relief when the hotel operator transferred her to Amie's room. When that call also went to voicemail, she hung up without leaving a message.

Better to go there and see her in person to find out what brought her here.

It could be purely coincidence, she reasoned. Amie could have decided to escape from the publicity for a few days. She chose a beautiful tropical island. Nothing sinister about that. But traveling alone? No, not her style.

Her gut told her that Amie Watson was in danger. Unfortunately, her instinct couldn't tell her why.

She checked her watch as the late afternoon sun dipped low on the horizon. It would be dark in another hour, and she didn't want to take a ferry back to the larger island alone at night. She went out onto her terrace and looked at the resort's manicured grounds leading to the beach, where a lone vervet monkey skittered at the edge of the surf. She thought about Omaima's last moments on the sand.

The hair rose on the back of her neck. Shivering with a sudden chill, she went inside and locked the terrace doors behind her.

Early the next morning, she called Amie Watson's cell phone once more, but when the call went straight to voicemail, she decided to go back over to St. Kitts. She phoned David to check on Boomer but didn't tell him anything about her plans.

"He's fine," David said. "No worries. I thought you were done down there."

She made a split-second decision to avoid mentioning Amie Watson. She knew he'd try to stop her. "Something came up, but

I should be finished in a few days."

"Okay, boss. Just come home soon, okay? We miss you."

"I will. Believe me, I miss both of you, too. I have a few more things to do here and then I'll be on my way," she promised.

The boat ride over to the larger island of St. Kitts took longer than usual because a family with a small child boarded the craft in front of her. Midway there, the little girl began to vomit from seasickness and the water taxi operator slowed for a few minutes to offer her embarrassed parents assistance in getting her and the craft cleaned up. By the time she got off the boat, hailed a taxi, and traveled to the Marriott, it was eleven o'clock and Amie had left the hotel, according to the solicitous desk clerk who rang her room.

"My lady, Miss Watson did not say where she was going, but I can tell you that she asked me about the ferry and the water taxi service to Nevis. She said she wanted to visit someone there this afternoon."

Rita's heart raced as she ran through the lobby and rushed outside to hail a cab to retrace her route.

An hour later, exhausted and sweaty from her travels between the islands, Rita rang the doorbell at the medical school. Although she didn't know why, she felt an urgent sense of intuition that Amie would be there.

When no one answered, she tried the handle and the door swung open. "Hello, anyone here?"

There was no reply, so she stepped into the reception area where her stomach lurched when she noticed Omaima's name plate still sitting at the front of her unoccupied desk. She reached into her purse to double check that her phone's ringer was on vibrate, took a deep breath, and made her way to the door at the rear of the hallway where she'd photographed the body bag several days earlier. She wanted to see for herself that it had disappeared. As she turned the knob, she felt someone come up behind her. She froze.

"You know you're not supposed to be snooping around in here," he whispered. "Will you never learn, Miss Locke?"

She had no time to turn around before a sharp blow to her head knocked her to the floor, where she landed face down. Momentarily dazed, she realized she'd foolishly walked right into a trap. She struggled to turn over and free herself from his grip, but the man crushed her with his brute strength as he knelt on her back. As she fought to breathe, she felt a sharp stab of pain in her arm. Within seconds, everything went black.

CHAPTER SEVENTEEN

Rita's head hurt and her mouth tasted bitter when her eyes flickered open. She was groggy and confused, much as she'd been when she was hospitalized months before. She was lying down on something soft and comfortable, and she liked it, so after a few moments, she drifted off to sleep again.

Must be a dream. Back in the hospital, she reasoned. Don't care.

Sometime later, she dreamed she was swaying on a swinging cradle, rocking back and forth, comforted by the dark. This was a wonderful place, wherever it was, and she felt so safe and warm. That is, until the sound of men arguing in the distance woke her. Afraid to make a sound, she forced herself to remain motionless. She strained to listen to what they were saying, and although she could make out the words, she didn't recognize their voices.

"I did not bargain for kidnapping and murder when I agreed to get involved in this," one man shouted. "All I agreed to was to look the other way and now look at what you've forced me into. I can't afford for something like this to get out. It will mean my job."

Did she know that voice? The speech pattern sounded vaguely familiar to her.

"Look, I didn't kill her...don't try to pin murder on me. It's too late to back out now. You've been on board with everything... every time a fat deposit...in your account. These people pay big money, and for as long as they're paying it, we're...collect it, my friend," the other replied. "If you're not with us, you're against us, and you know what that means."

The other man's voice lowered, and Rita strained to hear. This time she made out only a few words, "threaten me..." and "what to do with snoop."

Her blood chilled, and she shivered. They were fighting about her.

But then she heard one of the men say, "do with them."

Who else were they fighting about? And where was here?

She wanted to kick herself for her stupidity in prowling around the medical school. No one, not David, not her editor, not her friend Kathy, knew where she'd gone in search of Amie. She felt so tired, so confused. How long had she been asleep? How long since she'd eaten a meal or had something to drink? Had drugs been used on her?

Who knew what these men were capable of? Maybe they thought she was dead, and if that's what they believed, possibly she was safe from further harm. If they left her alone, there might be time for someone to come to her rescue. But who?

Confused and exhausted again, her last thought before she fell asleep was that she was on her own.

Rita held her breath as she heard someone walking toward her in the dark. She tried to sit up but couldn't manage it. Still, she balled her fists, ready to lash out in self-defense if necessary. Weak or not, she wouldn't give up without a fight if the arguing men were coming for her.

"Rita, are you awake? Are you okay?"

She'd heard the breathless, whispering voice before, and recognized Amie Watson. She tried to speak but could manage only a raspy cough.

"Thank God, you're still alive," Amie said.

Unable to focus, Rita blinked several times before she made out Amie's silhouette in the darkened room illuminated only by a single dirty bulb dangling from the ceiling. Where was this place?

"Sit up against the wall if you can. I have water, but not much. Here, you can have it," Amie said, holding a half-empty bottle to Rita's parched lips.

Rita dragged herself up into a sitting position and took the water greedily, choking as she tried to swallow. Her throat felt raw. When she could speak, she demanded to know, "Where are we? How did I get here? What the hell is going on?"

The other woman leaned back against the wall and let out frustrated sigh. "That's the problem. I don't know where we are, how I got here myself, or what is going on. I must have been drugged. When I woke up about twenty minutes ago, I was lying on that cot over there with a bottle of water next to my hand."

She pointed across the room. "You were out cold. And just in case you're wondering about it, that door is locked from the other side. As soon as I could steady myself on my feet, I tried it. There's no way out."

Rita interrupted her. "Who brought you here?"

Amie leaned forward. "I don't know. I was in and out of a fog, kind of a drug haze, you know, like after surgery. I heard men yelling at each other. I didn't recognize their voices, but I heard your name."

Rita understood the hazy feeling. Nevertheless, she demanded answers. "And what? What did you hear? What did they say?"

Amie hesitated but then answered in a whisper. "I'm not sure, but I think one of them said something like he wasn't going to be satisfied until you were silenced once and for all."

Rita knew. Her words tumbled out in a rush. "Amie, it was James Foster. It had to be him. He's threatened me more than once. I'm convinced he and Shane Gilliam are in this together, but I believe James is the man who attacked me in my home and nearly killed me, and now, he's apparently trying to finish the job and get rid of you, too."

"No! I know James' voice and it wasn't him," Amie insisted.

Rita ignored her and continued to rant, accusing Foster of murdering both Bob Watson and Cindy Ekas, until Amie burst into tears. She cried so hard; she couldn't speak for several minutes.

Finally, Amie whispered, "You're wrong about them. Shane is Bob's good friend from high school, and as for James, why would you think he'd do something like this? He's not even here. Please, he's not a killer." She drew in a shuddering breath. "You're going to think I'm awful, so soon after Bob, but he said he loves me, and, and...I think I love him."

Amie lay curled up on the cot in the corner. She'd been asleep for more than an hour since her emotional breakdown. Rita, her head aching, shivered in the cold room. They'd talked for what felt like hours, and Rita's mind raced with what the other woman told her.

The month before, right around the time they'd discovered the empty coffin that was supposed to be the final resting place for David's grandmother, Amie had stumbled upon some paperwork in a wall safe in the coffin room. She hadn't been aware her late husband used the safe, which had been installed by her father when she was a child. Back then, she explained, many people paid in cash, and her father routinely kept large amounts of money on hand because he had little faith in banks.

"He was a child of the Great Depression and had heard horror stories from his parents and how much money was lost when banks failed and closed. He wanted to hold his money in his hands, not just see it as numbers on paper," Amie explained.

After her father died, and her husband and brother took over the business, they emptied the safe, and split the money three ways, with a third for Amie and Bob, a third for Daniel, and a third going to her sister. She didn't know whether the safe had been opened or used at all in the years since.

"I remembered the combination because it was a play on our birthdays. Myself and my brother and sister," she said. "Out of curiosity, or maybe to feel closer to my dad after losing Bob, I opened it. The problem is, I'm not sure what I found."

Rita had held her breath. "What? What are you talking about?"

Amie looked away, unable to face Rita as she answered. "I found a list."

Rita leaned forward. "And… What was on it?" She coaxed the distraught woman in a gentle tone. "Please, Amie, tell me. You can do this."

Five seconds passed before Amie whispered, "It was a list of bodies. About a dozen. I think it was a list of people who were supposed to be buried but then weren't."

Rita gasped, and her blood ran cold. "Amie, are you sure? It simply could have been a list of people who were laid out and then buried by the funeral home, some kind of record you didn't understand clearly. You told me yourself that you never got involved in the daily operations of your husband's business.

What makes you think that?"

Amie hesitated again for a few seconds as if considering how much she wanted to reveal. "Well, David Hatfield's grandmother's name was on it. So were the names of people who were supposed to be buried in the two other caskets that were empty when exhumed." She rubbed her eyes and let out a deep sigh. "I'd imagine it's only a matter of time before other people come forward and there are more."

Rita's lip quivered at the mention of her fiancé's name. How she regretted not telling him where she was going. *One of these days your independent streak is going to be your downfall. Hopefully not today.*

"And if you found this list weeks ago, why haven't you gone to the police?"

The other woman laughed softly. "And say what? Hey officer, I'm sorry, but I think my husband was taking jewelry from corpses and doing something with them instead of burying them, so let's just make this whole ugly scandal worse and close the doors to this place once and for all so I can yank my son out of school and ruin all the progress he's made in the last two years."

She shook her head. "I can't do that. Almost immediately after Bob died, the publicity cut into our business by more than half of what we had last year, and my brother is losing his mind and having fits over every article that appears. I'm not an accountant, but I know enough to realize if this continues, we'll barely be able to pay our bills, let alone my son's school tuition, which is due again in a few months."

"Aren't you afraid that keeping the information from police will make them think you were in on it?"

Amie gasped. "Oh, my God, I never thought of that."

Rita studied the other woman's face and, despite the dim bulb, could make out that it was pale and drawn. She feared she knew the answer to the question she was about to ask. "Who have you told about this list? Does your brother know?"

Amie shook her head again and then looked at the floor. "I didn't tell him yet because I didn't want to upset him. I had to know for sure what it meant. I wish I had because maybe he would have helped me to understand it and explain what's going on. I planned to tell him after I returned from the island."

"Speaking of which, why did you come here?"

"There was an address on a slip of paper attached to the list, and I didn't recognize it. I couldn't think of anyone Bob may have known in the Caribbean, let alone on a small island like Nevis."

She explained that she'd had to look up Nevis on a map because she'd never even heard of it. She'd hoped to visit the island to find out more about the list. "I wanted to prove that I was wrong about what I suspected. The only person I confided in was James, and all I told him was that I had to come here because it might help to solve Bob's murder. We argued about it."

She said he'd tried to convince her to let him come along after he finished with a funeral, but she changed her flight to an earlier one and left without him.

Rita's mind raced.

"Where was the address in Nevis? The medical school?"

Amie's head snapped up. "Medical school? I don't know anything about a medical school. When I got to Nevis, I took a taxi to the address, and it turned out to be Shane Gilliam's home. I had no idea he lived here."

She said he wasn't there, but his housekeeper called him.

"I assumed he was at work. He told her to ask me to stay for lunch. I felt like a fool, showing up unannounced at someone's home in another country. I didn't know what to do."

"What did he say when you saw him?"

"That's just it, I never did. I had an iced tea while I was waiting for him, but I started to feel sick, dizzy actually, and I asked the housekeeper if I could use the restroom. I thought maybe I got some bad fish at dinner the night before. I don't remember anything else until I woke up here, wherever here is."

She looked around the darkened room which had concrete block walls similar to those of a basement or garage. "I don't know how I got here."

Rita's stomach turned. It was no coincidence that she and Amie Watson had been drugged and held captive in the same place. She shook her head, both amazed and sympathetic at the other woman's naivete.

"Amie, Shane Gilliam is how you got here. He must have had the housekeeper slip something into your drink."

Amie rolled her eyes in disbelief. "But why would he want to do that to me? I recognized his name as one of Bob's good friends, but I'd never met him. Bob talked about the fun he had with him when the subject of high school came up."

She said they apparently lost touch when her husband went to mortuary school and started his career at the funeral home.

"It seems awfully far-fetched that he'd drug me and kidnap me out of the blue when he had no idea I was coming. For what reason? That's the stuff you see in bad movies."

Rita blew out a deep breath. This would be hard for Amie to take, but she had to hear it sooner or later. "I believe he and Bob were still in touch, and if I'm right, they were in business together."

"What kind of business?"

Rita debated whether she should voice her suspicions aloud. After a few seconds, she blurted it out. "Bodies. Shane needs cadavers for students to play with and cut up at his medical school. I believe Bob provided them. And now, you have a list of names to prove it."

Amie gasped and held her hands up to her throat as if she couldn't breathe. She shook her head, and her eyes filled with tears. "Cut them up? No, you can't say that. You're wrong, Rita. That list has to be something else. He would never. You know nothing about the kind of man Bob was..."

Approaching footsteps sounded outside the door. "Shhhh," Rita hissed. They stared, frozen in silence as the door swung open with a loud creaking noise. Someone, without saying a word, shoved a metal tray and an empty bucket through the doorway, scraping them along the floor and leaving both a few feet into the room. They couldn't see the person and were too afraid to move closer. The door closed as quickly as it opened, and in a few seconds, the sound of the footsteps died away.

Rita pushed the bucket toward a far corner. "You know what that's for, don't you? It means we're not getting out of here anytime soon so that's our 'powder room.' We're going to have to get over any sense of modesty, if you know what I mean."

"Ugh, I'm not sure I can do that," Amie said. "I don't even like to use public restrooms."

"Well, if we're here long enough, you'll change your mind sooner or later." Rita scooted over toward the tray, which held a bottle of water, a bowl of cold rice and beans, and a plastic spoon. "Here," she said pushing the tray to Amie. "Take half and leave half for me. We better eat if we're going to stay alive and make it out of here. If we do, maybe we can make some sense of this mess."

About an hour after their sparse meal, they took turns using the bucket to relieve themselves. They avoided talk of Bob and Shane, coming to an unspoken understanding that they'd never agree on their relationship. They decided to keep track of time from then on. Rita checked her watch, which had numbers that glowed in the dark, and they began to mark the hours. They were both tired from whatever drugs had been used to sedate them, so they took turns sleeping in four-hour shifts, and for the next twelve hours, remained undisturbed.

Close to the twelve-hour mark, they heard footsteps approaching once more. They'd already placed the empty tray near the door, so they quickly moved to the farthest corner of the room and huddled there together as the door swung open. They didn't make a sound.

Dark, weathered hands, the tops of which were wrinkled with a maze of protruding veins, reached inside, pulled the tray across the floor, and then yanked it out the door. A few seconds later, the tray slid back into the room. On it was a bottle of water, two crusty rolls and a few slices of cheese.

Without speaking, each took a roll and some cheese. Rita opened the bottle of water, poured half into the plastic bottle they'd shared earlier, and kept half for herself. They ate in silence, set the empty tray closer to the door, and sat down on their cots.

After a few minutes spent brooding, Rita stood up. "We can't just sit here, waiting for scraps of food every twelve hours," she insisted. "We have to do something to save ourselves. The next time that door swings open, I'm going through it."

Amie gasped. "Why would you do that? Whoever is giving us food must want to help us by giving us a chance to survive. If we try to force our way out, whoever put us in here is going to kill us."

Rita knew she spoke the truth. Risky, yes, but a gamble she was willing to take. “I’d rather go down fighting than sit here waiting to die. We haven’t heard any voices for more than sixteen hours, give or take, so I’m hoping whoever brings us food is the only person around. Who knows if anyone else is anywhere near us? I say we come up with a plan and get ready to rush the door whenever it opens again.”

Amy wrung her hands and looked around the room. Her voice shook when she answered, weakly, “Okay. I don’t know what you want me to do, but I’ll help you.”

Rita walked over to the door and felt along both sides of the walls surrounding it but could not find a switch to turn the light out. She wanted to make sure Amy hadn’t missed it. Then, she focused on her cot, thinking for a few moments. “You’re right. The switch must be outside the door. Let’s push this under the light bulb so I can unscrew it. You won’t mind sitting in total darkness, will you?”

Amie shook her head but said nothing. Together, they moved the cot a couple feet from where it stood until it rested directly under the light fixture. Rita climbed up on it, wobbled on her tip toes, and used the hem of her dress to unscrew the hot bulb. Despite the material, it burned her fingers, and she let go. It ricocheted off the cot and hit the floor, where it shattered into tiny pieces. She jumped down.

“Help me push this back to where it was. I think it should be about two feet away from where it is now.”

Amie stumbled and bumped into Rita, who lost her balance and nearly fell over. When they regained their footing, they shoved the cot back to its original spot. “Now, hold my hand, and I’ll guide you over there to sit down.”

They inched their way slowly to the corner, their shoes crunching on the broken bulb. Rita's shin smacked into the corner rail of the cot, causing her to swear and wince in pain. Her head pounded and the aching in her legs brought tears to her eyes. She felt along the cot for the head railing. When she found it, she moved to the head of the cot and told Amie to sit down. "If I'm right, the doorway is about ten feet to the left of this corner. Hopefully our eyes will adjust to the dark soon. When we hear footsteps, you're going to have to be ready to run and to fight. Can you do that, Amie?"

She answered Rita in the darkness. "I'll try."

"No, put it this way: you have no choice but to be able to do it. When that door opens, hopefully whoever opens it will have another tray of food. The room will be pitch black, so he'll stop and try to turn on the light. When that happens, I'm charging through that doorway. The hands that pushed that tray in looked old, and I'm banking on that as the key to overpowering him–at least I think it's a guy. I hope you're going to be behind me, for your own sake."

"I said I'll try," Amie whispered. "I'm not much of a fighter, though."

Rita grabbed her arm. "Listen to me, Amie. You can do this, but you have to be ready when I say 'go!' or it won't work."

For the next eight hours, they took turns sleeping in shifts. Refreshed and a little stronger after that, they listened, silently praying that their plan would set them free and save their lives.

CHAPTER EIGHTEEN

They waited.

An hour, then another, and two more. Fixed in silence, they strained their ears for the telltale sounds of shuffling footsteps from whoever had delivered the previous two trays at twelve-hour intervals. The thirteenth hour passed, and then another, each counted on the lighted dials on Rita's watch.

Amie whispered in despair, "I think they've left us here to die. No one is coming back."

Rita tried to make her see reason. "Why would they do that? Someone pushed food into the door, so tell me why they would feed us and then kill us."

"Well, maybe you're right," Amie conceded.

Rita ignored her, deep in thought. She knew that the element of surprise could be the difference between life and death, but only if someone returned while they still had enough strength to fight. Two sparse meals and a few sips of water in the past twenty-four hours, on top of whatever sedation drugs they'd ingested, left them both weak and nauseous.

Amie started to speak, but then cut herself short as if she'd reconsidered what she'd planned to say. Another hour passed in silence. The only sounds were creaking springs on their cots whenever they shifted their weight.

Fifteen and a half hours after they'd developed a plan, Rita heard a shuffling noise coming from outside the room. She jumped up from her cot and cocked her ear toward the door. "Get ready," she hissed to Amie. "Move, now!"

The cot creaked when Amie got up and moved behind Rita, who stood facing the door. Rita took a deep breath. This was their make-or-break moment, she thought, mouthing a silent prayer. It had to work.

The doorknob turned and when the door opened, a thin shaft of light pierced the darkness. "Go!" Rita pushed forward with all her strength, barreling into a small man's stomach.

"Wha…oof," he said.

She slammed him with her hands and knocked him to the ground. "Run, Amie! Follow me."

Together, they raced for their lives down the hall of what appeared to be some type of garage or warehouse. When they came to a doorway, Rita grabbed the knob and twisted it. She looked into a room that contained several large wooden crates the size that she'd seen on the porch of the medical school. Two dusty windows lined with cobwebs showed what looked like early evening sunlight into the room that had no other entrance. She turned around and slammed it shut.

"We can't get out this way," she said. "Let's try the other direction."

Amie said nothing but followed Rita's commands. Finally, at the end of another long hall, they reached an exit door. Just as Rita made it outside into a gravel parking lot, she heard a piercing scream and turned around to see Amie being dragged backward into the concrete block building. She looked around and recognized the space as the lot adjacent to the medical school.

A battered car sat parked just outside the door with its engine running and the driver's side opened. She assumed it belonged to whoever delivered the meager meals.

Rita debated turning around, but knew she was too weak to fight whoever caught Amie. Opting instead to seek help, she jumped into the car behind the steering wheel, and pushed the gas pedal to the floor, sending a cloud of dusty gravel spewing behind her as she sped away.

She was free, but she'd lost Amie. She'd have to go back.

First things first. She needed food and another, better plan. Because she was unfamiliar with driving on the left side of the road, she swerved and jerked awkwardly as she drove away from the medical school, thankful there were few cars on the roads. She debated stopping and trying to flag someone down, but she didn't know who to trust.

After a few minutes, she realized she'd been driving in circles and was lost with no idea how to get back to the center of town, or to her resort. She felt hungry and confused. She tried her best to study the trees and bushes on either side of the narrow, winding road, and finally, she slammed on the brakes, bouncing in her seat when she parked in a cloud of dust.

Out of the car, she went to the left side of the road and stepped a few feet into the trees. She lifted the hem of her filthy dress, gathering it to catch berries that she'd noticed hanging from several low-lying bushes. When she'd grabbed thirty or forty berries, she held the dress carefully so as not to dump or smash them and made her way back to the car. She sat down with them in her lap as she drove off.

Gooseberries, she knew, were safe to eat because she'd tried them at a restaurant on a vacation to the Caribbean about seven years before. She wanted to gobble them but ate slowly so as not to make herself sick. She needed the sugar, and the juice would help to stave off dehydration until she could get a meal and find someone to help with Amie.

After another couple miles of driving through sparsely populated areas thick with vegetation, she managed to find her way back to the edge of town just before dusk. She pulled over and quickly searched the car for money. There was enough in the glove box to buy a cheap meal, so she ditched the car in a public parking area and then bought a sandwich and a bottle of lemonade at a beach shack a few minutes before it closed for the night.

Now, she needed clean clothes and a plan to help Amie. She was afraid to go back to her resort and risk being captured. She thought about going straight to the police but decided against it because, without her purse, she had no passport or means of identification, no money, no phone, and had just stolen a vehicle. She doubted that anyone one in law enforcement, especially the impatient Inspector Stringer, would believe her story about being kidnapped and drugged. *No doubt, he'd have me committed or slam me in jail immediately. I need access to a computer so I can email David to let him know I'm alive and to get me help from the newspaper and law enforcement. But how?*

At dark, she walked back toward a cluster of brightly painted homes between the beach area and the center of town. Limping through alleys, she looked over walls and through fenced courtyards, hoping to find what she needed. Finally, after combing three streets, she noticed a clothesline line loaded with clean laundry in the back courtyard of a small pink home where lights blazed through a kitchen window. She could see a man, woman, and two children at the table, probably eating dinner. Her mouth watered at the thought of a hot meal. Houses on either side were dark, so she crept up to the low wall, climbed into the courtyard, and crawled on her hands and knees to the clothesline.

She mouthed a silent prayer while reaching up and taking down what appeared to be a long sundress and a billowing scarf, begging forgiveness for stealing and hoping that the dress would fit her small frame. A dog barked in the distance, which sent her scurrying out of the yard, over the wall, and down the street, clutching the clothes as if they were valuable treasures as she hobbled to the beach.

Stripping down, she put her toes into the surf where it met the sand and tried not to think of the fish and other creatures hidden in the ocean's dark waves. The warm, salty water rushed over her body when she walked into it to wash away the grime of several days' captivity. Back on the beach, she let the sultry tropical air dry her skin before slipping on the dress and winding the scarf at her waist as a belt. She spent the night leaning against a palm tree, sleeping off and on in short intervals as she developed a plan to rescue Amie.

By morning, she was ready.

Dressed in another woman's clothes, she boldly walked from the beach to the center of town, located the wood frame building that housed the public library, and followed the librarian inside when she arrived to open it at nine. She faked a bright smile and forced herself to sound relaxed and cheerful when her insides were quaking with fear. "Good morning. Might I be able to use one of your computers to send a quick email? I left my purse and phone at the resort and just remembered I need to tell my secretary in the United States something right way."

She named the resort where she'd stayed previously and chatted about how much she loved the island. Within a few minutes, the librarian offered her a pastry and a cup of coffee and set her up at one of two computers in the library's study center. She accessed her email account and, with her fingers flying across the keyboard, sent a detailed message to David that she also copied to George Carr at the state police station and her editors at the newspaper. She explained everything that had happened, hoping they'd believe her and send help.

"Unfortunately, I can't wait for a reply to this. There's no time. I have to do something to get Amie Watson out of there, and soon. Too many hours have passed, and for all I know, whoever dragged her back into the garage may have hurt her. I'm going to go to the police station to see Inspector Stringer immediately after I leave here. Hopefully, he'll believe me and help us. Please, do anything you can from your end," she wrote. She added a personal line to her fiancé, not caring whether her editors or Carr read it. "I love you, David. I'm so sorry to have gotten into such a mess again. Please, if anything happens, take care of Boomer, and forgive me."

She logged out of her email account, thanked the librarian for her hospitality, and headed for the police station.

Inspector Stringer sat back in his chair, tipping it onto its rear wheels and rocking up and down, as he listened to Rita's story that began with her visit to the medical school and ended with her escape from the building behind it and her night on the beach. When she finished, he threw his head back and looked up at the ceiling, roaring with laughter.

When he stopped laughing, he wiped his eyes with a handkerchief pulled from his shirt pocket and shook his head. "Oh, Miss Locke, that's a good one. You've certainly got a talent for telling fantastic stories to get out of trouble. I'll admit, you're a very creative journalist."

She sat back in her chair, stunned. Creative? He didn't believe her. And what did he mean by trouble?

Just then the phone rang, and he reached for it. "Excuse me, but I'm expecting a call. I'll be right with you." He turned away from her to face the window as he spoke. "Oh, yes, here at the station just as we'd anticipated. Yes, please, feel free to stop in, doctor, and we'll take care of that report you filed. We'll be here."

Her breath caught in her throat. He'd referred to the caller as *doctor*. Right then she knew he'd been talking to Shane Gilliam, and they were discussing *her*. Thank goodness she hadn't told him about the emails she'd sent to David, her editor, and the state police. It was best that he remained unaware of that because he and Shane were either friends or business associates, and she knew he couldn't be trusted to help her rescue Amie or get back to the United States. She tried to think of a plan to get away from the inspector, and by the time he was hanging up, she gave him a broad smile. He couldn't know what she suspected. "Inspector, may I use your ladies' restroom before we finish our talk? I'm sure you can help me with this, but first…" Her voice trailed off, and she smiled again.

He gestured toward the hall. "Oh, my dear, of course. Just outside my door and to the left. If you'd like, I'll go upstairs to our lunchroom and get us a cold drink while I'm waiting for you to come back."

She stood and smiled once more, still playing stupid. "You're so kind. That would be wonderful. I'd love a cold Diet Coke if you have it. The heat today is unbearable." She walked slowly to the door, opened it, and turned to the left. "Back in a few minutes."

He followed her out the door, and she listened to the sound

of his footsteps growing quieter as he walked in the opposite direction. When he left the hallway to ascend the stairs, she turned around and moved as fast as she could past his office door, through the main lobby and out into the street, never stopping to look back.

He could not be trusted. She was alone, and on her own.

Sticking to side streets and alleys, she half-ran, half-stumbled most of the way back toward the medical school in the boiling midday sunshine. If the police here were corrupt, she had to get to Amie as quickly as possible. After several blocks, her leg throbbed, and she had no choice but to slow her gait. She stopped to catch her breath in some thick bushes shaded by three towering palm trees across the alley from the school where two cars sat in the parking lot. When the rear door of the school opened, she ducked to the ground and watched Shane Gilliam get into one of the cars and drive away.

This was her chance.

She left her hiding place and went to the door of the concrete garage building where she last saw Amie. She tried the handle and was shocked when it turned easily, and the door swung open. Slowly, she sneaked inside and made her way to the door she'd barged through the day before. She tiptoed, moving as soundlessly as possible, until she reached it. Of course, it was locked. She tapped on it lightly several times but got no response. *They may have taken Amie somewhere else by now. Or maybe she's in no condition to answer me.*

On a whim, she felt along the top ledge of the doorframe, which had always been her grandma's favorite spot to hide her extra housekey for teenage Rita, who forgot to keep track of her keys. When her hand touched the metal key on the right side of the frame, she mentally thanked her grandmother before inserting it into the lock. She made her way to the doorway of the room where she'd been held captive. Peering inside, she could see that the cots remained, but Amie was nowhere to be seen. Just then, she felt a hand grip her shoulder. She froze.

"Well, if it isn't Rita Locke, Pittsburgh's finest investigative journalist, lost and alone so very far from home. Thank you for joining us, Miss Locke. Tell me, what's your story now?"

She knew that voice.

She turned and tried to wriggle away from the hand that clamped down even tighter as it spun her around. When she stopped, she was facing Shane Gilliam's icy blue eyes. Behind him stood Inspector Stringer, dangling a pair of handcuffs from his index finger.

"You! Where's Amie Watson?" she demanded. "I know she's here somewhere, so don't tell me you don't know. What have you done with her?"

Shane let out a little chuckle. "Pardon me, Miss Locke, but you're not exactly in the position to make demands and ask questions right now. First off, you're trespassing on private property, my property. Then, there's the matter of the car you stole yesterday, and oh, don't let me forget, my employee that you assaulted when you were attempting to break into this building."

She glared at him. "Me? I didn't assault anyone. Break in? How dare you say that after you knocked me out and locked me up here."

"Tsk, tsk. I have no idea what you're talking about. To me, that's pretty far-fetched, but then you are quite the storyteller. Looks like you're in quite a bit of trouble, wouldn't you say so, Wade?"

When he called the inspector by his first name, Rita's heart sunk. The situation was exactly as she feared.

"I'm not the one who should be worried." She spat out the words. "Did you think your little gang could get away with stealing jewelry from the dead? And do you think people won't be horrified when I publish my story and they find out what you've done with me and Amie and what you're doing here with stolen cadavers under the guise of running a medical school?"

The two men broke into laughter. When they stopped, Shane looked directly at her. "First, I think it's hilarious that you believe you're ever going to write another story for that rag newspaper you work for. But let's just suppose for the sake of argument that you do. What are they going to do? Run me out of Pittsburgh again? In case you haven't checked a map lately, this sweet little island is far from the reaches of U.S. law enforcement."

He chuckled again. "God, Rita, I thought you were smarter than that, or maybe you bumped your head a little too hard when you had a late-night visitor at your house." When her eyes widened with recognition, he went on. "Surely, by now you figured it out that this isn't about a couple of chintzy gold chains and rings that simpleton Cindy stashed in her safety deposit box, and it's certainly not about anything those fools playing doctor are doing with their dime store scalpels in my anatomy classes. The bodies they're playing with are nothing more than busy work activities to keep them occupied and out of my way."

Inspector Stringer cleared his throat and warned, "Shane, that's enough. You've said too much already."

If Shane was going to tell her more, he'd changed his mind about confessing when the inspector spoke. "Never mind. All you should worry about is what happens next."

He turned to the inspector. "Wade, tell me, what should happen next? Should this pretty little redhead go to jail for all she's done, or should I keep her here with me? Hmmm. Tough decision."

The inspector moved closer to Rita, yanked one arm and then the other behind her before clamping the handcuffs on her hands. "I believe for now; she should come with me."

He shoved Rita toward the door, but Shane blocked him from leaving.

"No, Wade, on second thought, she's staying here. We need a little more direction from our connection before I decide what to do with her."

"Shane, this is a mistake…" Stringer said.

Without another word, Shane dragged her away from the inspector and shoved her onto a chair. He reached into his pocket and pulled out a vial and hypodermic syringe.

"You can't do this," she said, trying to shrink away from him. "You're not going to get away with this."

"Shane, stop," Stringer shouted. "I'm not…"

It was too late. Shane stabbed the needle into her arm. In the moments before she lost consciousness, she realized she would have been safer in jail.

CHAPTER NINETEEN

Rita blinked from the burst of sunlight when she opened her eyes and tried to focus on the room. Moaning, she rolled over on the lumpy bed and winced when she tried to move. She had a splitting headache and her arms burned, still bound with the cuffs behind her back. More than anything, though, her leg pounded with pain.

"Where are we," she croaked, her throat dry and parched. "How did I get here?"

"I don't know where we are, but it's bad, Rita." Amie Watson's eyes filled with tears as she whispered from the opposite bed. "Worse than anything you or I could have imagined. After the guy dragged me back into that building yesterday when you were running away, he called someone on the phone. You were right. Within a few minutes, Shane Gilliam came rushing in, furious with him. I thought he was going to kill the poor old guy with his bare hands, but instead he shoved him out the door and told him to get to a hospital to get the cut on his head sewn up because he was bleeding all over the floor."

She said she tried to fight him off, but she couldn't match his brute strength. He shoved a needle into her arm, and she fainted. "I don't remember anything after that, until I woke up here last night." She moved her left arm along the bed rail to show Rita she'd been handcuffed to the metal bedrail. "Anyway, this morning the old guy came back and brought me a tray of food and a bottle of water. I got a good look at him this time, and I think he looked familiar, but I don't know where I've seen him before. He watched me eat but didn't say a word."

Rita stopped her. "Have you seen Shane today?"

"No, but I heard him talking to someone in the next room a little while ago, just after he brought you in. I acted like I was asleep. Were you awake enough to see who was with him? Do you know who it was?"

Rita took a deep breath before she answered, fearing that Amie would panic when she learned police would be of no help to them – ever – because of Inspector Stringer's involvement in the scheme. She didn't want her to lose hope of making it home to see her son again. She eased her way into the conversation.

"Well, it seems as though the police inspector and Shane are buddies. He's in on whatever Shane Gilliam is doing, but I get the feeling they're not in agreement as to what to do with us."

She explained that the inspector tried to intervene on her behalf with Shane.

"I believe, in Stringer's eyes, Shane is going too far, but he's in too deep to stop him."

Amie sat listening to Rita's theories. When she finally spoke, she looked at the floor.

"Rita, there are some things I need to tell you," Amie said. "There's more. I found more than just the list."

"Go on," Rita said, almost fearing what she was about to hear.

"There were other papers in Bob's files, but I didn't know

what to make of them because it didn't have our names or the business name on them. Now, it's all starting to come together and make sense to me."

Thirty minutes later, Rita felt sick to her stomach as she tried to digest and understand what Amie had been telling her and put it together with what Shane had let slip. It appeared that one or more bodies may have been sent from the United States to the medical school via the Mason-Watson Funeral Home. However, she realized that the school was just part of a more extensive clandestine operation, if the tidbits of information Amie had been able to piece together were accurate.

Amie explained that she didn't understand what she'd discovered, so she showed the information to her brother.

"He looked upset, but told me not to worry about them, that they had nothing to do with us. He said he'd handle everything," she said.

"What kind of papers were they?"

"They looked like invoices from laboratories, with staggering amounts of money on them. The invoices listed body parts – arms, legs, torsos – sold by a company called GW Collections to tissue donation banks. I don't know anything about the company, or who owns it, but if the numbers I saw were correct, they've been raking in hundreds of thousands of dollars a year," Amie said.

Rita figured it out immediately, but said nothing, making a mental note that the GW could stand for Gilliam Watson. "Go on," she said.

Amie explained that she also found a bill from a private air transport company for GW Collections that she gave to her brother as well. "I can't remember the location for the trip. He took one look at it, and he tore it up. He said it must have been sent by mistake and that if I got another one, to give it to him and not to worry about it."

She described Daniel's reaction as "totally in character for him" because he always acted as her protector when they were growing up.

"Now, with all that's happened, I know Bob was involved in something awful, and Daniel is trying to protect me from it because he knows I can't afford to lose the business. He's always been there for me."

Rita realized that Bob Watson had to have provided Shane with the cadavers used at the medical school without gaining permission from the deceased's families. She doubted that Shane paid him much, if anything, for those bodies, based on their lengthy friendship. She suspected Watson had been making the bulk of his money through other illicit means.

She'd done several stories over the years on organ donation awareness and medical tissue banks and learned enough about the process to understand that accredited tissue banks around the world relied on donations, rather than purchased tissue and body parts. She knew that if donated tissue had been removed and preserved within twenty-four hours of the donor's death, it would be viable for transplantation. In most cases, donated tissues were removed from the deceased donor in surgical operations immediately following death if the donor died in the hospital. When a donor died elsewhere, the process would have been handled together by the funeral director and medical examiner upon receiving consent from the family.

Without consent, removing body parts and tissue from a corpse became a crime. Selling them made it even worse. She reasoned that selling them to unaccredited tissue banks with no other means to obtain products meant big money.

Amie was right. Her husband had been involved in something awful if he'd been harvesting tissue from the deceased brought into his funeral home without receiving consent from family members and then selling body parts. Bob Watson was much more than a jewelry thief. He was a butcher for hire.

Rita's mind raced.

She'd stumbled across the biggest news story of her career, and she might not live long enough to write it.

Amie continued, "From what I overheard earlier, to me it appears that Shane seems to be the coordinator of the whole scheme because he was screaming at someone that he 'brokered the deals and brought in the money' and that he'd make the decisions from here on out. He said he wasn't going to be told what to do or be pushed into a corner, and if anybody tried, he'd kill them."

"Think, Amie, who was Shane talking to? Did you hear any names?"

Amie shook her head. "Truthfully, I couldn't tell if he was speaking to someone in the room with him or talking on the phone. I thought I heard another muffled voice, but it could have been the old man that brings the food."

Rita thought for a few minutes. If Shane was the mastermind, and the deal maker, he most likely paid the police inspector, and possibly immigration officials at the airport on the larger island of St. Kitts, to look the other way when bodies were shipped into Basseterre for the medical school. Thinking back to her encounters with Wade Stringer, she marveled at the inspector's acting ability when he'd tried to help her, and particularly, when he first appeared shocked by what Shane had been doing at the medical school. He deserved nothing less than an Oscar.

"Amie, the medical school is nothing more than a diversion, although a somewhat profitable one for Shane and for the island. First and foremost, the school is a great way to legitimatize

Shane's professional credentials when he brokered the deals to sell human tissue. I doubt anyone would question him concerning his professional background because it's not every day that someone fakes being a doctor and gets away with it."

How many families had this operation affected? Rita's stomach clenched when she thought about the empty coffin that was supposed to have been the final resting place for David's grandmother. Hopefully, he'd never know. If he ever learned his grandmother's body had been mutilated by students at a shady medical school or chopped up and sold for parts, it would kill him.

For some other families, however, the truth could be even more devastating. She didn't want to imagine the horror of discovering your loved one's body parts had been cut off and sold for profit without your knowledge. What secrets had been hidden beneath the soft satin layers of coffin blankets or in cremation urns?

"Okay, Amie, let's say Bob had been providing bodies for the school and body parts for the tissue selling scheme. There's no way he'd have had enough of them because not every body would have been delivered to your business within the narrow window for viable harvesting, correct?"

She didn't wait for an answer. "And, it would have been difficult for him to whisk bodies out of coffins and hide them somewhere until he could ship them offshore. That means someone else was involved, and, whether you like it or not, that someone is James Foster. I know you care for him, but that explains why Daniel was so upset when he saw those invoices. He had to have been sick when he figured out what they'd done to tarnish your father's legacy."

She heard Amie's sharp intake of breath but went on. "Don't you see, Amie? Bob and James were friends. Bob and Shane were friends. James has his own funeral home in Butler County that could have provided additional bodies and tissue. It only makes sense that they'd be in on this together to share the rewards. What I don't understand, though, is why Bob and Cindy were murdered if everyone was making money."

Amie's voice caught in her throat as she whispered, "I understand perfectly. They died because of me."

Amie stared at the ceiling and didn't look at Rita as she talked.

"We were having money troubles for years. We had only Bob's income because I spent most of my time taking care of our son. He was a handful as a baby and a toddler, but as he grew older, it became clear to us that he needed more than we could give him. I found the school he needed, and I'm the one who pressured Bob into finding the money to pay for it."

Her eyes filled with tears that overflowed onto her cheeks. "I think I told you that I never finished college, but I never told you I quit because I was pregnant. Well, we had a little girl who lived only a few days because of severe birth defects."

She explained that the baby's death sent her into a deep depression that required hospitalization for two months. After that, she never returned to school to earn her degree, nor had she worked during their entire marriage. "We decided that if we were fortunate enough to have a child, I'd stay at home. When we had our son, that decision turned out to be the best choice for our family because of his developmental problems.

"There never seemed to be enough money. In my father's day, the business made substantial profits, and we lived an affluent lifestyle. In recent years, though, more families turn to the cheaper option of cremation and the funeral business is very competitive. My husband wasn't a strong competitor."

She went on to say that she fought with her husband because she felt he wasn't providing enough money, wasn't marketing the business well. “He was quiet, and maybe too shy to deal effectively with the public in the way my father had. I pushed him and pushed him to make more money so we could afford to send our son to the best place in the state for children with severe autism. I gave him an ultimatum about two years ago and told him I'd leave him if he didn't turn things around. I never would have gone, but he didn't know that.

“Within a few months' time, we had the tuition money and were caught up on bills,” she said. “I never once asked where the money came from. I think I didn't want to know.”

Rita listened but said nothing for a few seconds. “Okay, fine, but how does that make you responsible for their murders?”

Amie took a deep breath. “In late December, just after Christmas, Bob came to me one evening as I was getting ready for bed. He said he'd done something he wasn't very proud of, and he didn't know what to do about it. I laughed at him and told him that unless he was talking about another woman, nothing he did would upset me. I brushed it off as one of his weird moods.

“The next day I asked him what he wanted to tell me, and he said it wasn't important anymore. The phone rang, and I took the call when I recognized the school's number. Our son had slipped on ice and fractured his wrist, so I packed a bag and left within an hour,” she said. “When I got home three days later, we never spoke about it again.”

She surmised he'd been trying to tell her about the scheme, and that he was trying to get out of it because his conscience got the best of him. She'd always put her son first, and her husband second, she admitted.

“He started it to make more money for me, and when he ended it, he was murdered. He would have needed help, so I feel as though Cindy stepped in because she had been a family friend forever and was so loyal to him. She would have helped him with the bodies, and I have no doubt now that she was hiding the jewelry removed from them for him. She died because she knew too much."

She stared into Rita's eyes. "And if we don't get out of here soon, we're going to die, too, aren't we?"

CHAPTER TWENTY

Dusk fell and the room grew dim. They heard shuffling footsteps outside the door. When it creaked open, Rita let out a deep breath in relief. It was the old man with a tray, and not Shane Gilliam or Inspector Stringer.

He stopped in the doorway and hit a light switch, illuminating his face, where a bandage covered most of the right side of his forehead. Shocked, she recognized him immediately as the friendly water taxi operator who had transported her between the islands during her stay. She wondered, for a moment, how he'd gotten involved in this mess, but then realized he was a necessary element in the operation because his taxi could have been used to transport bodies from the docks in St. Kitts to Nevis.

"I'm sorry for hurting you," she said. "I didn't mean for you to fall. I was just trying to get away."

He grunted but said nothing as he placed a sandwich on the small table next to her bed, along with a bottle of iced tea. He leaned forward and undid the handcuffs, allowing her to rub her wrists for a moment before he took one of her hands and cuffed it to the bed's metal railing. She took a long gulp of the tea while watching him place food on Amie's bedside table.

After Amie thanked him, Rita tried to talk to him again, hoping to illicit a response. "Thank you for feeding us, especially after what happened yesterday. We appreciate your kindness. I, um, know you must be in an awkward position here…"

He snapped. "Enough. I will not listen to more from you today. She is gone, and it is your fault."

She looked at his face and noticed his eyes were rimmed in red. "My fault? Who's gone where? What have I done?"

"My precious Omaima, my beautiful niece, is dead because of you and your meddling. She told me when she came home that day all about you, how she thought you were so pretty and so smart when you visited the school. She wanted to have your bravery and confidence someday. She wanted to make money and travel," he said, his voice breaking with emotion. "Now, she is in the mausoleum, her beautiful face going nowhere ever again."

Tears streamed down his cheeks. "The medical examiner told me today that her body was filled with bad drugs that would have put her to sleep, name of Ativan. She never touched anything, not even a glass of rum punch on her birthday. Drugged, tied up, and left to take her last breaths of sand and ocean water until her lungs were full. The parrot feather, a sign of evil obeah, all because of talking to you."

Omaima was his niece. Did he not understand that he was working for the person most likely to have killed her?

"Sir, please, listen to me. You must believe me. Don't you see? If Omaima had drugs in her bloodstream, they had to have been given to her by Shane Gilliam. He used them on me, and he used them on Amie," she said, pointing across the room. "How do you think we got here? Why do you think you've been instructed to keep us here? He's going to kill us, too. And someday, because you know too much, you're going to be one of his victims as well."

He said nothing and showed no emotion. He focused on her eyes as he listened to her explain why she'd come to the island

and why Omaima's impromptu tour of the medical school ultimately led to her death. "She was targeted because she allowed me to see what was going on here, not because I asked questions. She didn't know it at the time, but I was going to write about the school for the newspaper to tell everyone that Shane Gilliam is not a doctor and shouldn't be anywhere near a medical school or medical students. I saw horrible things there for myself. He's obtaining bodies illegally and letting students cut some of them up under the pretense of teaching anatomy. He's selling other bodies and their parts for huge profits."

When she'd finished, the old man shook his head and pulled a rumpled handkerchief from his pants pocket. "He told me someone hurt my girl because of you." He gestured toward Amie. "And her."

His eyes watered. "And now, you tell me he is a butcher. That he's the one? My beautiful Omaima died because of this man who pays me? I only helped him to keep you until the inspector took you away to jail."

She had to make him understand. The words spewed from her mouth in rapid fire succession. "I don't know for sure who killed Omaima, and please, understand that I am so sorry that your beautiful niece died. She was so bright and had so much to offer the world. I liked her the moment I met her."

She took a deep breath and looked at the door, fearful that she'd be overheard. She lowered her voice to a whisper. "They're not taking us to jail. He wants to hurt us. And the police here are involved in some way, if not all of them, at least Inspector Stringer is part of this."

He hung his head as she went on.

"Two other people were murdered over this in the United States. The school is just a cover for a much bigger operation there. He's making tons of money working with someone there to sell body parts..."

"Enough! Please, I can't listen anymore," he begged, covering his ears to block what she said. Without saying another word, he trudged out of the room, flipped off the light, and slammed the door.

More than an hour passed before either of them said anything. Amie spoke first, her voice a low, tired monotone in the dark. The single question shattered the silence. "What do you think he's going to do?"

The grim reality of what she'd asked broke Rita's concentration. She'd been imagining various scenarios concerning what would happen if the distraught uncle confronted Shane. He'd probably end up dead as well because these people apparently had no qualms about killing anyone who dared to get in his way.

"I don't know. I don't want anything to happen to him, that's for sure. Maybe I said too much, but I was simply trying to get him to understand..."

Footsteps in the hall silenced her mid-sentence. When the door creaked open, she held her breath.

Without a word, the old man moved first to her bed, and then to Amie's, using a screwdriver on both to loosen the metal screws that held the railings in place. He was helping them.

"There is a party tonight to celebrate the school at the big resort on the beach. Dr. Gilliam and Inspector Stringer will be there because alcohol will be plenty, and so will the young ladies. Wait one hour and then push the rails and slide handcuffs off. It must look as though you freed yourself. Run, and get out of here as fast as you can. Tonight, for sure, will be your only chance. I prayed about this, and I cannot let you suffer the same fate as my beautiful Omaima. Run to my taxi at the docks. Name of Yellow Bird. It has gas and the key to start. Handcuff keys and a little money on seat. I don't know how to use it, but I left Omaima's phone there. Take it, and get off this island before daylight, my ladies. If not, you are dead, too."

Rita couldn't believe what he'd said. "What about you?" she asked. "Shouldn't you come with us? We can get help. Won't they come after you now?"

He turned to leave the room but stopped at the door. He shook his head. "About that, I do not care. I am old and alone now. While they are sleeping off their party headaches, I will visit my Omaima with flowers in the morning. After that, whatever will be, will be."

They watched the wall clock. Sixty minutes ticked away, one by one, as they waited together in the dark, whispering plans. Rita believed they were being held somewhere near the school but had no way of knowing for sure. It wouldn't be until they made it outside to the street that she'd be able to figure out where to go to find the taxi operator's boat. She tried not to think about him, knowing that the risk he took by helping them could mean the end of his life if Shane figured it out.

When an hour passed, they did as he'd ordered. She'd tugged at her railing, shaking it back and forth with all her might until the screws fell to the floor. She slid her handcuffed hand off the rail. Freed, she hobbled to Amie's bedside, her leg pounding as she helped to rock the rails there until they clattered to the floor as well.

"God, I hope no one heard that," Rita muttered. "Let's go. If we get separated, head to the waterfront. Use alleys and try to stay hidden until we find each other. I remember his taxi. It's blue with bright flowers painted on the front. Hopefully, there's a streetlight nearby so we can see it."

Amie nodded, her eyes wide with fear. "I'm ready, but I'm sticking with you this time. I can't do this alone. I trust you. Please, Rita, help me to get back to my son."

Together, they fled.

They'd been held in a home only two doors down from the medical school. Once they made it to the street, Rita recognized it from the school brochure, which advertised it as a temporary dormitory for students who had yet to obtain permanent housing in Nevis. Despite the late hour, she grabbed Amie's hand and pulled her into the alley behind the home where they could remain unseen by any passing cars or nosy neighbors. They wound through the back streets, some of which Rita remembered from her earlier escape, until they arrived at the docks. Only two lights illuminated the wooden plank platforms that ran in front of at least twenty similar water taxis. After ten minutes of searching, they located the old man's boat and clambered aboard awkwardly, sending it rocking back and forth in the black water.

"Can you drive this thing?" Amie asked. "I wouldn't know what to do."

Rita shrugged with false bravado. "How hard can it be? Once it's fired up, I'd imagine it steers like a car, and right now, I don't think we have much of a choice other than to go for it." She felt around in the dark until she scooped up a set of keys from the seat. She tried three before the handcuff fell off her left hand and landed in the bottom of the taxi. She freed Amie and then pocketed the money and phone for use later before she raised the small anchor from the water just as she'd seen the taxi operators do when she'd traveled between the islands.

"Reach under your seat for a life jacket and put it on. I know there's one under every seat because the old man told me so during his emergency safety spiel when he first brought me from St. Kitts to Nevis. When you get it on, sit down and hold on," she said. She reached under her own seat, grabbed the life vest, and strapped it around her waist before inserting the key into the ignition.

"All I can say is that I'm grateful that Yellow Bird here has a gas pedal instead of a throttle because I'd probably send us overboard."

The engine started, rumbled, and then petered out. She pressed her foot to the gas and tried again with the same result. The pungent odor of gasoline burned her nostrils. *C'mon, c'mon, she begged. Don't flood out. If we don't move, someone is going to hear this. We've come too far to fail now.*

Finally, on the third try the engine started to purr. Slowly, she eased the taxi away from the docks and headed out into the open water. About two hundred yards from shore, she killed the engine and dropped the anchor back into the waves. Her plan was to remain just a short distance offshore for an hour or so until daybreak, when she'd have a better chance of making her way along the coast toward St. Kitts, which lay nearly three miles away.

Floating and rocking, she tried to think. The old man had given them less than a hundred dollars, which was enough for a few meals at beach shacks, but not enough to pay for shelter until they could find a way to leave the larger island for home. *As if we could. We have no identification and no passports.* They'd probably be arrested on the spot if they even tried to go near the airport. She powered up the phone he'd given them, and found that it worked without a password, but there wasn't much battery life left, and he'd not given them a charger. She noticed that the signal was weak out on the water, so she turned it off to preserve the battery.

At dawn, she shook Amie's shoulder to wake her. Amie had been snoring, and although she'd napped herself for a few minutes, Rita feared getting caught too much to sleep any longer. "It's time to move. Get ready and hold on."

She raised the anchor once more, sat down behind the wheel, and turned the key to start the engine which, thankfully, fired up and purred as she maneuvered the craft along the coastline for a while. Finally, going for broke, she pushed the gas pedal down further and headed, hopefully, in the direction of Basseterre in St. Kitts. Waves slapped the boat as she increased speed.

"Slow down," Amie begged, her eyes wide with fear. "Don't go so fast!"

Rita shouted over the noisy engine. "I want to get there as quickly as possible before anyone realizes we're gone and how we got away. I can't imagine the old guy is going to report his boat stolen too soon, but I don't want to take the chance. I don't want anyone waiting for us at the dock in St. Kitts, for pity's sake." She looked at the sky. "It's probably close to six now. We don't have time to waste."

Sometime later, Rita realized they were lost.

She could see land, and knew it was St. Kitts, but they weren't anywhere near Basseterre or anything she remembered on her previous water taxi rides to the island. She saw a few houses sprinkled on the hills around the coast, but no town and no docks. To her right, she noticed a small stretch of isolated beach flanked by jutting rocks on both sides. She looked at the fuel gauge and saw the tank was almost empty. The beach ahead appeared to be the best choice to stop. Hopefully, from there, they could make their way onshore for help.

“We’re going in there,” she shouted to Amie over the roar of the engine, pointing toward the beach. “No other choice because we’re almost out of fuel, and I don’t know where we are. I’m going to take it in slow and try to get as close to shore as possible but I’m afraid we’ll hit rocks if we go in all the way.”

She let up on the gas and steered toward land, moving slowly across the water. About a hundred yards from shore, she heard a screeching noise, and the boat jolted forward abruptly when it hit a large rock jutting only a few inches above the surface of the waves. Amie screamed as the craft rocked violently and began to tilt. Rita killed the engine and leaned over the side of the craft, where a gaping hole sucked water into its belly. She’d been right to think the rocks could cause a problem. “Oh shit, Amie, we’re in trouble. This thing is going down in a few minutes.”

They were going to have to swim. She looked around for something to keep the precious phone safe and dry from the saltwater that would render it useless. She found a used plastic bag on the floor, probably left over from a passenger’s lunch sandwich. Wasting no time, she yanked the phone and money from her skirt pocket and sealed them inside the bag before stuffing it into her bra beneath the life vest. Still wearing the long dress stolen from the clothesline, she wrapped it high around her waist to keep her legs from getting tangled in its folds. She looked at Amie, who appeared ready to cry. “Keep your shoes on,” she commanded, noting that Amie’s shorter sundress wouldn’t be a problem.

As the boat floated toward shore it took on more water, so she turned to Amie, who looked terrified. “Listen to me. Just stay calm, ok? We’re not that far from shore, and you’re not going to sink with that life jacket on. The only things we have to watch out for are any rocks that we can't see right now. We're going to ease into the water gently and take the advice they give to whitewater rafters. If you get into trouble, sit down and float. Don't try to stand or you can get caught on something," she ordered.

Amie nodded but said nothing. A few minutes later, as the water taxi sunk deeper onto its side, they were in the ocean, paddling toward the shore.

CHAPTER TWENTY-ONE

Rita screamed in pain when a sharp rock tore into her left leg, leaving a trail of red spilling into the water behind her. Somehow, she made it to the beach gasping and choking while Amie helped her onto the sand. Through tears, she watched as Amie quickly removed her own life vest before kneeling and undoing the straps on hers. "Raise up," Amie said. "I'm going to pull this out from under you."

When she was freed, she felt Amie tugging on the bottom of the dress she'd tied around her waist. Amie gripped the fabric and tore a long piece from the hemline, which she used as a tourniquet to staunch the bleeding.

"You need a doctor, and soon. We have to get help. That gash is going to need stitches or you're going to bleed all over this island," Amie said.

Rita gritted her teeth and powered up the phone she'd pulled from her bra. There was a signal, but a weak one. He wouldn't recognize the number, but hopefully, he'd answer the call.

One ring, two, and then a third. She waited, holding her breath, through a fourth and a fifth until his voice came over the line when the call went to voicemail. "David, it's me. I'm somewhere on a beach in St. Kitts, and I'm hurt. Please, I need help."

She told him as much as she could about what had happened to them, where they were, and what she'd suspected about Shane Gilliam, James Foster, Bob Watson and the police inspector. When she hung up, she called her editor's number at the paper. It was too early for him to be at his desk, but she couldn't remember his cell number. She told him everything she'd already relayed to David, adding an apology for becoming part of the story she'd been covering, ending just before the phone's battery beeped, signaling that it was close to running out of power. Sobbing in despair, she shut it off, preserving what little juice it had left. She stuffed it into the plastic bag with the cash.

"Rita, I don't want to, but I have to leave you here," Amie said. "If you can make it up to those trees, you'll be in the shade. I'm going to see if I can find a house, maybe get someone to help us. Give me the money. There might be somewhere around here to buy food or first aid supplies."

Rita handed her the bag with the phone and the cash and half crawled to the swaying palms. When she reached the welcome shade, she closed her eyes, exhausted. "Go," she said. "But be careful who you talk to. We don't know who we can trust. Remember that."

Amie nodded. "I will. Please stay here and don't move so I can find my way back to you. I'll be back as soon as I can."

By nightfall, Amie hadn't returned, and Rita was losing hope. She hadn't had anything to eat since the old man brought them sandwiches the night before, and the bottled water he'd left for them in the taxi sunk along with it. She was sweating profusely and had muscle cramps from dehydration. Blood crusted and turned brown on the folds of the material Amie tied around her leg. It burned, and she wondered whether the salty ocean water had helped it or hurt it. She'd passed a few daylight hours watching two lizards crawling along the sandy shoreline, and in the distance, she heard odd cackling, crying noises that frightened her until she remembered the island's monkeys. No doubt the trees and the hills were full of them. The only critter she liked was Boomer, and her beloved little Yorkie was more than two thousand miles away.

As she drifted to sleep, lulled by the sound of waves crashing onto the rocks, her thoughts wandered to Boomer. Poor little guy. Alone again. She hoped he'd found his way into David's heart, and that he'd have a home there after she was gone.

Rita's body burned with fever. Blisters covered her lips, and the parts of her shoulders and upper chest left uncovered by the dress were fiery red from hours of unfiltered morning sun blazing through the sparse leaves of the palm trees. She watched helplessly as yellow fluid oozed from the material wrapping the gash in her leg. In front of her, stunning turquoise waves lapped the edge of the shoreline, taunting her. *How does that old saying go? Water, water everywhere, but not a drop to drink?* She couldn't remember where she'd heard that, but the words rang true. She'd do anything right now for a sip of water to ease the raw pain in her parched throat.

Where had Amie gone? Why hadn't she returned? Most likely, she was lost. She closed her eyes.

Hours later, when the sun rose directly overhead, she heard voices coming from somewhere in the trees and tried unsuccessfully to stand up. "Here, over here," she croaked, unable to scream. "Help me."

She rolled onto her side, squinting as she looked up into the trees when she heard twigs snapping in the thick vegetation behind her. A minute or two later, two men emerged, scuffing the sand as they made their way toward her.

"Well, Miss Locke. We've found you safe and sound, although your leg is looking a little worse for wear. And now, my dear, I must inform you that you are under arrest."

Rita shivered. Inspector Wade Stringer stood above her. Beside him stood Shane Gilliam, who raised his hand in mock salute.

"Under arrest for what," she managed to whisper.

"Oh, for a number of things," the inspector said. "Let's start with theft of a watercraft, then assault for your attack on a school employee, and, oh, don't forget, false statements to law enforcement authorities. Last, but not least, violating immigration laws by entering our country unlawfully. Although, if you can produce your passport and proper identification, the last charge will be dropped."

She gaped at him. He'd changed his attitude from the last time she saw him, when he'd tried to stop Shane from drugging her. How much money had it taken to make him align himself even more closely with Shane?

"You can't be serious. How much is he paying you? You know exactly how I got to the island, and you know it was legally. And as for how I ended up with no identification, you know it wasn't through any fault of my own. My things are probably locked up in your office right now."

He smirked. "Now my lady, whatever are you talking about?"

"You know damn well what I'm talking about," she hissed. "You'll never get away with this. I've already told people in the

United States what you're doing here, what you've all done."

"Perhaps all of that is true, my lady, but we're not going to debate travel logistics here, out in the scorching sun, although I will tell you that there's nothing anyone in the United States can do to help you now. You're in my jurisdiction and presently in my custody, so it matters not at all that you've managed to phone someone in your country for help," he said. "That blonde fool you were with made a phone call as well, from what I understand."

Rita spat out the words, her voice stronger, fueled by anger. "She was trying to help me. Where is she? What have you done with her?"

At that, Shane Gilliam laughed. "Relax, no one has done anything with her, at least not yet. She's pretty enough, but so stupid. She made her way to a house on the hill, where the people were kind enough to give her food, water, and bandages for you. Then, she made the mistake of a phone call, and now we are here. You forget, our federation of islands sits close together, and our friendships with people on both St. Kitts and Nevis are strong."

Rita knew then that Amie's foolishness had given them away by saying too much in front of the people who helped her. Who had she phoned? They must have overheard her and called the police.

Inspector Stringer held his right hand out to help her up from the sand. With his left, he gave her a bottle of water. Weak, she had no choice but to take it and lean on him for support as he led her deeper into the palms with Gilliam following closely behind them. As she moved, the cut on her leg burst open and began to bleed again, leaving a trail of red running down her ankle and onto the ground.

She hated herself for what she was about to say, but she felt she had no choice.

"I need stitches in this, and probably an antibiotic. I've had a fever since last night, so I'm sure it's already infected. Please, take me to a hospital, and I promise, I'll take Amie, leave, and never look back," she begged.

Gilliam broke out in a fit of laughter matched almost immediately by the inspector. "Why would I take you to a hospital when I'm a *doctor* who owns a medical school? Don't worry, Rita, between myself and my *first-year* students, I'm sure we can patch you up and give you a shot or two until we get some direction as to what your future entails," he said. "And as for Amie, you're probably not going to see her again anytime soon."

He'd barely finished speaking when his phone rang. "Yes, we located the package, but we're not sure what you'd like done with it because it is damaged, slightly hurt during its recent journey. Yes, it can be repaired. Whatever you say. Same terms as before, deposits in both accounts for our trouble." He hesitated for a few moments, listening. "I don't care if you don't have it. Find it somewhere."

He ended the call abruptly and turned to the inspector. "Check to see that you have received your deposit later today."

When they reached the edge of the trees, she saw a police car parked along the two-lane road. "If you are smart, you will say nothing," the inspector said, gripping her arm tightly. He patted the gun holstered at his waist. The uniformed officer who waited behind the steering wheel said nothing as Stringer shoved her into the back seat and sat beside her. Gilliam took the front passenger seat.

"Drive on, please," Stringer told the man. "We must get this poor woman medical treatment immediately. If you would be so kind to take us to the docks in Basseterre, we will return her to Nevis as quickly as possible for treatment at the medical school."

They rode in silence for fifteen minutes, winding along the coastline until they reached the docks in the center of town. The inspector never eased his grip on her arm when they got out, walked to a waiting water taxi, and climbed aboard for the two-and-a-half-mile ride to the smaller island. She thought about screaming for help but realized no one would listen to her. She was bleeding, filthy, and sunburned, and the dress she'd stolen hung in shreds around her legs.

I probably look like a lunatic. Who would believe me? I almost can't believe this is happening myself. I wanted to write a story to expose Shane Gilliam for what he truly is, and now, I'm nothing but one of his pathetic victims, caught up in lies and fraud.

Upon arrival in Nevis, the inspector helped her out of the boat, led her to the dock, and turned to Gilliam. He spoke loudly enough for the taxi operator to hear. "This is where I must leave you. I'm turning custody of the prisoner over to you so that she can receive the proper medical attention she needs. I'm sure she will be in good hands."

He turned and walked away in the direction of his parked vehicle.

"You smell," Gilliam announced. "Take a shower and put on these clothes." He shoved a pair of green surgical scrubs into her hands and pointed her to a bathroom down the hall from the room she and Amie escaped from two days earlier. "Don't get any ideas about going anywhere, because I'm sure you can tell I've got people all over the islands who are willing to help me. They love me here for the money that's been flowing in since I opened this school," he said. "For some reason, my connection wants you alive and healthy, so we're going to take care of that cut before the infection gets any worse."

The shower felt like heaven and hell at the same time. Tepid, soapy water did wonders for her itching scalp and sunburned body, but she gritted her teeth when the first razor-like drops reached the wide cut in her leg. Gingerly, she used a soft washcloth to scrub away the blood and yellow pus that crusted around it until it came clean. It wasn't extremely deep, but it was several inches long, and she could see that it would need at least eight or ten stitches to close. When she finished, she dried herself with a towel hanging on a bar next to the shower, pulled on the scrubs and fluffed her hair. Gilliam waited in the hall.

"This way," he said, pointing to the room where the rails had been returned to the beds. Once in the doorway, she saw the nervous young man who'd greeted her at the medical school the morning Omaima's body had been discovered on the beach. He smiled in recognition, but she shook her head and rolled her eyes toward Gilliam to stop him from saying anything. She limped to the bed.

"Young Robert here is going to sew up that nasty cut and give you an injection of antibiotics while I go next door to get you some lunch," Gilliam said. "I'll be back in ten minutes, Robert, so please wait here with our patient. She's under arrest by the Nevis police, and they've placed her under our care. I wouldn't want her running out without eating and hurting herself even more. She needs her strength."

He walked out, and when she heard the exterior door close, her words came in a rush. "Robert, he's holding me here against my will. My name is Rita Locke, and I'm a reporter from *The Journal* in Pittsburgh, Pennsylvania. I'm not under arrest. I was abducted while working on a story about a murder that occurred there."

He said nothing as she rattled on.

"Gilliam isn't a medical doctor. He and the murdered man, a funeral director, were selling bodies and parts and making tons of money, and I think he's responsible or knows who is responsible for killing Omaima. Please, help me to get out of here."

The young man's eyes widened with fear, and his face had turned white. The syringe he held in his hand started to shake as he looked toward the doorway in despair.

"Lady, if he's not a doctor, you're in trouble. I know nothing about giving shots or stitching someone up, and I sure don't know anything about selling bodies and body parts," he whined. "And I don't know how to get you out of here. This guy is crazy."

She barked at him. "First, stick that needle into my arm. I'm not going to die from an infection because you're scared. If you can't do it, give it to me."

Trembling, he held out the syringe that she prayed contained an antibiotic and not a sedative. She grabbed it, yanked the needle cover off, and closed her eyes as she jabbed it into the fatty tissue at the top of her wounded leg. Her eyes watered with tears from the sting of the needle as she released the liquid into her thigh. She pulled it out, capped the point and handed it back to him.

"Now, get your needle and thread. We're going to teach you to sew."

She lay back on the bed, leaning on her elbows. She shrieked in pain, precariously close to fainting, when he stuck the needle into the broken flesh at the top of the wound and pulled the thick, black thread into a crude first stitch. He backed away in fear, but she praised him and waved him back toward her. "Good, that's good. Keep going, even if I beg you to stop."

Her face poured sweat and tears streamed down both of their faces as he continued. His hands shook, and his teeth chattered with fear. "I can't…I can't do this, please," he begged. "I'm not cut out for this."

"Robert, don't you dare stop. I can't walk around with an open wound. Keep. Going." She gritted her teeth and closed her eyes as the needle and thread tore through her skin.

Two stitches, a third, and then a fourth, brought the skin tighter. By the seventh, she felt dizzy and ready to faint from the agony, but she urged him on. "Almost done, please, make it quick. Just go for it," she moaned.

By the ninth stitch, the wound was closed in a jagged map of black thread, and he was crying. "That's it, knot it and cut it off." Soaked in sweat, she sank down onto the pillow and closed her eyes, grateful the worst was over. "Thank you for being so brave."

He wiped the tears from his cheeks with the sleeve of his white lab coat. "Me? Brave? Lady, I've never met anyone as tough as you. Tough. As. Nails. If you can do this, I can figure out a way to help you get out of here. Give me some time…"

The sound of the front door closing stopped him mid-sentence. Gilliam walked into the room, smiling. "All done here?" When Robert nodded, he continued. "Great. Rita, here's a cup of tea and some soup. Just what our young Dr. Robert ordered, am I correct?"

Robert nodded again but said nothing. He backed out of the room and took only two steps before Rita heard him retching in the hallway.

"Shame. He's not going to make it through medical school if that's how he reacts to a small cut," Gilliam said, shaking his head. "And you know all about people who don't make it out of medical school, don't you Rita?"

He laughed as he turned toward the door and called out to his student, "Robert, clean up that mess in the hall, for God's sake.

I'll see you in the anatomy lab later. You, my young friend, need practice...and a much stronger stomach."

He cuffed one of her clammy hands to the bed railing, winked at her, and left.

Rita took a few sips of tea and ate most of the vegetables in the soup before pushing the tray onto the bedside table. She wondered, could she trust the kid to help her? Her life lay in his hands. Exhausted, she pushed the thought from her mind. Too tired to care about the throbbing pain running up and down her leg, she closed her eyes and fell into an exhausted sleep.

CHAPTER TWENTY-TWO

Over the next two days, Rita endured several more antibiotic injections, all administered by a trembling Robert under Gilliam's watchful eye. Her wound, despite its ragged closure, appeared to be healing well, and her fever and pain subsided, thanks in part to the ibuprofen tablets the young man slipped into her palm when Gilliam wasn't looking.

And Gilliam was always looking.

She cringed the first time she'd asked to use a restroom.

"No chance, honey. Here's your new bucket. I'm sure you know how to use it," he'd cracked. He shoved a bedpan onto her bed and chuckled as he walked out of the room.

"I'll be close by, but call young Robert when you're finished."

She couldn't bring herself to make eye contact with Robert when he came to pick up the pan fifteen minutes later. He took it away without saying a word, a ritual repeated more times than she cared to remember.

With Gilliam always hovering nearby, there was no opportunity to speak to Robert alone again, so she had no way of knowing whether he'd been successful in reaching anyone at the paper, or in fact, whether he'd even tried.

On the third day, she began to despair. She thought she heard voices coming from another room down the hall but couldn't make out whether one of them belonged to Amie. *What happened to her? Where had they taken her?*

Evenings were quiet, with no sign of Shane or Robert, who kindly left the bedpan on the edge of her bed at the end of each day in case she needed it overnight. She imagined that the door was locked, and she was forgotten until morning. Knowing Shane's romantic proclivities, based on his relationship with Kathy, she felt he had a woman, or more than one, to keep him busy most nights.

To occupy her time, she went over and over the facts and information she'd gained since the first morning on the scene of Bob Watson's murder. She thought back to the explosion that killed Cindy Ekas, the jewelry discovery, and then the brutal attack at her home. Back then, she'd never have imagined Shane Gilliam to be a part of those events, nor would she have believed him responsible for killing Omaima or holding them captive. She wouldn't have pegged him as capable of violence.

Fraud? Absolutely. Selling body parts? Possibly. But murder, assault, and kidnapping? No, he appeared too pretty to get his hands that dirty.

If she was right, he was the front man, and he let others, like Inspector Stringer and James Foster, do the dirty work and clean up the messes. She had no idea how or why Cindy ended up with the jewelry, which she assumed had been taken by Bob.

Was it at Shane's direction? Foster's? Why had Cindy kept it? She mulled over her situation.

This is one of those sensational, once in a lifetime crime stories that journalists dream about writing. Tom Moore and Bill Martin are probably having a field day with this back at the paper, if that kid got through to them. Hopefully, David listened to my message about Shane and the inspector and talked to the police in St. Kitts. The force on Nevis is controlled by Stringer. It's not that law enforcement authorities can fly down to the Caribbean and start arresting people, but they can catch Shane if he ever decides to return home.

Tears trickled down her cheeks. She missed her parents, David, and Boomer. She wanted her life back, and there were so many stories she'd yet to tell. She fell asleep berating herself for her stupidity. *I'd much rather be writing this story, than living it, but once again, I didn't listen, and I got too close. No headline is worth dying for.*

Hours later, she awoke to the sounds of footsteps and scratching outside her door. She held her breath. They'd never bothered her at night. Someone was coming for her.

"Rita! Red, are you in there?"

David? She had to be dreaming. "Yes, yes! Please, get me out of here."

The scratching grew louder and suddenly, the door burst open into a shower of splinters. David rushed to her beside in the dark. "Oh, my God, you're okay." He scooped her into his arms and tried to lift her from the bed.

"Owww, wait, my arm is cuffed to the bedrail," she cried. "I can't get up."

He ran back to the doorway, knelt on the floor, and searched though the smashed wood for the screwdriver he'd used to pry the door open. When he found it, he used the flashlight on his cell phone to illuminate the screws that held the rail in place. He loosened them, pulled the rail away from the bed and freed her arm. "Let's go. I don't know how much time we have. My rental car is parked down the street."

"Wait," she begged. "There are other rooms. Please, we have to look for Amie Watson. She's here, somewhere, I know it."

Together, they checked two other dormitory-style bedrooms and the bathroom on the first floor. She followed David as he raced up the stairs with the screwdriver, taking two at a time. He opened two doors, revealing bedrooms with two empty cots each, and then found a locked door at the end of the hall. "Call to her. See if she's in there," he ordered.

"Amie, it's Rita, if you're in there…"

Whispered pleas interrupted her. "Yes, oh God, get me out of here."

David pried the door open, ran to the bed, and repeated the process to free Amie from the railing. "Let's go. It's nearly dawn, and we have no time to lose. We have to get to the airport."

"Where are we going? We don't have passports. We're not flying anywhere without them," Rita said, her voice frantic with despair.

"Oh, yes we are, thanks to your publisher, his private jet, and a number of well-greased palms," David announced. "The deal is, though, the plane takes off unseen, before morning, or we're stuck. It took some time to get here from St. Kitts because I had to wake up a water taxi driver and bribe him to make the round-trip at this hour. We're running out of darkness. Now, go!"

They slipped out of the front door unnoticed. He sprinted away from the house, dragging her along with Amie's help. By the time they'd gone the two blocks to his rental car, Rita was gasping.

She was shocked to see Robert waiting in the car with the engine running. David pointed toward him, explaining to Rita, "From what I've heard about Shane Gilliam and that damn crooked inspector, this kid can't stay here after helping me to find you, so he's going with us."

Robert smiled and saluted when he saw Rita. "There's Ms. Tough as Nails. I knew you'd make it."

David jumped into the front passenger seat, while Rita and Amie climbed into the back. Robert wasted no time in gunning the engine and racing to the dock where a young man dozed behind the steering wheel of an ancient red water taxi. Robert popped the trunk of the car, grabbed his computer bag and a small suitcase, and the four of them crammed into the boat that should have held only two passengers and the driver.

Rita held her breath as they crossed the channel, afraid to believe that she'd managed to get away. No one spoke during the brief voyage. When they reached St. Kitts, David handed the driver an envelope, shook his hand, and pointed to another rental car parked at the docks. Robert stowed his gear in the trunk, and they sped the few miles to the airport in the minutes before sunrise.

There was no time to lose.

When they arrived at the airport, they left the car parked in a front lot. David led them to a small, adjacent hangar about two hundred yards from the main terminal. He rang a buzzer and knocked on a side door, which opened a few seconds later.

A young black man wearing a security guard's uniform looked around the parking lot, presumably to make sure they hadn't been followed. He waved them toward a door on the opposite end of the building. "Your aircraft is re-fueled and ready, sir. Make haste, before you are seen."

David held Rita's arm as she limped painfully, and Amie, her eyes streaming with tears, stuck close to Robert, whose smile grew wider as they made it to the runway, where they saw the light jet with the words *News One* painted in bright letters on its side.

Robert whistled when he saw the aircraft. He pulled out his cell phone and snapped a quick photo before ascending the stairs. "Man, I don't feel so bad about having to leave now because we're traveling home in style. My parents will never believe this."

A single flight attendant stood at the open jetway door at the top of the steps. "Please, folks, let's move along. Our captain just informed me that we are two minutes to take off. Find a seat and buckle up as quickly as possible."

A minute after the steps were raised and the door closed, the sun began to climb above the horizon. Rita felt the wheels lift from the runway and the aircraft start its ascent into the clouds.

They were going home. Thanks to the generosity of her publisher and the courage of the man she loved, her ghastly ordeal was over, and she'd live to write another day.

After a brief refueling stop in Puerto Rico, the jet took off once more enroute to Pittsburgh. On the way, David did the best he could to fill in the blanks concerning the events of the last two days.

"I went to the paper, and to the police when I got your email. Thank God you copied your editors and George Carr on it because I was about ten minutes away from hysteria when I tried to explain things to them. Of course, George wanted to jump on the next flight to rescue you, but his hands were tied because of jurisdictional limitations."

Rita nodded. "I know that, but I love him for wanting to try."

He continued, unable to hide his excitement. "We called authorities here but kept hitting brick walls. Seemed like no one would cooperate or confirm anything. Finally, Tom went to the publisher who called me and immediately put his jet at my disposal. Can you believe that? Never met the guy before, but I'll say he's awesome. It's not every day that someone gives you a damn airplane."

Rita let a tear trickle down her cheek. So much to be grateful for. "I can't even imagine what this must be costing him."

David laughed. "Honey, it's way out of my price range, that's for sure. Anyway, I had no clue where to go or what to do until our friend Robert here called the paper and told us what you'd been through and how to find you. It took us two days to come up with a plan, and I have no idea how much money your publisher threw around or what he did to get people to look the other way, but here we are."

Finally, he took a deep breath. "Red, I hope you've had your share of thrills for a while. I don't think I could go through something like this again."

"Well, there's more to this," she said, looking directly at Amie. "There's a killer out there somewhere, and he's not going to be happy about this, based on what we know."

For the next hour, David and Robert sat listening to her explain what she knew for sure, and what they strongly suspected about the clandestine operation run by Bob Watson and Shane Gilliam. When she finished, she drained a can of Diet Coke provided by the flight attendant. Never before had her favorite drink tasted better.

David wiped his forehead with a handkerchief pulled from his jacket pocket. The heady excitement he'd experienced had evaporated upon hearing her story. He turned to her, pleading, "Red, tell me this isn't what happened to my grandmother. Please, tell me you're wrong."

She leaned back against the cushioned leather seat and closed her eyes. "I'd like to, but I believe, because she'd been embalmed, that her body was shipped to the medical school on Nevis, or possibly another medical school somewhere offshore. Most of the schools in the Caribbean don't have the facilities, nor governmental permission, to use cadavers in their instructional programs. They rely on illegal means, sort of a black market, to obtain them. If she didn't go to Celtic Cross, I'm afraid she went somewhere else. I'm so, so sorry."

He didn't answer. Five full minutes passed before he spoke directly to Amie. "Amie, I'm not blaming you for this, but I will say that your husband was pure evil to do something like this to my family and to other families without our permission. And for that, I'm sorry, but I dearly hope he rots in hell."

Amie nodded in agreement, trying unsuccessfully to choke back tears. "He wasn't the man I believed him to be. That said, I still want to know who killed him, for my son's sake."

Rita touched the other woman's arm. "And for ours. We'll never be safe until the killer is behind bars."

"I'm glad you said that," David said. "Because now I can tell you the plan."

"Plan? What plan?" Rita demanded.

David blew out a deep breath, a familiar tactic Rita recognized as his way of stalling when he didn't want to say something unpleasant or upsetting. "Well, George Carr doesn't want anyone to see you or know where you are once you're back in the United States. He believes that when Shane Gilliam finds you're not on one of the islands, he may be desperate enough to look for you stateside."

Rita's head snapped up. "Why would Shane do that?"

"Several reasons. For one, George is certain Shane is dealing with a partner, most likely whoever killed Bob Watson and Cindy Ekas."

"I think he's working with James Foster." She glanced toward Amie, whose face reddened. "I'm sorry, but I still think he's the one who killed your husband."

Before Amie could reply, David continued, "Whoever it is, Carr believes Shane is going to want to silence you before that partner turns on him. Two, if Shane wants to continue that body broker scheme, or whatever you want to call it, it could be that he's going to be looking for someone else to work with. He knows western Pennsylvania, so there's no better place for him to start making rounds of funeral homes to drum up more business. And three..."

She cut him off.

"Three, if he wants to shut us up, George plans to use us for bait at some point, am I right?"

He hung his head. "I'll admit, I don't like the thought of that at all, but you can't hide forever, and you'll never be safe until the killer is in prison and Shane is no longer a threat. Jesus, Red, look at all you've gone through in the past few months."

He placed his hand on her arm and studied her face. "How many times do you have to come close to dying? How many times do you think you can escape danger? We're never going to have any kind of life if we're looking over our shoulders forever."

Rita pondered the theory for a moment. She doubted it would work, knowing Shane might not be foolish enough to leave the protection he enjoyed offshore. "So, we go into hiding and they stake out baggage claim and watch airports? How long would that last, and what makes you think police have the kind of manpower for something like that?"

David looked into her eyes. "Not long at all, especially when you write the front-page story that police are close to arresting a suspect in the homicides of Bob Watson and Cindy Ekas. As much as they don't like it, Tom and your publisher agreed with

Carr to let you do it for the sake of the greater good. It won't be much, and it can't include anything about the jewelry or the exhumation petitions, and most of all, it can't mention anything to do with Gilliam or his school. You're off that story now, too, according to Tom."

She groaned. She'd known wondered if this was going to happen ever since that dead parrot ended up under her sheets, but she'd refused to quit pursuing her investigation. "Of course, I am. What else is new? Why don't I just hand someone else a Pulitzer while I'm at it?"

David continued, "Tom said just a few inches, or whatever you call it, quoting police and using some of the stuff you've already written. When we arrive at the airport, there will be a car waiting to take you and Amie somewhere safe. Robert, you have identification to fly home to Michigan, am I right?"

The young man sat up. He'd been listening intently, engrossed in the conversation, and appeared thrilled to be included. "Yeah, but I don't have enough..."

"That's what we thought," David said, pulling a wad of cash from his pocket. He peeled off five one-hundred-dollar bills. "Go to the ticket counter, buy a seat on the first plane leaving for Detroit, and go home. You left the letter explaining to Gilliam that you changed your mind about becoming a doctor, right? And you bought the ticket from St. Kitts to Miami on your credit card and left the receipt in your room as instructed?"

"Yep. Told him I was going to Florida to stay with my girlfriend. Thanked him for everything but said I didn't have the stomach for medicine," Robert said, beaming with pride at his subterfuge. "I took my computer and most of my clothes. Only left a couple pairs of shoes and a jacket in the closet and trashed the rest in a dumpster a couple blocks from the school before I met you last night. He won't think anything of it. Three other students quit last week."

"Good, I doubt he'll put two and two together. There's no reason for him to suspect you helped Rita, and if the money I spread around the two islands helped at all, no one will talk about the way we left," he said.

Amie, who hadn't said a word, leaned forward toward David. "What about me? Where do I fit in here?"

He looked at his feet for a few seconds before responding. "Of course, you'll be staying with Rita in a safe place. Police think it's for the best that you don't go home yet."

She raised her hands waving them at his face, "Oh, no. You're not keeping me away from my business, and certainly not from my son. No way. I won't do it. I haven't seen him in weeks, and I have to go to Philadelphia."

David rolled his eyes toward the ceiling. "I told George Carr you'd never agree to this, and I was right. He said if you insisted, he would make the necessary arrangements to have your son brought to you for a brief overnight visit in a safe place."

"What about James, or my brother? My business?"

He took a deep breath and shook his head. Police already had the funeral home under discreet surveillance for the protection of her brother and their occasional part-time employees. "They're going to have to wait, unfortunately, because your business is at the center of this situation, and police don't want to place your brother or anyone else at risk."

"You mean I can't even call him?"

"No, the less he knows, the better for his personal safety. This only includes your son. The school will be informed that he is being removed temporarily in connection with your husband's death." He explained that she'd have twenty-four hours with the boy before they take him back and explain to the headmaster that the risk to his safety is gone.

"That's the deal, the only way to see him. Amie, it's for your protection, and his. Right now, there's a target on your back the same as Rita's. Don't be foolish."

CHAPTER TWENTY-THREE

Rita and Amie were blindfolded on their way to the safe house, which George Carr described as located, "somewhere in the mountains above the quiet Westmoreland County town of Ligonier." She felt the blindfolds were overkill, but he said it would serve to prevent them from accidentally divulging their location to anyone.

Two days after their arrival, Rita used quotes supplied by Carr to write and file a brief story indicating that state police were close to making an arrest in connection with the murder of Bob Watson. It was vague, but hopefully enough to convince people that she was alive, well, and back at work. She'd used David's phone to call her parents to let them know she'd returned safely from her island assignment. Carr had given her an untraceable, throwaway cell phone to call her editor and to keep in touch with him. When he left, he took the computer laptop she'd used to file her story. "Extra protection," he'd said. "It's not that I don't trust you, Red…or well, yes, it is because I don't trust you to keep quiet about where you are and stay out of trouble."

She punched in her editor's number after she called her parents.

"Red, it's good to hear your voice," Tom whispered. He

explained that the newsroom was full of reporters and editors that afternoon. "You doing okay? I understand you had a hell of a ride down there."

"Yeah, I'm good. Listen, I'm sorry for what I put you through. I can't say much now, but let the big guy know I appreciate everything and that I'll hopefully get to thank him in person soon," she said. "I can't imagine the amount of money it took to get me out of there. That's it for now, boss. Can't call you again. Gotta be careful."

"Right, got it. Be safe."

She hung up, missing her job and their Pittsburgh newsroom almost as much as she missed Boomer and sleeping in her own bed. She was grateful to have been able to see David and talk to her parents, but she wanted more. She wanted normal, and wouldn't have minded a little dose of boredom, if she were being honest with herself. Thrilling exploits were for the people she wrote about, not something she wanted to participate in. Excitement, she concluded, is overrated.

The cabin they were staying in had every luxury, including flat screen TVs, a fully stocked chef's kitchen with a wine refrigerator and bar, three bedrooms, and a hot tub on a deck overlooking a mountain stream. She wondered if it belonged to her publisher, thinking again how thankful she was for his help.

Amie spent her time reading a book and working on crosswords in the largest of the three bedrooms, where she'd had a full twenty-four hours enjoying the company of her son, Dale, watching movies and building puzzles. Rita sensed he was a little upset from the long ride to meet them, although he appeared to understand that his mother was happy and that he'd be seeing her at school soon. Dale spoke a few words but communicated largely through a private sign language shared only with his mother.

When George Carr arrived with the female troopers who would return him to school, Dale waved happily, clutching a new box of Legos as he got in the car. Amie told him the troopers were teachers, and because the women were dressed in plain clothes and drove an unmarked vehicle, he appeared to be at ease with them.

After that, the days dragged on. Rita began to believe that the monotony and boredom were worse than anything they'd suffer if discovered. They'd been waiting for six days when Rita's phone rang.

"He's back," Carr said. "We got a call from immigration that he boarded a plane this morning, and our guys were waiting for him when it landed. Rented a car at the airport and is driving toward the city. They're tailing him now. I'll keep in touch."

Her heart pounded, and she screamed for Amie when she hung up the phone. "They were right! He came back, and they're watching him. God, this might be over soon."

The following morning, police followed Shane Gilliam to the Mason-Watson Funeral Home, where a viewing and service were taking place under the direction of James Foster and Daniel Mason. Carr told Rita that he stayed only a few minutes before getting back into his rental car and driving off, according to the surveillance detail assigned to tail him.

Upon leaving there, Gilliam cruised Rita's neighborhood, driving slowly past her townhome twice before moving on. Finally, he ended up in the city, where he parked in a public lot across the street from *The Journal*. He remained there for the rest of the day, leaving only when night fell and most of the newsroom staff streamed from the building.

"It's apparent to my team that he's searching for you," Carr confirmed. "We're just waiting for him to make a wrong move, and then we'll swoop in. I have a feeling he's probably getting impatient by now."

Rita woke from a deep sleep when the phone buzzed on the nightstand early the next morning. Groggy, she grabbed it, swiped her finger across the screen, and answered, "Yeah, George?"

"We picked up Shane Gilliam last night in your townhome and charged him with breaking and entering," he said.

"Thank God. It's over."

"Well, Red, there's more to it. We also charged him with attempted homicide because troopers caught him in the act of cutting the gas line. We believe he was trying to kill you, much in the manner that Cindy Ekas died. Girl, I told you there was a target on your head," he said.

She shivered, recalling the charred rubble that had been Cindy's business. Carr's elaborate precautions paid off. "Hey, in case I forget to tell you when I see you, thanks for all you're doing for us."

"Part of the job, Red. Thankfully, you weren't anywhere near the place because, if you'd turned on a light switch or lit one of those candles on your coffee table, you'd be singing with the angels right now."

She tried to contain herself, but her words spilled out, "What about Foster? Did you get him? You know they're in on this together."

He cut her off. "Red, I know you think you have this solved, but we've got nothing concrete on him, and I don't have any reason to pester a judge to issue a warrant to search his place."

"Aw, c'mon George, you know I'm right this time. Get us out

of here already. I'm about to go stir crazy."

He reminded her that she could be totally off base, that Shane Gilliam's partner might have nothing at all to do with the funeral business. For that reason, he believed they should remain hidden and safe. "Give me a little more time. It could be that we should be looking for someone at one of these tissue banks. There's one in Pittsburgh, and I'm going to send a couple of guys there tomorrow to do some digging around."

She had to respect his opinion, even though she didn't agree with it. "Okay, fine. Great. When can we come home? I want my life back, and Amie is starting to get antsy again about seeing her son. Gimme a timeline, please?"

He whistled. "Woman, you are the most impatient female I've ever met, unless you count my wife when she wants to go shopping. You, of all people, know how things work. Give me some time with Gilliam, a couple of days, and maybe we can get him to talk. Until then, stay put."

Rita made a pot of coffee before rapping on the master bedroom door to wake Amie, who was overjoyed to hear about Shane Gilliam's arrest. She threw a tantrum, though, when Rita told her they had to remain at the cabin indefinitely.

"Why? He's arrested, in jail, and it's over. I'll give it another day, but after that, I'm out of here and nothing you or George Carr or anyone says or does is going to stop me from going home to my life and my son," she shouted. "My brother can't run everything alone. I haven't talked to him or James since I left for the islands. They're probably worried sick about me."

She went into her bedroom and closed the door, but it didn't muffle the sound of her crying.

Nothing Rita said would calm the distraught woman. They spent most of the day alone in their rooms. It was chilly out, but Rita cooked two steaks on the outside deck grill and made a salad. Amie refused to eat anything, so Rita ate alone at the kitchen island, finishing the meal with two glasses of wine from the bar.

Later that evening, she noticed the light shining through a crack at the bottom of Amie's door but did not see her before she showered and went to bed shortly before midnight.

When she woke up the next morning, Amie's door stood open to reveal her bed had been made. She went to the kitchen to find her and discovered that the throwaway cell phone she'd left on the kitchen island had disappeared. Immediately, she rushed to the hall closet, opened it, and saw that Amie's jacket and boots had been removed.

True to her word, Amie was gone.

Rita paced the floor. The isolated cabin did not have a landline, and she had no way to alert George Carr without a computer.

She had no way to communicate with anyone and no means of transportation. If she left and started walking, Carr would be furious when he found out, and she had no desire to violate his trust and ruin their friendship, not after everything he'd done to help her. She was stuck there, unable to do anything but wait.

With each hour that passed through the morning and afternoon, her frustration grew. She reasoned that Amie clearly wasn't thinking rationally, otherwise she never would have set out on her own.

After five games of solitaire and two DVD romance movies, she stretched her legs and went into the kitchen in search of food. She boiled a small pot of water for pasta, smothered the cooked noodles with a microwaved jar of sauce, and ate at the island, uncorking the bottle of wine she'd started the night before. When she finished, she washed the pot and the other dishes, picked a random book from a shelf in the living room, and went into her bedroom to read. An hour later, bored, she filled the bathtub in the master bathroom with bubbles and soaked until the water cooled.

Under other circumstances, the electronics-free peace and solitude might have been a welcome respite. In this case, she felt anxious and trapped like a caged animal.

The next morning and afternoon dragged on. More mindless television, another boring book, and no one to talk to. She scribbled a few notes on a tablet from the kitchen desk, a list of potential wedding guests, kinds of flowers she might like, names of possible bridesmaids. *Good lord, weddings involve too many details. It might be simpler to convince David to elope to a tacky chapel in Las Vegas.*

Surely police would be there in the morning. Her gut told her Carr had to have tried to call her by now. He would have realized something was wrong when she didn't answer.

After a hot shower, she climbed under the soft down comforter on her bed and fell asleep listening to faint chimes of the grandfather clock in the corner of the living room.

Rapping at the front door woke her in the middle of the night. She grabbed her robe, wrapped it around her shoulders and rushed to open it.

Shocked, she took a step backward when she saw Daniel Mason instead of Amie.

"What are you doing here," she demanded. "How did you find me?"

"Calm down, Miss Locke. Amie told me everything that happened and gave me directions on how to find you." He stepped inside the door without invitation and scanned the living room. "I apologize for the late-night interruption, but she felt awful about leaving you here. She asked me to come and bring you back right away."

He explained that Amie planned to visit her son in the afternoon, so he told her to stay behind and get some sleep. "She was so worried about you, I offered to make the drive for her. She checked with Lieutenant Carr, and he said it's okay for us to meet at the station tomorrow morning before she goes."

At that, a warning bell went off in Rita's head. No way would Carr do that. Her gut told her something wasn't right. She hesitated, backing away from him. She smiled, hoping he wouldn't realize it was fake.

"It's not that I don't believe you, but you have to understand that I'm not comfortable leaving here until Lieutenant Carr comes to get me and tells me it's okay. He'd be furious with me," she lied, inching toward the door. "Thank you, Daniel, for your trouble, and please, tell Amie I appreciate your offer of help, but I'm fine here." She tried to push the door to close it, but he planted his foot firmly in the doorway to keep it open.

"Well, have it your way," he said, the tone of his voice becoming menacing. "We can either leave together or stay here alone together. Your choice."

Just as she started to answer, he reached into his pocket and pulled out a gun. He pointed it at her face. "Maybe this will help you decide. What's it going to be?"

Stunned, she backed away from him. Why was he doing this? She remembered Amie's comments about the PTSD he'd suffered with since returning from combat and sensed it was better to cooperate with him rather than challenge him. "What? Okay, okay, put that away. Let me get some clothes on."

"Don't try anything stupid. It's too late in the evening and my patience is wearing thin. Leave the door open and hurry it up. I don't have all night."

She pulled on a pair of jeans, a sweater, and ankle boots, all the while looking around the bedroom for a weapon. Desperate, she found nothing there to match a loaded gun. She glanced at the nightstand where she'd been writing wedding planning notes. At least she could leave a clue as to what had happened to her.

She grabbed the pencil, flipped to a blank page, and wrote down his name.

He'd moved to the doorway and was about to enter the room when she walked toward him, praying he didn't look at what she'd written. "I'm ready, I'm coming."

"Go," he ordered. "Outside."

Her heart pounded as he forced her into the passenger side. "Move over," he commanded, holding the gun on her until she slid over behind the steering wheel. "That's right, you're driving. Again, I'm warning you, don't try anything stupid unless you want a bullet in your head. Maintain the speed limit and don't try to be cute by flashing lights or swerving at other cars."

She drove in silence, trembling. She knew exactly where he wanted to go.

CHAPTER TWENTY-FOUR

When she drove around the corner to the front of the funeral home, he barked, "Around to the rear. First door." He pulled a remote-control garage door opener from the sun visor above her head and the door opened. "Inside."

She pulled in and parked, watching the door go down in the rear-view mirror. Trapped again, she realized her captor was a cold-blooded killer and that he had murdered his own sister's husband.

And if he'd already hurt Amie, he was a killer with little else to lose.

He led her through the hallway directly to the coffin room, where she saw a row of floor-length ruffled nightgowns in pastel shades of lemon, peach, turquoise, and lavender, hanging on a rack against the wall. She'd seen similar ones before and had helped her own mother pick out a frothy pink confection to bury her grandmother years earlier. She remembered her mother's logic in making the choice. *Grandma wanted to wear pink, her mother explained, and these are more beautiful than any of her everyday clothes.*

Her heart ached at the memory, and she turned her eyes away from the rack. She shivered with chills. No one used those creepy death gowns anymore.

He noticed her reaction and started to chuckle. "What's the matter, honey? Something scare you? Don't you like this room? I understand you've been caught snooping around here, so I'd imagine you feel pretty darn comfortable."

He motioned to the rack, sweeping his hand in a gesture of largesse. "Take your pick, Ms. Locke. You can have your choice of any of those."

She shrank away from the gowns. He continued, cruelly teasing her with sick sarcasm. "Personally, with your natural red hair color and green eyes, I'd say the lavender will be most flattering, although I'm no fashion expert. I'd have liked to have seen those long red curls you used to have flowing around your shoulders, but I guess this new cut will have to do."

He held the gun to her head and used his left hand to grip her arm, his fingers tight and bruising, as he led her to the rack. She dragged her feet until he yanked her to stand in front of it. "I said pick one. Now."

Her fingers shook and her legs turned to rubber as she fought panic. She had to do something to stall for time, anything to buy her precious minutes that might mean the difference between living and dying at the hands of this madman. "Where's Amie? What have you done with her? Is she okay? I need to see her."

"I haven't *done* anything with my sister, you fool, and I'm not going to do anything to hurt her. Here's the thing, Ms. Locke. You're not in a good position to make any demands at the moment, are you? I will tell you, though, that Amie is presently indisposed, and that you will not be seeing her now, or at any time in the future."

"That's where you're wrong," she insisted. "She's going to wonder where I am eventually, and you're going to get caught."

"No honey, that's where *you're* wrong. When she wakes up, she's going to think that you are alive and well and leaving us all alone for a change and that her involvement in this mess is over. I'll see to that. Now, listen to me," he demanded. He used his free hand to shove her face first into the rack, sending its wheels rolling backward toward the wall and her to the floor. He ripped the lavender gown from its hanger and tossed it to her. "Put it on."

She stood and did as he'd ordered, pulling the sweater over her head, and replacing it with the filmy gown that hung two sizes too big over her shoulders. When the hem hit the floor, she stepped out of her boots and slipped off her jeans.

She leaned down and was picking up a boot to replace it on her foot when he threw his head back and laughed. "No need for shoes. Don't you know we don't bury people with shoes?" He chuckled again when he saw her shocked expression. "And don't worry about the size of that dress. All I need to do is tuck it under that sweet little rear end of yours, and it'll look just fine. For all the snooping you've done, I guess you've never peeked under a coffin blanket, have you?"

She squared her shoulders in defiance. "You're not going to get away with this. If you turn yourself in now, I'm sure Lt. Carr and the district attorney will work together to get you a lighter sentence…"

He cut her off. "That, my dear, is where you are wrong. I *can* and I *will* get away with this because you will not be here to testify against me. We all know the dead don't talk. Look at Bob, for example, and Cindy. I got away with that, didn't I?"

He waved the gun at her face. "And if I'd used this instead of my fists and a hammer, we wouldn't be debating this issue right now, would we? My mistake was to *leave* you for dead, but not *ensure* you were dead. Well, honey, I don't make the same mistakes twice."

Chills sent her teeth chattering. *He's a maniac. Think! Say something to stop him. Anything.*

She blurted out, "State police are probably already on their way, here, you know. I haven't spoken to them in two days since Amie left, and Lieutenant Carr will be wondering why he hasn't heard from me…"

He shook his head. "Aww, wrong again, Ms. Locke. Your good friend heard from you twice yesterday and once today."

"How? Amie took the phone with her."

"True. Amie walked for a few miles when she left the cabin but then called me to pick her up. I brought her here, poor thing. She was so tired, especially after I gave her one of my special injectable cocktails, that she went straight to bed."

He pulled the throwaway phone from his pocket. "She's still upstairs, sleeping it off. In fact, when she went to sleep yesterday morning, she left this on her nightstand." He scrolled through recent messages. "You texted your buddy George Carr yesterday morning at eleven to let him know you had a migraine and wanted to nap through the afternoon. Then, you texted him last night to let him know you felt a little better and that you'd talk to him tomorrow. In case you're wondering, he wants you to feel better, and he'll let you know what happens with Shane."

Fear overtook her. She swayed on weak legs, nearly collapsing to the floor when she realized George Carr knew nothing and would not be looking for her. This time, there would be no escape.

Daniel went on, obviously enjoying both her physical reaction and the absolute power he held over the situation.

"Shane, that fool. I can't believe he couldn't do what he needed to do to keep you out of our way. If he'd have handled it on the island, no one would have had a clue where you'd gone. All that pretty boy had to do was think of a way, but the sniveling coward was afraid to piss off that damn blackmailing inspector who kept threatening to blow everything. Apparently, the inspector liked the money he got for turning his head to the school, but he didn't sign on for murder."

Rambling, he mumbled under his breath, "If I hadn't flown back to the islands to take care of things, that receptionist of his would still be giving free tours to nosy reporters."

She realized then that he, and not Shane, had murdered Omaima. He'd kill her, too.

She tried a different tactic and pleaded with him, hoping to change his mind. "You don't have to do this. I promise, I'm not going to write anything about you. I can't anymore, because it's a conflict of interest, and my editors won't hear of it, and…"

He gritted his teeth. "You think I'm afraid of a news story? Well, aren't you just full of yourself? You've already ruined this operation. I don't have the materials I need to supply to my buyers, and without them, the money stopped. The good *Doctor* Gilliam is in police custody right now, most likely singing like a bird to get off the hook. This isn't business anymore, Ms. Locke. It's personal."

She cringed. "What about Amie? Surely you haven't…you won't do anything to hurt her. I know she cares about you. What about her little boy? If anything happens to her, he'll be an orphan. He'd never understand…"

With that, he flinched, blinking his eyes before looking away from her. He gritted his teeth. "Leave my sister out of this. She never should have sided with you." He turned back toward her and took her arm once again. "Enough talking. Let's find a pretty box for you. So many to choose from."

Her comment to George Carr came back to haunt her as they strolled around the room. He stopped two feet away from the silver casket with mirrored ornamentation, the one she'd liked on her first visit there.

"Hmmm, wood or metal, Ms. Locke? These are some of our finest models. This one, in particular, is a stunning example of master craftsmanship, wouldn't you say?" He rested his hand on the silver coffin. "What do you think? Do you want it?"

She cringed, looking away from the coffins that filled the room. She had to keep him talking. Where was Amie? Wasn't there anyone else around? "You don't need to do this. You're just upset, Daniel. I think you need help. Please, stop this, and I promise you I'll do everything I can to try to get you the help you need," she begged.

"The only thing I *needed* was more money. Bob was afraid of getting caught, or maybe he had a guilty conscience and thought he was headed for hell." He waved the gun in the air, and she flinched. His desperation chilled her blood as she shook with fear.

He turned the gun on her once more. "He wanted to quit and made the mistake of telling me that Cindy agreed he should. That woman was as loyal to him as a dog, and she knew too damn much about what he'd been doing."

She said nothing as his voice trailed off. He looked around the room. "And now, you and that rag you work for put the nail in the coffin." He threw his head back and laughed. "Ha, ha. Pun intended! Just a little funeral director humor to lighten the mood."

"Daniel, why did you need money? There's a great business here. Why would you need more?"

He pulled her away. "No more talking. This is the one," he said, patting the silver coffin. "Open it. I'm sure you can. In fact, I'm sure you know all about how coffins work from the shit show with your boyfriend's grandma, don't you? Another fiasco, thanks to Cindy hanging onto that jewelry when it should have ended up at the dump. I wanted Bob to get rid of it, sell it even, but he was too afraid some pawn shop owner would rat us out."

He waved the gun at her, and she slowly raised the lid. "Get in," he barked. He rubbed his free hand along the sleek white material lining the interior. "Look at that beautiful lining. It's not every day you see such detail in the tufting."

She felt faint with panic. She couldn't do this, couldn't willingly climb into a coffin and lie down on a bed of satin and lace and wait for him to seal her inside to die. For a moment, she wondered whether she should try to run and force him to shoot her. At least it would be over in a few seconds.

As if sensing her dilemma, he dropped the gun and scooped her into his arms. She clawed at his face and pummeled his chest until he tossed her inside, shoved her down, and slammed the lid. She tried to raise it, but it wouldn't budge. She was no match for his brute strength.

He's so strong. He's holding it down.

Instinctively, she let out a shrieking, guttural scream. "Noooooo! Please, don't do this. Daniel, please."

He did not respond.

She pushed up against the lid again and then tried kicking with her feet, but it didn't move. To calm herself, she tried to remember exactly what happened the morning of the exhumation for David's grandmother. Coffins, if sealed properly, were airtight and could not be opened without a tool. That much she knew for sure. She focused her thoughts on the process, trying to remember step by step what the two cemetery employees did that day after they lifted the coffin above ground. She closed her eyes and pictured the scene: on each end of a coffin was a small round hole, normally closed with a plug during visitations at the funeral home. The men removed those plugs and then inserted a thin metal rod into each hole to crank open the lid.

In order to seal the coffin she lay in, Daniel would have to use a similar crank to render it airtight. Would he do that? Or did he mean to frighten her into silence?

She fought terror and claustrophobia to slow her breathing in an effort to conserve oxygen, telling herself that someone would stop him and find her before it was too late or that he'd reconsider suffocating her. She strained to listen for footsteps, for voices, for anything or anyone who could get her out, but all she heard was a faint squeaking noise near her feet, and then, a few minutes later, at her head.

Terror gripped her stomach. When she found her voice, she screamed again.

He'd wound the metal crank into the plug holes, sealing her in and sealing her fate.

How long would the air inside the coffin keep her alive? Fighting to remember, she recalled that at most, if she remained perfectly still and managed to stay calm, she had about five hours of oxygen. Or was it four?

No one knew she'd been taken from the cabin. No one suspected Daniel Mason. No one would look for her in a sealed coffin in a funeral home in the middle of the night, or ever for that matter.

It's over.

CHAPTER TWENTY-FIVE

As the minutes ticked away, Rita tried without success to avoid thoughts of her parents, and David, and the people and things she'd miss, the experiences she'd never have, the places she'd never see. She found a certain irony that she had a bucket list but never stopped working long enough to do anything on it. She'd never toss a coin into a fountain in Rome, or honeymoon in Paris, or hike in Alaska. She'd never win a Pulitzer, write a novel, or retire.

She'd read somewhere that when you are at the end of your life, you don't wish for more time at work, you wish for more time with your family and friends. That was true. Why hadn't she figured it out sooner?

Funny, right now I could care less about work, about the all-important front-page stories that have ruled my life since my first day in a newsroom.

Morbidly, she remembered a sick joke that went something like whatever you're wearing when you die becomes your ghost outfit, so always dress nicely. She felt the chiffon lavender gown. God, why couldn't she be wearing her jeans and boots? *Not cool, Rita. Not cool at all.*

Shifting thoughts, tears slid from her eyes, down her temples and into her hair when she thought of David, and how much she loved him. They'd never had the chance to plan their wedding. She'd not yet said 'yes to the dress' like the tearful brides on silly television reality shows. They hadn't chosen a wedding date, so at least he wouldn't have that memory to think about when looking at a calendar.

She would have loved to hold her father's steady arm walking down the aisle of their church. She imagined her mother in the front row, chic in a tasteful mother-of-the bride ensemble, most likely her favorite cornflower blue, and dabbing her eyes with pride. Her parents would never get over losing their only child. Nor would they ever know the joy of holding a grandchild.

Lying as still as possible, she thought of Boomer, and how much she'd come to love the little Yorkie. What a gift he'd been. Hopefully, he'll be a comfort to David.

And then, there was the story.

Who would find her? What would be the outcome of this sordid mess? Would a young, savvy detective on Carr's force nab the killer and solve the cases, figuring out at some point that she'd been abducted from the cabin and left to smother in an expensive box, or would she simply disappear and become yet another body sold for parts? What would they write about her after she was gone?

More importantly, how long had she been here?

She reached above her head and tried to rip the tufted lining with her nails, reasoning that she might be able to tap on the lid and alert Amie, an employee, anyone to her presence. The lining was too thick, her nails too short to make a difference.

She made mental lists of childhood friends, movies she'd seen, books she'd read, boyfriends she'd loved, anything to occupy her mind as the minutes passed. She imagined and counted pairs of shoes in her closet, the number of purses on her shelves.

She took a deep breath of stuffy, stale air. Was she imagining it, or could it be getting hotter? She ran her hands along the sides of the lining. The satin under her clammy fingertips no longer felt cool to the touch.

She wondered how it would feel at the end and hoped the lack of oxygen would cause her to drift off into a painless sleep. The thought of struggling for her final breaths terrified her even more. When she felt her chest begin to pound with building panic, she let out another desperate, blood curdling scream.

No one came to her rescue. No one heard. She started to sob.

Drenched with sweat, she managed to count to ten and took several calming breaths to steady her heart rate. By then, she knew, at least two hours or more had to have passed, most probably shortening her time to less than three. It all depended on the person and the circumstances she'd read, trying in vain to remember the formula for liters of oxygen, the size of the coffin, the time inside.

Finally, she decided she didn't want to know. Math had never been her strongest subject, and she certainly didn't want to spend the last minutes of her life doing something she'd hated.

Time swallowed the air around her and, at some point as her chest grew tight with pangs of fear, she began to pray—for her parents, for David, for Kathy, for her coworkers. She begged forgiveness for everything she'd ever done wrong, even though she'd never intentionally hurt anyone. Her language wasn't always the best, but she'd always tried to be kind, donated whatever she could to the less fortunate, and apologized when she'd made a mistake. She told the truth in her writing and always maintained a sense of fairness. And in the end, she thought, wasn't that the way everyone should behave?

Her skin felt clammy as sweat trickled from her temples onto the pillow behind her. She began to feel woozy, but relaxed and comfortable. How much precious air had she swallowed?

Exhaustion overtook her, and defeated, she gave up. So, this is how it's going to be, she thought, as her eyelids drooped.

Muffled voices from somewhere in the distance woke Rita.

Was she dreaming? She struggled to clear her mind and open her eyes. Again, she heard men talking.

Weak and groggy, she fought to scream but lacked the strength to do more than moan. She tried to raise her arms and scrape the lining once more. *Please, you have to help me.*

She faded into darkness once more. What was that pounding, she wondered, so tired. She reached up and rapped on the ceiling. *How am I supposed to sleep with all this noise?*

Bright light covered her, and cool air rushed at her face. She moaned. "She's here, she's in here. Rita, can you hear me?"

Her eyes fluttered but she was tired, and too weak to open them or answer.

"She's alive. Where is that ambulance? Get that ambulance here, and fast," George Carr ordered. "Rita, stay awake. You're going to be fine, honey. It's all over."

Yes, it's over, she thought, drifting away again. *Am I in Heaven, or Hell?*

She woke to harsh sunlight streaming into the room across her bed, where David sat on one side and George Carr on the other. A man she didn't recognize, wearing a white coat, stood near her feet. She looked around and realized she was lying in a hospital bed.

Intravenous tubing pumped fluid into her veins. She reached up and felt the tubes at her nose and smiled. Oxygen. After what she'd endured, she'd never take the fresh air for granted again.

"It's about time, sleepyhead," the lieutenant joked. "How am I supposed to get moving on this case if you're going to sleep the day away?"

"How did you find me?" she whispered. "How did I get here?"

David moved his chair closer and grabbed her hand. His eyes brimmed with tears. "Amie. She called police when she woke up and realized what had happened. If not for her, honey, you wouldn't have made it. You were losing consciousness when they found you. The doctors who treated you last night said you wouldn't have made it much longer."

"Thank God, where is she? Please, I have to thank her."

David looked toward the foot of the bed. "Is it okay, Dr. Wilkins?"

The doctor nodded. "As long as it doesn't upset her too much. Take it easy on her, okay? Whoever pulled her out of that box made it just in time."

He turned to go but stopped when he reached the door. "Make it quick. The nurse will be in to check her vitals in a few minutes." He left the room.

David took a deep breath and squeezed Rita's hand. "Honey, he shot her. It's a long story, and I'll tell you all the details later…"

"Oh, no, please tell me now," she begged. "What happened? Is she still alive? Did they catch him?"

Carr leaned forward. "Calm down, Red. Maybe your young man here doesn't realize you only function properly when you know every last tidbit of information about every damn thing possible. Allow me?" He looked at David, who smiled and spread his hands wide.

Carr took a deep breath. This wasn't going to be easy. "Amie told us she was asleep when you arrived, but the sound of the garage door opening woke her up. She expected Daniel to come upstairs to the apartment to talk about her plans to visit her son, and when he didn't, she went down into the hallway. She heard him talking in the coffin room and waited outside the door. When she realized he was talking to you, she knew he'd brought you from the cabin."

He explained that Amie overheard him confessing to killing her husband and Cindy Ekas. "When you screamed, she ran upstairs and called me. She was telling me what she'd heard when he rushed into her room. Last thing I heard before the phone went dead was a gunshot."

She gulped and closed her eyes. "Oh my God. Please, tell me she's not dead. Tell me that monster didn't kill her."

David leaned forward. "She's alive, but she lost a lot of blood in the hours afterward. She was in surgery most of the night, and although they're holding out little hope, there's still a slim chance she'll make it."

Rita tried to make sense of what he said. Amie had been through so much, and now she'd risked her life to save her. She turned to Carr. "Hours? If she called police, how long did it take for you to get there?"

He blew out a deep breath. "We had cars there within a few minutes, but we couldn't get inside the building. As soon as Daniel heard the sirens approaching, he started shooting up the neighborhood and insisting he had two hostages. He said if we stormed the building or tried to get in, he'd kill you both. Because I'd heard a shot earlier, I knew he was armed, so we didn't take the chance."

He explained that police waited more than forty-five minutes for a SWAT team and a hostage negotiator to arrive on scene.

Police evacuated the neighborhood and had the place surrounded. "We got James Foster on the phone, and he tried to talk to him. In fact, the poor guy was begging Daniel to let an ambulance crew in to help Amie, but Daniel wouldn't agree to it. It took two hours, but somehow, the negotiator finally talked him into surrendering. Apparently, the guy has experience in dealing with veterans and said the right things. When Daniel came outside, we rushed in."

They found Amie in a bedroom in the upstairs apartment, bleeding from a gaping chest wound. "We couldn't find any trace of you," he said.

They searched the building from top to bottom, the upstairs apartment, the visitation rooms, the kitchen, the office. "There was no sign of you anywhere, so we thought Amie was mistaken, that he hadn't taken you. I was ready to leave the coffin room when I stopped to take a final look, to see if there was something we missed.

"All the coffins on display were opened to reveal their luxurious interiors," he said. "Except for one. It made me sick, but I knew somehow you were in it. I pounded on it, ready to lose my mind, and I yelled for the other guys to come in."

He said he heard her tapping from within.

"Thank God, you must have heard me pounding and tried to answer back. We looked around for ten minutes before we found a crank to open it. One of my guys had been present for two of the exhumations and knew what to look for and how to use it, because I wouldn't have had a clue as to how to do it otherwise."

He closed his eyes. "There you were, dressed like an angel in lavender," he said. He wiped tears from the corner of his eyes. "When you moaned, I knew it would be all right. You're the toughest woman I've ever met. I was raised by one, and I married another, but they couldn't hold a candle to you."

She reached for his hand and squeezed it. “Thank you. Thank you for everything you did to save me and for always bailing me out of trouble. I promise, from now on, I’m going to listen to you…”

He cut her off, smiling, “Red, don’t make promises you’ll never keep. As soon as you’re up and back on the crime beat, those promises will go out the window, right David? And now, I’m going to leave you two alone. I have suspects to interrogate and a court case to put together. Red, I’ll be talking to you to get your official statement in a day or two. Until then, relax. Let me know if you get any word about Amie, please? When, and if, she’s able, I’m going to need a statement from her as well.”

He squeezed her hand and leaned over to kiss her forehead, which shocked her. Normally, he was nothing but professional. When he noticed her expression, he chuckled. “Yeah, that won’t happen again. I guess you caught this tired, old man in a weak moment. Days like these are making retirement look pretty darn good to me right now.”

He winked at her, and nodded at David, then lumbered out the door.

Rita and David spent the next twenty minutes talking. He climbed onto her bed, and she curled into his arms comfortably as she laid her head on his chest. “Red, please, let’s get married as soon as possible, okay? I can’t stand being away from you…”

He stopped talking as Dr. Wilkins walked into the room. “Everything looks good, and I think you should be able to go home tomorrow. All of your bloodwork and other tests look fine, and the heartbeat is strong. You’ve been through a lot. Dehydration is nothing to treat lightly, especially in your condition. You’re going to want to take it easy for a while. Rest, eat, and take your vitamins.”

"Heartbeat? What heartbeat? Condition? Vitamins?" She looked at the doctor as if she couldn't comprehend what he was saying.

"Holy shit," David whispered. "I guess I should have told you first."

"Your pre-natal vitamins," the doctor continued. Her mouth flew open, but no words came out. He looked at her shocked expression. "What? You didn't know you were pregnant?"

When the doctor left the room, she tried to absorb the news.

She could feel her heart pounding in her chest until her ears started to ring and she felt dizzy. The room spun around her. Nothing made sense.

When she could focus, she looked at David and started to laugh. He watched her, obviously afraid to say anything, as she began to cry. Still, he never let go of her hand as tears trickled down her cheeks in a flood that left her heaving and sobbing, unable to talk.

Finally, she fell silent. It took a full five minutes after the doctor left before she was able to speak coherently.

She touched her stomach and looked up at him. "How? I've never been regular since the miscarriage, but how did I not know this? How did I not feel it?"

He shrugged and shook his head. "Honey, I have no clue. Last night, after you were asleep, Dr. Wilkins came in to talk about the baby. Could have knocked me over, I was so shocked. I knew you couldn't have been aware of it, or at least, I hoped that you weren't keeping something from me."

She listened as he told her they suspected she was about four months along, according to the ultrasound performed the evening before.

"You're telling me I missed an ultrasound test. Jesus, was I that out of it?" She couldn't believe what she was hearing.

"Red, listen to me. You almost died. That maniac tried to suffocate you to death, and he would have succeeded if George hadn't figured out that one closed coffin looked out of place in a room full of empty boxes," he said, his voice breaking with emotion. He wiped a tear from his eye with his sleeve. "He saved you. He saved both of you."

He explained that as they were running tests, bloodwork revealed the pregnancy. "That's when I got scared," he said.

She sat up, startled. "Of what? I thought you wanted kids. If you don't want to be a dad..."

He drew back as if slapped. "Oh, you've got it all wrong. Nothing like that. Red, you told me you'd been sedated on the island more than once, remember? Who knows what he used? Propofol? Ativan? Drugs like that kill people when they're not monitored by medical professionals. Can you imagine what they could do to a baby?"

She shuddered. She didn't want to think about it.

"After that, you were hurt and pumped full of something you thought were antibiotics by a kid who had no business studying medicine anywhere, let alone in a sham school owned by a fraud on a tiny island in the Caribbean. I was terrified, but only because I wouldn't be able to cope with the sorrow you'd feel if you lost another child. I wouldn't know what to do for you."

His eyes filled with tears that matched hers. She was afraid to ask.

Finally, she spoke. "What did the doctor say? Tell me. You said I'm four months along. Is this baby going to live? Has my job ruined everything for us?"

He smiled. "If Dr. Wilkins is correct, and it's four months, it would have been around the first time…we, um, after you got out of the rehabilitation center. Remember that first time when you were feeling better, and we opened the wine after dinner?"

She blushed, remembering.

"From what he said, the baby appears to be healthy, although he recommended that your obstetrician do further genetic testing in a month, so we know for sure. I didn't have the heart to admit we were clueless about the pregnancy, so I played along like I knew. I sure wouldn't want him to think our little girl is going to be raised by idiots."

She squealed, "Girl? We're having a girl?"

"Yep. The doctor said he didn't see anything to indicate otherwise."

She narrowed her eyes, trying to determine whether he was happy or disappointed. Most guys wanted sons. "Yep? Is that all you have to say?"

"Nope. If you'd let me finish, I was going to say that I hope she has red hair, just like her mother. Although, I'd be happy if she didn't have your temper, because I have a feeling it'll be two against one. I doubt any man alive could handle two of you."

CHAPTER TWENTY-SIX

Rita cried into her pillow when the attendant wheeled her back to her room.

Facing discharge the next morning, she'd persuaded doctors to allow her to see Amie Watson, who lay unconscious in the hospital's intensive care unit, where the pumping whir of her oxygen machine and incessant beeping of monitors surrounding the bed reminded Rita of her own hospital stay in the days after the attack at her home.

They'd been through so much together, and she dared to hope they might become friends when this ordeal ended. Nevertheless, the nurse assigned to Amie told Rita that she had not regained consciousness since the surgery, and when she tried to read the nurse's expression, she found it devoid of hope. She hoped Amie's prognosis wasn't that dire.

A single dim light shone above the bed. Plastic tubing ran into Amie's mouth, nose, and arms, providing nutrition, medication, and lifesaving oxygen. Heavy bandages covered her upper chest above a thin hospital gown. Leaning forward in her wheelchair, Rita reached for Amie's hand, cool and chalk-white against the thin cotton blanket. She squeezed it gently, praying for some reaction as she whispered her gratitude.

"Amie, honey, if you can hear me, I want you know that I'll always be grateful for what you did for me. You told me in Nevis that you're not brave, not sure if you can fight. You *are* brave, and you have to fight to get back to your son. Please, you can do this."

She searched Amie's face for a reaction, but there was nothing. The machines beeped a rhythm with the beating of her heart, while the oxygen machine hissed its steady flow.

When the call came, Rita had been at home for three days, resting comfortably with Boomer and making lists of things she needed to do before she was cleared to go back to work. Now, she forgot all about arrangements for maternity leave, wedding plans, and outfitting a nursery.

She hung up the phone, overwhelmed with grief so heavy it made her chest hurt.

Amie Watson had died in her sleep the night before, according to her sister, Barbara Mason. Plans were being made to bury her in a plot beside her husband. There would be no service. Her sister said it would be too much to bear.

Tears stung Rita's eyes, and she balled her fists in anger. In murdering his sister, Daniel Mason now had a mother's blood on his hands. The list of his victims grew with each passing day.

She inquired about Amie's son. She remembered how his face lit up when he first saw Amie at the cabin. How would that poor child, already burdened with the loss of his father, handle losing his mother?

Barbara confided that she dreaded having to break the news of his mother's death to him. On top of that, as his legal guardian, she had to make major logistical changes in his life and move him to another state.

"I'm going to take Dale home with me," she explained "There's a very good residential school near the hospital where I work that will meet his needs. By taking care of the legalities after Bob died, Amie made it easy for me to assume his care. She always put Dale first."

She said Amie would have approved of her decision to move him to that school as long as he would get the opportunity to continue to make advancements. "Since he'll be close, I'm going to be able to see him on weekends and monitor his progress. I've already contacted the headmaster there, and I'll make the arrangements to transfer him when I go home next week."

Rita's heart broke for the child.

After Amie's death, Rita's testimony was the only thing standing between Daniel and prison, or worse. George Carr, when taking her official statement for his report, said prosecutors were considering filing a petition to seek the death penalty.

"Good," she'd said. "Based on everything he's done he deserves it, in my opinion. I know he's probably mentally ill, but I can't, and I won't feel sorry for him. He's caused so much pain..." Her voice trailed off. The memory of lying in the coffin took her breath away.

Just the thought of sitting in a room without windows, or watching the doors close on an elevator, or flying on a plane, made her feel physically sick. The first time it hit her was the day of her hospital discharge. When David pushed her wheelchair into the elevator on the fourth floor, she found it hard to catch her breath. By the time they reached the first floor, hysteria set in, and she emerged in the throes of a full-blown panic attack.

David wanted to call her doctor for help, but she refused.

"Please, just take me home,' she begged.

Never before had she suffered from claustrophobia, but now any hint of confinement, real or imagined, made her shake with terror.

And at night, in her dreams, she clawed and fought to breathe, buried alive.

Rita's face heated with frustration. After a week at home, her first day back at work couldn't get much worse, thanks to the latest news from George Carr.

"Red, we can't prove Shane Gilliam conspired with Daniel or had anything to do with the murders of Bob Watson and Cindy Ekas because he has solid alibi witnesses in the Federation of St. Kitts and Nevis who are willing to fly here to testify that on the nights they were murdered, he was there at the medical school."

She gritted her teeth to avoid shouting. "And just who are these witnesses?"

"Well, for one, Inspector Wade Stringer of the Nevis police force," he said.

"Of course, and you know as well as I do that they're in this together and that he's lying to save his own ass, too."

"Yes, I do, and I know it's likely Stringer would lie under oath, that is, *if* we had the power to make him come to the states to testify, which we don't. He carries a lot of weight down there, Red, probably from greasing government palms. You know how much I hate a dirty cop, but there's no use fighting it."

She already knew the authorities stateside could do nothing to Shane based on her claims that he held her against her will on the island. Indeed, Carr confirmed that Shane told everyone he simply provided her with free medical care at his school when he and the inspector found her sick and hurt after she wrecked a stolen water taxi.

"I'm sure he made it sound as though he'd done the police, and me, a lowly criminal, a gracious favor," she hissed.

Carr added that they had no concrete evidence to support any criminal charges against Shane for anything other than the break-in at her townhome.

"Whatever. Listen George, I'm not upset with you, I'm just so frustrated that this guy will end up with a slap on the wrist before this is all over. That said, I gotta go before I say something I'll regret."

"Sure, Red. Just know that we're trying."

When he hung up, she slammed the phone down on her desk, where it landed with a loud thud that echoed across the newsroom. Several reporters glanced up, their faces curious, and her editor turned away from his computer and rolled his chair toward her.

"Geez Red, who peed in your cornflakes this morning?" Tom asked.

"Nobody likes a comedian," she said, scowling. "That was George Carr, so you'd better get Bill over here to listen to this. He's going to want to do a story."

Tom whistled and motioned for Bill Martin to join them. She liked Bill, but it killed her to give up solid news stories, even when she knew she had no choice.

"What's up?" Bill asked. "And why can't the cops start calling me on this instead of you?"

She chuckled. "Hmmph. Simple enough. They don't call you because I've trained them to call me first. It's all about cultivating sources, my friend. Someday the master will teach you how it's done."

He smiled and flipped open his notebook. "Whaddya got for me?"

"It's about Shane Gilliam, and what's going to happen with his case, or should I say, what's not going to happen with his case."

She relayed what Carr said and added that because Omaima Alwen died in a foreign country outside U.S. law enforcement jurisdiction, there also was nothing American authorities could do to pin her death on Daniel Mason, she said. Carr theorized that Mason flew to the island via a private charter, killed the young woman, and then returned home.

"Even if authorities here found records to support that theory, anything that happened on the island is out of our hands. Police in Nevis aren't pursuing him for the killing either, most likely thanks to the intervention of the very corrupt Inspector Wade Stringer."

She went on to explain that the medical student, Robert Caruso, told Carr he'd be more than willing to testify as to what Shane had made him, and other medical students, do at St. Brendan's, as well as what he'd witnessed with both Rita and Amie Watson there. Unfortunately, another would-be witness, the water taxi operator who helped them, suffered a heart attack and died several days after Rita and Amie fled the island, according to the inspector.

"But again, their testimony would be useless here."

Search warrants served at the Mason-Watson Funeral home, as well as those served at James Foster's Butler County facility and Daniel Mason's place in Washington, turned up no records regarding sales of body parts, transactions with tissue banks or invoices from medical transport companies, according to police. The documents Amie said she'd seen were nowhere to be found, and she was not alive to testify as to what they contained. In addition, police had no proof that Shane knew anything about Bob Watson removing bodies from coffins prior to burial.

"It's all supposition and hearsay, according to Carr. Once again, Shane Gilliam is coated with Teflon, and he's going to slip away once more. All they can get him on is the break-in at my house because the prosecutor said being able to prove the charge of attempted homicide is a longshot," she said.

She added that Carr told her Shane has no prior criminal record, stole nothing from her townhome, and offered to plead guilty to the break-in in exchange for a sentence of six months in the county prison to avoid a trial.

"Carr said prosecutors are going to run with it. He made the phone call as a courtesy to me. That maniac is going to walk in a couple of months."

Tom whistled through his teeth. "Calm down, Red. You know the law. At least it's something. You exposed what he did, so hopefully, people will be warned."

She knew that the information she'd given Bill about the medical school and the stories he'd written based on her reporting and eyewitness accounts made headlines across the country from Pittsburgh to New York to Los Angeles for weeks. The Associated Press picked up the photos she'd taken and they, too, had been publicized all over the country and internationally.

In that, she found some small measure of satisfaction.

Tom reminded her, "He's not going to be able to get away with anything like this again."

She shook her head in frustration.

"I know him. Too well. Trust me on this one, that pretty boy will walk, and six months from now, he'll pop up somewhere else in the world wearing that damn white lab coat, playing doctor again."

Tom raised his hand. "Rita, stop. Let. It. Go. We're a newspaper here. It's business, not personal."

She turned away from him and muttered one last comment under her breath on the way back to her desk.

"Says the man who has never been suffocated in a coffin."

CHAPTER TWENTY-SEVEN

Five months later, jury selection began early in the triple homicide trial of Daniel Mason, who faced multiple counts in the deaths of Bob and Amie Watson and Cindy Ekas.

Rita, in her ninth month of pregnancy, struggled to ignore her aching back and swollen feet when she parked her Jeep in the public lot across from the Westmoreland Courthouse. When she approached the security stand, the elderly guard rushed to grab her satchel as she moved to place it on the conveyor belt at the x-ray machine. "Red, I don't know why you're carrying that heavy thing around in your condition," he muttered. "You ought to be home with your feet up, no matter what the district attorney says. This is no place for you."

"Aww, you're a sweetheart, but don't worry about me," she told him. She held up her left hand, where a sparkling diamond band circled her ring finger. "If it makes you feel any better, I'd imagine my husband will be here in a little while to make sure I'm behaving."

Her mood grew somber as she looked toward the staircase she'd used on her way to cover so many murder trials over the course of her career. "They need me if they're going to put this guy away for good. You have to understand, I can't let him go free."

He shook his head but waved her through the security gate and handed her the satchel on the other side. "Maybe tomorrow you should lighten this bag up a bit," he said, getting in the last word.

Despite her physical discomfort, she climbed the stairs to avoid confinement in the elevator. Several months of counseling to overcome her claustrophobia and nightmares helped somewhat, but as yet, therapy sessions hadn't alleviated her worst fears.

She waved at Bill Martin and several other reporters as she slipped into a seat at the back of the courtroom. Carr sat at the counsel table with the prosecutor, Franklin Hardt, on the right side, and the defendant and his attorney on the left, all with their backs to the door. When she saw that the defendant had hired Norman Davis, one of Pittsburgh's best and most expensive defense attorneys, she bristled with anger. She knew Barbara Mason was completing inventories at the Mason-Watson Funeral Home and at Daniel Mason's business for liquidation sales to settle the Watsons' estates and to amass assets for her brother's mounting legal bills.

Rita smiled when Common Pleas Court Judge Lydia Duff, seated on the bench facing her, nodded ever so slightly to acknowledge her presence. She'd covered many cases in Duff's courtroom before, and they had a relationship of mutual professional respect.

She'd listened to the two attorneys question at least a dozen prospective jurors about their backgrounds, their views on capital punishment, and other legal concepts when David slid onto the bench next to her and gave her a pointed look. He tapped his watch. "Enough," he whispered.

Rita ignored him for another hour until her back pain forced her to give in. Pouting, she handed him her satchel and followed him out the door and down the stairs. Most days, she loved everything about being pregnant and couldn't wait to be a mother. However, today, she didn't want to be coddled. She wanted to watch every single moment of this trial until the monster had been put away for good.

Three days later, a jury of ten men and two women, as well as two female alternates, were seated and ready to hear opening arguments in the case. Reporters gathered in the back of the room, and Rita suffered pangs of jealousy when she slipped into her front row seat next to David. She'd much rather have been in the press gallery covering this sensational case, rather than serving as the prosecution's star witness.

Already, she'd missed writing about the lawsuits filed against the Watsons' estates by David's family and several other families whose relatives' graves were found empty upon exhumation. It could be years before they'd recover any monetary damages, not that they cared about cash. All they truly wanted to know was where their loved ones' bodies had gone and why their final resting places had been disturbed.

Several relatives of people who had been buried from the funeral home came forward with necessary proof to claim the pieces of jewelry recovered from the safety deposit box. Rita knew that more than a dozen rings, a necklace, and two watches remained in a storage room at the state police station. She expected more families would come forward after the trial.

Rita rubbed her fingers over the diamond and pearl locket she wore around her neck. David's mother had given it to her the night before their wedding, which they'd kept to a small family affair with a simple church service and dinner at a local restaurant. She cherished it, knowing it belonged to David's grandmother.

"It's precious to me, and I want it to remain in the family," her mother-in-law insisted. "I can't bring myself to wear it. After all you've been through, I wanted to give it to you."

"All rise," the court bailiff shouted. "The honorable Judge Lydia Duff now presiding."

Rita used her hand as leverage to push herself up from her seat when the judge entered the courtroom from a side door and ascended the bench. *I feel like a beached whale. I can't wait to have this baby and get rid of this belly.*

"Please, be seated," the bailiff said. She sank back onto her seat, grateful for the respite.

A rear door to the left of the judge's bench swung open, and Rita closed her eyes. She hadn't seen him since he closed the lid of the coffin, leaving her trapped and screaming. *That was then, this is now. David is here, there are cops in the room, and this monster can't get anywhere near you. He's done hurting people.*

Forcing herself, she opened her eyes and stared boldly into Daniel Mason's face.

Over and over, so many times, Rita had been wrong.

She turned to look at the man sitting two rows behind her, his handsome face unable to mask the disappointment and sadness that clouded his eyes. For months, up until the time Daniel Mason showed up at the cabin, she'd believed that James Foster was the guilty one, the evil mastermind who murdered his friend, Bob Watson, set the explosion that killed Cindy Ekas, and beat her so savagely, all for the love of money.

Now, her face reddened with shame when their eyes met.

James nodded to her in acknowledgement. His jaw clenched, and she noticed his right hand tapping nervously on his thigh. He turned his head away.

Looking at James, Rita wondered how awful it must be to be the last man standing, so to speak. Bob was gone and Daniel faced the death penalty. His own business suffered from adverse publicity. More important, however, he'd truly loved Amie, and now she was dead.

Rita knew he blamed her for that. In truth, she blamed herself.

The prosecutor set up a chart on an easel that he used during his opening remarks. Commanding the courtroom with a booming voice, he took jurors through a timeline that began with the death of Bob Watson, then the explosion at the hair salon, and the discovery of the jewelry. He spoke about the attack upon Rita, the exhumations of David's grandmother and several others, and concluded with her abduction from the cabin and Daniel Mason's attempt to kill her. She knew that everything Amie discovered had disappeared, so she understood why he did not mention the body-selling scheme. He finished with Amie's shooting and a description of the police stand-off, ending with Rita's dramatic rescue.

"Ladies and gentlemen," he boomed. "Miss Locke survived the brutal attack at her home earlier this year that left her hospitalized in critical condition and then lived to be abducted once more by this man." He pointed to the defendant. "With the intent to silence her for good, he shoved her into a coffin, sealed the lid, and left her to suffocate to death."

Upon hearing that, one of the female jurors clutched her neck and shrank back into her seat.

Rita wished Hardt could have said more about Mason's involvement with Shane Gilliam, but knew he'd risk a mistrial without evidentiary proof that the defendant participated in his brother-in-law's body selling scheme.

Already mid-way through his sentence, Shane Gilliam could be called as a possible hostile witness for the prosecution, but she doubted his testimony would benefit the state's case much because anything he said about the scheme could open the door for additional charges against him. He'd be a fool to risk his freedom, so she expected him to shield himself with the Fifth Amendment to avoid self-incrimination.

The prosecutor's witness list included only Carr, several other state troopers, the coroner, two ambulance attendants, Dr. Wilkins, and Rita.

Hardt, in his opening statements, indicated that he expected the trial to be a short one. "However, we're going for quality, not quantity. We will be calling witnesses to tell you that Daniel Mason killed his brother-in-law Bob Watson because Mr. Watson wanted to end a side business relationship they'd shared. He lured Cindy Ekas to her death in an explosion. Then he murdered his own sister, Amie Watson, in cold blood because she tried to intervene and stop him from killing Rita Locke, a journalist who had been writing about and investigating the business operation. It's only through a miracle, a life-saving rescue by police, that his plan to kill Miss Locke did not come to fruition."

Norman Davis, in his opening statements, described his client as an honorably discharged Persian Gulf War veteran who suffered from Post-Traumatic Stress Disorder, a gambling addiction, blackout-inducing alcoholism, and paranoia resulting from severe anxiety as the result of his Army service. "We will provide you with medical and psychological records from the Veterans

Administration to show that Daniel Mason is struggling horribly from the effects of serving his country."

Davis said the defense will not dispute the defendant's role in shooting his sister. "However, we will prove to you that her death resulted from a terrible accident during an unfortunate episode in which Rita Locke unlawfully entered the Mason-Watson Funeral Home. Mr. Mason will testify that Ms. Locke, in a bizarre attempt to fabricate a sensational news story and fuel her career ambitions, climbed into a coffin, and shut herself inside to create drama, and that he unknowingly sealed that coffin while working at his business premises."

Rita's face flushed with anger that burned from her scalp to her neck. She whispered to no one in particular, "Lying snake."

Davis turned and shot her an irritated look, but continued, "Mr. Mason will also testify that he knows nothing about the death of his brother-in-law and had no involvement in the explosion at Cindy Ekas' salon, and we assert that any contrary testimony is purely speculative."

Carr, the prosecution's first witness, testified at length concerning the investigations into the deaths of Bob and Amie Watson and Cindy Ekas.

Rita was next up on the witness stand. Hardt delved into her professional background and showed her copies of several early news stories she'd done about the funeral director's slaying. "Please tell the jury, Ms. Locke, what processes you used to cover this homicide and whether your work compiling information for these stories differed in any way from other homicide stories you've written during your professional career, both at *The Journal* and any other publications you may have written for."

"No, it did not. I gathered information and reported only the facts confirmed through official sources. I interviewed Ms. Ekas twice before her death, and I attempted to talk to Amie Watson about her husband and the business, but we never completed the interview."

"And why is that?" he asked.

"I was attacked by a masked intruder at my home and suffered significant injuries that resulted in a lengthy hospital stay, several weeks in a rehabilitation center, and a few weeks of therapy and recuperation at home, followed by a period of time on desk duty at the newspaper," she said.

During cross-examination, the defendant's attorney asked, "So, you did not see the intruder's face?"

"No, Mr. Davis, I did not. I heard his voice, and that was a whisper," she said.

"Did you recognize it?"

"No, sir."

"Well, how can you be sure that Daniel Mason is the man who attacked you?"

"I can be sure because the man who attacked me used a hammer to twice fracture my skull. That information was never made public in any news story and was redacted from police reports. The day of Amie Watson's shooting, Daniel Mason referred to his use of a hammer against me. He told me he should have used it to finish me off."

Rita's testimony rounded out the trial's first day, and Duff excused the jurors, cautioning them to avoid newspaper and television coverage of the case. After the judge left the bench, the jurors exited from a side door, and the defendant was led out of the courtroom by a court officer. Rita, David, and the reporters in the press gallery were standing to leave when a uniformed state trooper walked up the aisle and whispered something to Carr and Hardt, who turned to Davis and did the same. Rita, in the front row, strained to hear them but couldn't make out a word.

When he stood, Carr turned to face her and smiled. "Call you later," he mouthed.

Three hours passed before the lieutenant's name appeared on her phone's screen. She swiped her finger across to answer it. "What? Tell me?"

"Well, it could be good news, or not so good news, depending upon how you look at it," he drawled.

"George Carr don't play games with me. Tell me what you know."

He let out a deep belly laugh. "Sorry Red, I'm in a teasing mood. Okay, here goes. Barbara Mason just left my office after making a very important statement to the Pennsylvania State Police concerning her brother-in-law's shady business dealings with her brother, several offshore medical schools, and a number of unaccredited tissue banks around the world."

"Shut. Up. How in the hell did that happen?" she asked.

"Barbara has been ankle deep in paperwork at both funeral homes for the last two weeks," he said. "Papers for the estate, papers for the sale of Daniel's assets, you name it. Well, she was looking around Daniel's place in Washington County yesterday, and she remembered that her father had a wall safe where he kept cash and important private papers. She knew Daniel had always tried to imitate their dad, so she began to look behind paintings, under cabinets, and…"

Rita interrupted him. "Please, don't drag this out. She found a safe, right? What was in it?"

"Bingo. Stashed behind one of those wall displays where they show you the material and the color of the box they're going to put you in. Can you believe it? She found paydirt under a little piece of coffin sticking on the wall. I'm talking lists of names and numbers of bodies sold to Shane and his cronies, names of people who were dismembered and sold to tissue banks, and names of the contacts at the banks they used, how much money they made, how it was divided, all..."

He paused when she sniffled. "Red, it's all here honey, neatly packed in a leather briefcase. In fact, Hardt and I have two clerks making multiple copies of the documents for the attorneys and the judge right now. Tomorrow morning, Hardt is going to present what we have and hope the court will let us continue the case after Davis makes a motion for a mistrial, which we know he will do. Hardt said he'll agree to give Davis time to review this new evidence since it is coming in after they've completed the discovery process. Hopefully, Duff will see it our way."

"What about Shane? Can you charge him with anything more?" She waited, breathlessly, for his answer.

"Possibly. The records show that he was living in the United States or traveling back and forth from here to the Caribbean while brokering several of these deals with tissue banks. Hardt's assistants are talking to people now who identified Shane Gilliam as their contact for the transactions involving body parts. Already, two are willing to testify that he sold them corneal tissue, torsos, arms, and legs. We've found nothing to show they had permission from any family."

She blew out a deep sigh. She hated to ask, but she had to know. "George, what about David's grandmother? Did you confirm anything about what happened to his Grandma Grace?"

He hesitated a few seconds. "Red, do you really want to know?

Maybe it's best to let it go."

"No, tell me."

He took a deep breath. "Each case was different. Various body parts from un-embalmed corpses of people who were supposed to be cremated were flown to a tissue bank in Europe within the proper amount of time for harvesting. The remaining parts of those bodies were destroyed here, in a crematory in Pittsburgh. And before you ask, we've found nothing to indicate the crematory owners had any idea the bodies they cremated had been sent there without the consent of family members. From a review of the lists, we believe because David's grandmother had been embalmed for viewing, her body ended up at the Celtic Cross Medical School."

She whispered, "Thank you for being honest."

Carr said the meticulously detailed records had been compiled by Bob Watson and included a letter he wrote but never mailed to Daniel saying he wanted to quit and didn't want to be involved in the operation anymore. "Bob said he was sorry he couldn't help Daniel pay his gambling debts any longer because he had to be able to live with himself. Looks like Daniel also has a bit of a problem with credit cards, and word on the street is that he's into every bookie in town for big bucks."

He said Barbara Mason found another letter addressed to Shane that implicated him as well. In that one, Bob told Shane that he could no longer allow students to practice on the embalmed bodies he'd provided, no matter how much his and other offshore medical schools were willing to pay.

"I'd say guilt got the best of him, and it cost him his life."

Questions flooded her thoughts. "How did Daniel get all this stuff? And why in the hell would he keep it?"

"We think Bob told Daniel he wanted to talk to him the weekend when Amie left to visit her sister. That explains the lack of forced entry and no evidence of a robbery. Bob's gun was in the corner, ready for firing. My theory is that Daniel came over, they argued, and Daniel blew him away. He had motive, means, and opportunity," he concluded.

As to why Daniel was careless enough to keep the damaging evidence, Carr couldn't say. "Who knows? Could be, he wanted to use it against Shane at some point," he speculated.

She whistled. "Boom. Done. I know I shouldn't feel this way because of David's grandmother, but I could scream right now because this story just keeps getting better and better. Bill Martin and the other reporters are going to go nuts when this comes out. Thanks, I'll see you tomorrow."

CHAPTER TWENTY-EIGHT

Hardt informed the court about the previously undiscovered documents before the jurors entered the courtroom the following morning.

As anticipated, Davis asked the judge to grant a defense motion for a mistrial. "Your honor, in the interest of fairness to my client, I have no other choice. After more than four months of preparations, it is totally unfair to spring this on us as proceedings are underway. We've just been handed a copy of this after-acquired evidence. We will need considerable time to review them and validate their authenticity to mount a proper legal challenge," Davis argued.

"Miss Barbara Mason, the defendant's sister, came to my office at the end of the day yesterday with a briefcase full of papers that she'd never seen before," Hardt said. "Neither she, nor any of us, knew the documents existed until she located them a mere eighteen hours before she brought them to me."

Duff listened to their arguments and indicated she'd take the matter under advisement. "Mr. Hardt, I'd like to meet with you, the witness, and Mr. Davis in my chambers in two hours to discuss this further. Mr. Hardt, can you have your witness available by then?"

"Yes, your honor, she is already on her way," he said.

The judge instructed the tipstaff to inform the jury to take the day off and wait for a phone call for further instruction before returning for service. Rita, David, and the other spectators filed out of the courtroom and into the hallway.

David held her arm as they walked down the marble staircase to the first floor. "Red, you've covered the judge before, what do you think she'll do?"

Rita thought for a few seconds because she knew judges and juries were highly unpredictable. "Well, it could go either way. This case is complex because there are multiple victims, locations, and events. I truly hope she doesn't grant the mistrial and make us all wait around for what could be months and months while Davis reviews the records. The best-case scenario, in my mind, would be a short postponement to give the defense some time to investigate."

She felt the baby kicking and rubbed her stomach gently. "If it's a postponement, I hope it's not too far off. I have a feeling baby girl is going to be here sooner, rather than later."

That evening, Carr phoned her at home to tell her Duff denied Davis' motion for a mistrial. Instead, the judge approved a two-week postponement before the trial would begin again with the same jury panel.

"It's not as bad as I'd feared," he said. "I worried that she'd go the other way. Barbara Mason's sincerity during the meeting in the judge's chambers sealed the deal for us, though. She said she'd be willing to testify under oath as to when she stumbled upon the paperwork while clearing out her brother's business."

Rita glanced at the calendar in her kitchen. "So, we're back in two weeks. Damn, George, I'm going to be cutting it close. My due date is just a few days after the trial resumes. Hope baby girl doesn't decide to come early, or you're going to have to haul jurors to the delivery room."

He laughed. "Red, if she's as impatient as you, she'll be here tonight. Just hang in there until we get it done, okay? You know how difficult it is to seat a jury in a capital murder case, let alone one involving three victims. Too many people don't want the task of deciding whether someone should live or die."

They chatted a few minutes more. When Rita hung up, she wondered what her decision would be if she had to decide Daniel Mason's fate. She shivered, remembering what he'd put her through and realized she'd have no trouble deciding at all.

Fourteen days seemed an eternity to Rita, who spent her time at the paper working on several feature projects on abuses in the state government's grant awards system and fraud in Pennsylvania's Department of Public Welfare. It wasn't as exciting as covering courts and crime, but the events of recent months, as well as her advancing pregnancy, resulted in her editors confining her to desk duty until her maternity leave.

For once, she didn't complain.

David's sister Chrissy helped her best friend Kathy organize a small baby shower for her family, close friends, and co-workers at her townhome the night before the trial resumed. After everyone left, she fell into bed, exhausted. Her back ached more than usual, and she couldn't get comfortable, even with a body pillow.

"I wouldn't be disappointed if the trial runs right up to my due date, and I didn't have to go back to work," she confided in David. "I'm tired. Now I know why most women start their families when they're younger than me. Doing this at my age isn't the smartest thing I've ever done."

He patted her stomach. "Listen up, baby girl. Mommy just admitted she's not always right, and that doesn't happen often."

She swatted his hand away. "She's not listening. The shower tired her out, too. Go to sleep."

When the trial resumed, Hardt called Barbara Mason as his first witness.

"Can you tell me, Miss Mason, why were you in the defendant's place of business?" he asked.

She looked at her brother, who turned his head away. "I was going through bills and invoices and cleaning out rooms because the Mason-Watson Funeral Home and the Mason Funeral Home are being sold and the contents of both liquidated," she said.

He pushed further. "For what reason?"

She looked directly at the defendant, who scribbled on a tablet and refused to meet her gaze. "Well sir, my sister and brother-in-law, who were partners with my brother, are dead, and I am the executor settling their estates. While examining records, I found that their and my brother's funeral homes are on the brink of bankruptcy as the result of a recent decline in business and Daniel's massive debts, so I have no choice but to sell everything to get out from under them. I also have legal power of attorney given by my brother to act on his behalf in business matters during his incarceration."

When she wiped a tear from her cheek, Hardt returned to the counsel table, pulled a tissue from a box at his seat, and handed it to her. "I'm sure this is very hard for you to talk about, so take your time. Can you tell us what you found at your brother's funeral home?"

"Yes sir. I found documents to show that my brother-in-law, my brother, and another man, Shane Gilliam, had been selling body parts to unaccredited tissue banks around the world. The parts were removed from bodies they'd been entrusted to cremate or bury from their funeral homes. Last year, they also sold at least a dozen intact, embalmed bodies to several offshore medical schools in the Caribbean for students to practice on during anatomy classes."

One of the female jurors let out a loud, 'Oh!' and then reached down to the floor for a plastic water bottle. She took a big gulp, after which she fanned herself with her hand.

Hardt paused briefly but then continued his line of questioning. "I know this is hard to talk about, but if they removed and sold body parts and tissues, what happened to the rest of the bodies' remains?"

"Most were cremated," she said. She looked at the floor, her face flushed.

He leaned toward the witness chair. "Did you find anything to indicate the decedents' families had given permission for either removal of tissue from bodies slated for cremation or donation of intact bodies for anatomical studies?"

She shook her head, then answered, "The families never knew any of this, not until the newspaper started running stories about exhumations and empty graves."

She hesitated for a few seconds and then looked toward the counsel table. A single tear ran down her cheek. "My brother and brother-in-law removed some corpses from their coffins within the few minutes after the funeral services ended and the time when mourners were getting into their cars for the procession to the cemetery. They put empty caskets into the ground and let people go on thinking that their loved ones were inside them."

Hardt held up a piece of paper. "Can you tell me, Miss Mason, what this is?"

She nodded. "It's a list my brother-in-law compiled of jewelry he'd removed from the corpses he sold rather than buried. It's his handwriting. I don't know for sure why he kept it, other than maybe he felt guilty."

Davis jumped to his feet. "Objection, your honor! The witness can't speak for the dead and is in no position to know what her brother-in-law may have been thinking at the time he compiled that list."

The judge leaned forward, nodding. "Granted. The jury will disregard that remark."

Barbara Mason remained on the witness stand for the remainder of the day as Hardt and Davis battled over nearly every scrap of paper she'd recovered in her brother's wall safe. By late afternoon the defendant shuffled his feet and shifted back and forth in his seat in obvious agitation as he listened to the mounting evidence against him. Twice, he turned back to look at Rita, glaring at her when their eyes met.

During cross-examination, Davis attempted to discredit the validity of the records and suggested that the witness stood to gain financially if her brother were convicted.

When her eyes welled with tears, the bailiff poured a cup of water from a pitcher on the end of the counsel table and gave it to her. She blew her nose and then took a small sip before answering the question. "Sir, I will be lucky if we can break even after all these debts and legal fees are paid. If anything, I will get a little help from the state for the care of my young nephew, who is disabled and receives federal Social Security survivor benefits as the result of his parents' deaths. Even with that help, I will be using some of my own money to care for him and pay his private residential school tuition because of my brother's financial mess."

Davis gave up. "No further questions."

Hardt then called Rita to return to the witness stand. "Can you tell me, Miss Locke, how did you come to be in possession of the jewelry removed from the corpses?"

She told him about her interviews with Cindy Ekas and the safety deposit key mailed to her anonymously. "I assumed it was a prank, most likely someone playing games with me to send me on a wild goose chase. But, when something *did* happen to someone who had been quite obviously terrified during my interviews, as Cindy behaved when I met her, I immediately went to the bank to find out what the box held."

He held up the note and the key, both held in a sealed plastic evidence bag. "Did Cindy mention either the safety deposit box or the key during your visits to her salon?"

She took a sip of water and shook her head. "No sir. We talked for a few minutes, but when I tried to get her to tell me anything about Bob Watson or his funeral home, she practically shoved me out the door to get rid of me. She said anyone could be watching us, and she didn't want to be involved in any discussion involving Bob's murder. I think she knew Daniel Mason did it."

At that, the defendant sprang up from his seat, leaped over the counsel table, and lunged toward Rita. He held a ball point pen above his head, as if ready to stab her with it.

"Stop, Daniel! What are you doing? Stop this," Davis shouted at his client.

Rita panicked and ducked, shielding her stomach. Several women in the courtroom screamed as George Carr knocked his chair over and moved to tackle Mason before he could reach the witness stand. As they wrestled on the floor, David followed on Carr's heels. When he reached Rita, he wrapped his arms around her, pulling her out of the chair and up onto the judge's platform. Finally, as a court constable whisked the judge off the bench and away from the chaos, two additional court constables who had been standing in the back of the room ran up the aisle and helped Carr subdue the defendant who was placed in handcuffs and removed from the courtroom.

The ink pen rolled away from Mason and across the floor, coming to a stop in front of Hardt, who stood frozen in front of the jury. Davis remained in his seat, his head in his hands. "It's over now," he muttered.

Carr stood, breathless and heaving, as he faced Rita and David. He looked around the courtroom, where papers lay scattered on the floor in front of the counsel table. Water puddled around Rita's cup that had been knocked over during the scuffle. "Red, you ok? Is that baby girl of yours alright?"

Her knees wobbled as she clutched David's arm. They made their way to the front row, and she sunk down onto the bench seat. Trembling, she struggled to find her voice. "Yes, I'm ok. Thanks to you, he never got close enough to lay a hand on me. I'm fine," she said.

"Good girl." Carr turned to face Hardt, who was gathering papers from around his feet. He sat down and poured a drink of water from a pitcher that somehow remained upright on the counsel table and took a long gulp. Breathing heavily, he reached into his jacket pocket and pulled out a white handkerchief which he used to mop his sweating brow.

"George, you don't look so hot," Rita said, leaning toward him. "What's wrong??"

He said nothing for a few seconds. Standing up, he mumbled, "Hey, I, uh, think I have a little problem here," he said. He grabbed his chest, closing his eyes.

Rita screamed as his knees buckled, and he collapsed to the floor.

Rita watched with horror as a burly court bailiff performed CPR on him in an effort to restart his heart and save his life. With each chest compression, her own heart pounded, and she willed him to respond. He'd looked so tired lately, she realized. Age, his weight, and the stress of his job had taken a toll on him, and now, the physical effort to tackle Daniel Mason had been too much for him to bear.

He did it to save me. Please, lord, save him.

"I'm still not getting a pulse," Hardt said. The prosecutor, kneeling next to Carr on the floor, held his fingers to the trooper's wrist as the bailiff worked. "I can't believe there's not a defibrillator in this building, of all places. Where's the damn ambulance?"

Rita watched in horror. How long had he been unconscious? She feared the worst.

A minute later, the doors to the courtroom burst open and two emergency medical technicians ran up the aisle. Immediately, they opened the case on their automatic defibrillator and swiftly attached the pads to Carr's chest.

"Stand clear," one of the men commanded. He shocked the trooper's heart once, and then a second time. "Okay, we got a pulse. Let's go."

Within two minutes they had him on a gurney and out the door.

Rita looked at David, and he nodded. She grabbed her purse. On the way to the hospital, she phoned Carr's wife, Susan.

Rita watched the clock for what seemed like hours, but only ninety minutes had passed since she last checked the time. It was just after 2 a.m. and Carr had been in the operating room for four hours. Susan had gone to the chapel to pray, and David slept in a recliner in the waiting room. Her nerves and her throbbing back wouldn't allow her to rest until she knew for sure he'd survived the emergency bypass surgery. She'd heard the doctor tell Susan that her husband's prognosis was grim, and it broke her heart to think her friend might not make it.

"Once we get through surgery, we'll know more after the first twenty-four hours or so," the cardiologist cautioned.

"Rita, wake up honey. It's time for us to go home," David said, shaking her shoulder gently. "C'mon babe, there's nothing more we can do here."

Her eyes fluttered open. Was it over?

"What? Where's Susan? Oh, God, David, is George dead?"

"No, no, honey, the surgery is over. The cardiologist just spoke with Susan, and they're letting her peek in on him for a few minutes in the cardiac intensive care unit on the sixth floor."

"How is he? Is he going to make it?"

"She said the doctor told her he's holding his own, and that time will tell. He's sedated, and on a ventilator right now. After she sees him, she's going to go home herself to rest. She'll call you tomorrow."

"Okay, good. He's tough. I know him. He can beat this."

When she tried to get up from the recliner, searing pain gripped her back and took her breath away. "Aaaagh," she moaned. "Help me up, would you? I can't do it."

David put one arm around her back and held her hand to raise her from the chair. When her feet hit the floor, another pain shot down her back and into her legs just as a flood of water gushed through her underwear and soaked her shoes.

"Oh my God, David. My water just broke."

CHAPTER TWENTY-NINE

Rita eased the phone from the drawer near her hospital bed, careful to avoid making too much noise. She glanced at her husband, who'd been dozing in a chair for the last hour, and then leaned over to peek at the sleeping infant swaddled in a bassinet at her side.

She'd been a mother for less than two days, but already knew she loved her baby girl with her whole heart and would do anything to protect her. Her tiny features were mesmerizing.

She scrolled through her contacts and punched in a number.

"Hey, Red, congratulations." George Carr sounded weak when he answered his cell phone. "David let my nurse know you were here. I've been worried about you. Are you okay?"

She laughed. "God, George, I only had a baby, even though she took her sweet time getting here. However, I see now why they call it 'labor.'

She told him she stopped counting twenty-four hours into her labor. Not long after that, her obstetrician decided it was best for both her and the baby to deliver her daughter by Cesarean section.

"Yeah, Susan told me your little one couldn't seem to make up her mind as to when she wanted to celebrate her birthday," he said.

"Minor details, though. You, on the other hand, saved my life from a maniac, damn near died of a heart attack on a courtroom floor, and underwent a six-hour heart bypass surgery a few days ago. How about I ask the questions? Everything okay?"

He let out a low chuckle and then whispered. "No, not really."

She drew in a deep breath, almost afraid to hear what he had to say. Just the day before, Susan said he was doing well and should be discharged in a few days with visiting nurses and physical therapists providing follow-up care at home. Had he been given bad news since then?

"What? Tell me what's wrong," she demanded.

"Well, for starters, the food in here sucks because they put me on a heart-healthy diet, which in translation means I can eat only those foods I hate. My physical therapist is obviously trying to kill me by making me walk up and down the hallway until my swollen leg throbs. I guess they had to go in through my leg to get a vein or something and use it for my heart or something. All I really want to do is watch the game on TV. I'd do just about anything for a pizza and a beer."

She giggled. "Sounds like you're a model patient. I have a feeling there's more, right?"

He hesitated a few seconds before he answered. "Well, every time my wife walks in the door, she's hounding me to file papers for my retirement, especially since this happened to me while on duty."

"And?"

"Last night, I told her I would. I'm sixty-eight next month. I'm tired, Red, and I'm too old to grapple on the floor with nut cases. I'm not going back."

Tears welled in her eyes and for a few seconds she couldn't say anything because she knew her job as a crime reporter would never be the same. Older cops like George Carr were becoming a rare breed, and she'd miss his shoe leather investigative instincts and his common-sense approach to catching criminals. Over the years, he'd helped her so much as a trusted news source, and twice in the last year, he'd saved her life.

She swallowed the lump forming in her throat. He deserved to enjoy himself, and if that meant fishing in the stream near his cabin in the Laurel Mountains instead of chasing criminals, he should do it.

She did her best to lighten the moment. "You're not old enough to retire, but I guess if you can't run with the young kids anymore, it's time to quit," she joked.

He growled at her. "Hey little girl, don't make me hobble up to that maternity ward."

She laughed. "You know I'm kidding. Anyway, you're going out with a bang, aren't you? I'm sure you've read the papers in between eating your veggies and parading the halls."

"Yep. Tell your buddy Bill Martin thanks for making me look good," he said. "With all the crap out there against the police, I kind of like being called a hero."

They talked for a few minutes about the conclusion of Daniel Mason's trial, which ended abruptly after the defendant's attack upon Rita. Mason, on the advice of his frustrated and very distraught defense attorney, entered guilty pleas to first-degree murder in the deaths of his brother-in-law, Bob, and Cindy Ekas, and to third-degree murder in the death of his sister, Amie, in exchange for a sentence of life in prison. Doing so, he avoided a new trial and the possibility of a death sentence.

Judge Duff also sentenced him to two consecutive terms of twenty years each on counts of kidnapping and assault for the attack upon Rita, as well as five years each on counts of conspiracy and mail fraud in connection with his role in the scheme to sell body parts and corpses.

"Too bad they couldn't get him on Omaima's murder or anything he'd done with Shane down in the Caribbean," she said. "Not all is lost, though, because part of his plea deal calls for him to testify against Shane for his role in the operation while in the United States. That's the only way Davis got the judge to approve the plea bargain. I think he was afraid that if the judge ordered a new trial, Hardt might seek death penalty again."

Carr whistled. "All wrapped up, neat and tidy."

She rocked the bassinet back and forth slowly when the baby began to stir. She looked at the wall clock at the foot of her bed and counted backwards. Time for another feeding in about ten minutes. "Yeah, but even if he's convicted, Shane isn't going to get much time, according to Hardt. Probably no more than five to ten years. Still, it's enough to keep him from playing doctor again anytime soon."

Carr yawned, and she could tell from his voice that he was fading when he spoke again. "So, tell me Red, are you going to give up the news business now that you're a mother?"

"No, but I'm taking a three-month leave. After that, I'll be back at my desk. My editor, Tom Moore and I have been talking about some changes on my beat. I've been there since I graduated from college, so it's about time. Plans are for Bill Martin to move to the crime and courts beat, and I'm going to move into more investigative and special, long-term projects work. Outside of the office, but with the paper's blessing, we may collaborate on a true-crime book about this mess."

He tried to whistle, but it came out sounding like a wheezy moan. "Impressive. Mommy's going to make the little one proud. Hey, you never told me the baby's name. What are you going to call her?"

She smiled when she answered, gazing down into the bassinet. She'd been waiting for him to ask. "We're calling her Georgia Grace. Georgia for the brave man who saved her mother's life, and Grace, after David's grandmother."

He didn't answer her. Surely, he couldn't be angry? Then, after a few seconds, she heard him make an odd honking sound, as if he'd blown his nose near the receiver. He was crying.

"George Carr, you old softie. I didn't mean to upset you."

He honked again, causing her to hold the phone away from her ear. "I'm not upset, Red. I just didn't expect…never imagined… hell, I'm honored. I can't tell you what this means to me."

Just then, an aide knocked at the door and stepped into her room carrying a floral arrangement. "Hey George, I gotta go. Someone's here. I'll give you a call in a week or so to see how you're doing." She hung up the phone and looked at the vase of pink roses, carnations, and hydrangeas. She couldn't imagine who sent them because the only people who knew she'd given birth, other than her doctor and the obstetrics nurses, were her parents, and David's mother and sister. Because she and David craved privacy after their recent ordeal, she hadn't told her co-workers yet. They weren't from the Carrs because Susan hand-carried flowers to her room the day before.

"Aren't they beautiful?" the aide asked. "Look, there's a tiny pair of pink crocheted booties tucked inside the flowers to hold the card."

"They can't be for me, can they? You must have the wrong room. Our family will be in later, so I doubt it's from any of them, and no one else knows we're here."

The aide moved to the windowsill and set the vase down. She reached into the booties and pulled out the florist's card. After she read it, she glanced at the whiteboard on the wall below the clock at the end of Rita's bed. "Oh, I'm sorry. My mistake. These are for someone named Rita Locke."

A sudden chill sent shivers up the back of Rita's neck. She still used her maiden name professionally, but she'd listed her married name, Hatfield, on her medical insurance cards and hospital admission records. Her hand shook slightly as she held it out to take the flowers. "No, you're right. That's me. Someone sent them in my maiden name."

After the aide left, she looked from David, still sleeping, to Georgia, who was making soft sucking sounds and squirming in her yellow striped swaddle. She pulled the card from the small pink 'It's a Girl!' envelope and shuddered when she read the typed inscription, a twisted rhyme that sent her mind racing.

"Wanted to let you know I haven't forgotten you or your stories, Miss Locke, or is it Red? We'll meet again when the cell door opens, and we'll have a blast until you're dead."

Had Daniel Mason sent this bouquet as one last sick threat to try to unnerve her? Well, his cell door wasn't going to open anytime soon, that's for sure. In fact, the sentences he'd received meant he'd most likely die of old age behind bars before he faced any possibility of parole.

She thought for a few moments. No, it couldn't have been him. He would have had to persuade someone outside the prison to order and pay for the flowers. James Foster wouldn't stoop that low, and she doubted that Shane Gilliam would be foolish enough to conspire with him on anything while awaiting additional charges of his own.

She read the card again, and this time, concentrated on each word in the rhyme until her stomach twisted with fear. No, this threat came from someone else she'd written about.

But who?

David stirred in his sleep and sat up. "Need anything, honey?"

"No, I'm good. She's still sleeping."

"Pretty flowers," he said, leaning forward to smell a rose. "Who sent them?"

"Just a friend," she said, hating herself for lying. "I don't think you've ever met." She tucked the card in her nightstand drawer, buying time until she could determine the sender.

After all they'd been through, she didn't have the heart to cast a shadow on their happiness by telling her husband that someone in prison, a criminal she'd written about, knew she'd given birth to their precious baby daughter less than forty-eight hours earlier. Or that he knew her nickname and exactly how to find her.

And that he wants her dead.

END

ACKNOWLEDGEMENTS

Before I sat down to write my first novel, *The Taker*, I thought all I had to do was come up with an idea, get the words on paper, live through some minor editing, and magically publish a best seller.

I didn't know what I didn't know.

With *Empty Boxes*, at least I knew what to expect.

This time around, there were endless drafts, rounds of editing, proofreading, pitching to agents, getting an agent, living through more edits, sweating through the submission process, and finally, signing a contract with a publisher. Oh, and then, there were more edits.

The idea is mine, crafted from years of experience while covering crimes and courts, learning from other journalists and legal professionals, and studying the habits of criminals. But the other stuff?

I had help. Lots of help.

You wouldn't be reading this novel if not for my dear friend, fellow author, and meticulous editor, Linda Rettstatt, who has sacrificed her time and sanity more than once to help me give birth to this work. Check out her more than fifty books, most of them women's fiction and romance, on Amazon. I'm beyond grateful for her insight and friendship.

Editor Beth Terrell-Hicks, who writes novels under the name Jaden Terrell, worked miracles with *The Taker* and polished the *Empty Boxes* manuscript until we made it shine prior to submission to agents. I'll always be thankful for the day I met her and dozens of other authors while networking and learning at Clay Stafford's Killer Nashville International Writers Conference. A word to the wise: It's held every August in Tennessee. If you write thrillers or mysteries, go there!

Finding unique names for characters always poses a problem for me, so I must thank those people who willingly let me appropriate their names for my characters. My dear friend and former newsroom colleague Cindy Ekas won a contest at my launch party for *The Taker* and generously allowed me to use her name without prior knowledge as to whether she'd end up as a villain or victim. My friend and powerhouse defense attorney James Davis offered his legal expertise when I was stumped by a question mid-manuscript and then also graciously let me use the name of his late father, Norman Davis, who had been a loyal friend to my late father-in-law. Thanks also to my oldest granddaughter, Chloe Studer, for the use of her name, and to my oldest grandson, Tyler Anthony Studer, for lending me part of his. I gave their characters interesting careers in *Empty Boxes*, and I can't wait to see what they become in real life. Two of my younger grandchildren, Lily and Braxton, lent their first names as well. A few friends and former newsroom colleagues might find variations or parts of their names in these pages, but I assure you that the story, the events within, and all my characters are purely fictional.

I'll always consider myself lucky for the day I met my agent, Dean Krystek, director of WordLink LLC, during a pitch session at Killer Nashville. He's a no-nonsense Army veteran who answers my calls and questions with honesty, humor, and kindness. He worked diligently on my behalf during the submission process and brokered the deal with Amphorae Publishing Group.

From our first meeting, publisher Lisa Miller and her team at Amphorae were excited about my work and included me in the editorial process. There's something wonderful about joining forces with a veteran/woman owned firm, and I hope ours is a relationship that continues for years to come. Kristina Makansi's cover art captures the essence of the story perfectly without giving [too] much away, and I truly appreciate her kindness in listening to my suggestions and creating art that blends visually with that of my first book.

I'm blessed to be surrounded by an amazing tribe of dozens of friends and supporters, who are too many to name individually, but they know who they are and that I love and treasure their friendship. I must, however, give special thanks to my tribal chiefs - Kathy Yourchik, Jamie Stringer, Jackie Murray Roble, Laura Ottenberg, Susan Nicholas, Jolene Hough and Monica Puskar - for blessing my life with their kindness and love. I don't know what I'd do without you.

Well, maybe that's a lie. I'd be lost without you.

Thanks, also, to my readers and supporters who purchased and read my first book. Your glowing reviews on Amazon gave me a boost of confidence and pushed me to learn more, write more, and venture into traditional publishing. You have no idea how much authors love great reviews.

Speaking of greatness, my childhood, and my life, for that matter, would have been dismal without the unconditional love of my father, Bob Acton, the original girl dad, my constant cheerleader, and my best friend since 1957. He encouraged me for years to write fiction, and you most likely would not be reading this if I hadn't decided to stop his constant prodding and give it a try. I hope I've made him proud.

My cherished daughter, Amy, and my stepsons Jake, Adam, and Nic, and daughters-in-law, Jennifer and Chrissy, have grown up to be wonderful, kind, hardworking people, and I'm enormously proud of them and their accomplishments every single day. On top of that, they've given me five beautiful grandchildren – Chloe, Tyler, Lily, Braxton and Lena – that I love with all my heart and plan to spoil rotten with gifts and treats and trips until my dying breath no matter what their parents say. They all learned early that the only rule at Grandma's house is that everyone gets what they want.

Thanks to my husband, Merle Harr, for loving our blended family, traveling the world with me, and supporting me in everything that I do, even if it means having to read another book. (He's not a reader, so his dream is that Hollywood will pick up the film rights and make a movie to spare him from having to turn another page. Hope it comes true!)

Lastly, love to my loyal companion, Louie, the sweetest, most high-maintenance poodle/bichon mix on the planet, who rests his chin against my laptop and snuggles by my side while I'm writing. That is, unless it's time for food, or a biscuit, or to run outside and chase a squirrel.

As you read this, I'm working on my third Rita Locke mystery, tentatively titled *The Last Obituary*. Look for updates on my website, robinactonbooks.com, or on my public Facebook page, Robin Acton, author.

ABOUT THE AUTHOR

Robin Ann Moore

Award winning journalist and author **Robin Acton** is known for her work in covering crime, courts and investigative projects for western Pennsylvania newspapers.

Acton interviewed everyone from presidential candidates to convicted murderers during a thirty-three year career that took her from crime scenes and courtrooms in western Pennsylvania to the mountains of Idaho, the Arizona desert, the streets of New York City, and the marbled halls of Congress in Washington, D.C. She has written extensively about crime, politics, government bureaucracy, terrorism, and both natural and man-made disasters, including the Sept. 11, 2001 crash of Flight 93.

Her 2021 debut novel, *The Taker*, was a Best Mystery finalist for the 2022 Silver Falchion Award given annually by the Killer Nashville International Writers' Conference.

A wanderer at heart, Acton loves to travel and has thus far visited forty-two states and fifty countries, with the rest of the world on her bucket list. She does her best writing poolside at her favorite spot in Aruba.

She and her husband, a retired Marine combat veteran, share a blended family that includes a daughter, three sons, five grandchildren, and a very spoiled Bichon, Louie.